Visit the author's Web page and place book orders at
www.booksurge.com

The Gas Machine

Blue Line Books
Printed in the United States of America

Cover Artist – Wayne Pickvet
Photographer – Shannon Strocel Funk

Library of Congress Control Number: 2002092060
ISBN: 1-58898-729-9

The Gas Machine

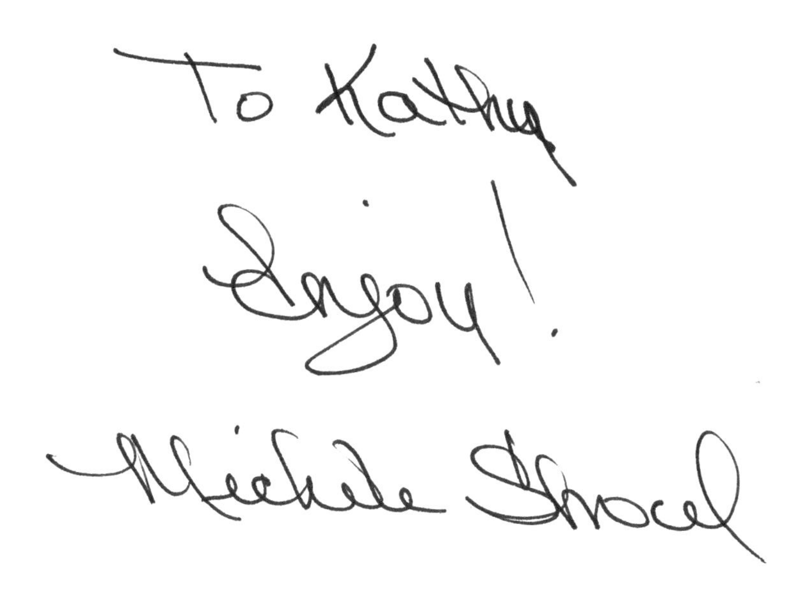

Michele Strocel

Blue Line Books

Acknowledgements

Thank you to all of my family and friends
who took the time and effort
to read my story at various degrees of completion
and for your suggestions and words of encouragement.

Special thanks to

Margaret Stephen McKay, for her help during two difficult years
Patrice LaCross, for her thoughtful encouragement
Cookie Wascha, for pointing me in the right direction
Misty Wilson, for words of advice and advice on words
Wayne Pickvet, for putting my words into a vision.

Dedicated with love to my husband and children

Dr. Anton "Tony" Strocel
Brian, Shannon, and Addison Young
Dustin and Becky Wilt
James and Shannon Funk

The Gas Machine

"And the Lord God caused a deep sleep to fall upon Adam..." Genesis 2:21
The first anesthetist did not need the gas machine to achieve a deep sleep.

Prologue

Early Friday Morning, October 22, 1976

Meet me at our place on 10 at 3

MJ smiled and wondered how he managed to surreptitiously pass the message to her. "Three o'clock, not three-thirty. Why the change in time?" she wondered, not that it mattered. She was just thankful that they could have a chance to be alone.

MJ knew that she must hurry because there was only ten minutes before the meeting. She signed out for a break at the X-ray desk but before she left the department, she stopped by the locker room to check her hair and make-up. She took the elevator to the tenth floor of Temple Memorial Hospital.

Temple Memorial is a large city hospital that has served the greater Flint area since the 1920s. The eleven-story facility was originally built with a V footprint consisting of two main corridors, the A and B wings. On most floors, the huge rotunda lobby at the point of the V contains an elevator bank, a nurses' station, and a stairwell tucked in a back corner. Later, an eleven story C wing was added changing the footprint to a Y.

The tenth floor houses the laboratory and the recovery room on the C wing, the operating rooms on the A and B wings, and occupying part of the rotunda area are the anesthesia lounge/locker room and surgery office. Because only emergency surgery is performed on the third-shift (11 p.m.-7 a.m.), the operating rooms require just three employees to be scheduled during that time period: a registered nurse (RN), an operating room scrub-technician (ORT), and a certified registered nurse anesthetist (CRNA).

As MJ exited the elevator, she looked around to see if anyone was there to observe her. The floor was quiet and the lights were dim. To the right was the C wing, where through an open door she could see the lab technicians busy at their tables. Also to the right was the door to the recovery room. It was closed for the night. Straight in front of the elevator door and across the rotunda area was the closed door to the anesthesia lounge. It was dark. No light could be seen through the crack under the door. To the left, the surgery office was empty and through the double doors leading to the operating rooms, the corridors were dark and quiet.

"No emergencies tonight, at least not yet," MJ thought as she quickly and quietly crossed the rotunda area to the back stairwell where she would wait.

She was sitting on the steps with her back to the door when she heard it open. She remained still, eagerly anticipating his tender kisses on the back of her neck. It was a scenario that had played out several times over the past three weeks. Finally, she was sure that she had met the man of her dreams, an eligible, handsome physician that was as infatuated with her as she was with him. She was so excited, her heart was pounding and she could hardly breathe. He did that to her.

"Lucky me," she thought as realities and fantasies of her doctor blended to completely occupy her mind.

MJ was quickly brought back to her senses, acutely aware that something was wrong, very, very, wrong. "Ouch! That's not a kiss," she thought as she quickly realized that she had just been poked with a needle on the back of her neck.

"Oh my God! What was that? What did you do?" she said as she tried to turn to face her attacker. Her question went unanswered. She began to feel strangely weak.

"What's happening to me?" Her voice started trailing off as the drug began to take effect. She was completely aware but could barely move and was having difficulty breathing. She was becoming paralyzed.

MJ could feel herself being lifted up to the safety railing of the stairwell that created a twelve-story triangular void from the eleventh floor to the basement. She could do nothing in her defense.

"Why are you doing this to me? What did I ever do to you?" She could only think the questions because not only could she not talk, she could no longer breathe. "Why me? Why now?" she thought as every cell in her body screamed for oxygen.

MJ could sense that she was being pushed over the railing before she began to fall. Her arms and legs stung with pain as they slapped into the metal stair rails when her descent to the basement floor seemed to accelerate.

Panic, pain, darkness, death.

Chapter One

Several hours earlier, Thursday Night, October 21, 1976

John Cavanaugh was sleeping soundly in front of the television. His wife, Mary, woke him, said good night, and sent him to bed. Then she turned out all of the lights in the house, except the small one over the kitchen stove. She left by the back door and walked three houses down the street to Kate McKenna's house. Mary used her key to let herself in.

"Hi, Kate!" Mary announced from the entryway to alert her daughter of her arrival. She removed her coat, revealing a terry cloth robe and pajamas. After she hung her coat in the front closet, she went to check on the children and found them sleeping peacefully in their room. She went to the guestroom to turn back the covers for the night. Mary would spend another night sleeping in her daughter's home.

"Hi, Mom. I'll be out in a minute," Kate called out in a hushed tone from her bedroom.

Kate finished dressing and went to the guestroom to visit with her mother for a few minutes before she had to leave for work. She had started working third-shift in the anesthesia department at Temple Memorial Hospital about a year ago, several months after the untimely death of her husband, Mike. Kate sat on the bed next to her mother and reached for her hand. "Mom, you know, you and Dad really are lifesavers for me. I don't know what I would do with the twins if you couldn't take care of them for me while I work."

"Well, it's not like it's such a hard chore. They're asleep

when I get here, and you're usually back in time to help get them off to school," Mary said, hoping to allay any guilt that Kate may be feeling for inconveniencing her.

"I know it's not hard work but it's time-consuming and disrupting for you. You and Dad are supposed to be enjoying your 'golden years' together and here you are, sleeping at my house. I just want you to know that I really appreciate everything that you and Dad do for the children and me. I don't want you to think that I'm taking advantage of you."

Mary smiled at her daughter. She knew Kate was an adult but in Mary's eyes, she would always be her little girl.

"Kate, you are my only child. Shelby and Shane are my only grandchildren. It's my job, my purpose in life, to care for my family. Now you go to the hospital and do your job, and I'll stay here and do mine."

"Thanks, Mom. I'll see you in the morning." Kate headed toward the door. "I love you," she said over her shoulder before she left the room.

The evening temperatures in mid-October in Michigan are often cool, and this night was typical. Kate opened the garage door before she started the engine of her white, 1975 Datsun 260 Z 2+2, which was sporting the new Michigan red, white, and blue Bicentennial license plates. Mike bought the car for her just days before he was shot and killed by a passenger in a car that he had stopped for a broken taillight.

The trip to the hospital was a short six blocks on the quiet tree-lined streets of her well-established neighborhood. As she drove to the hospital, Kate hardly noticed the splendor of the autumn leaves. Many of the leaves camouflaged the pavements, sidewalks, and yards while others still clung to the huge tree branches that canopied over the streets. The magnificent effect the foliage created, that of driving through a huge, golden tunnel, was lost to her because Mike was very much on her mind.

Katherine Cavanaugh and Michael McKenna, friends since childhood, had grown up in the same east-side Flint neighborhood where she still lives. Even though Kate was the smallest girl in her class, she was the only one who was tomboy enough to join the neighborhood boys in their games. When they were in elementary school, one of their favorite games was cops and robbers. The boys' roles changed from week to week between the good guys and the bad guys, but Kate's role always remained the same. Having read every Hardy Boys and Nancy Drew mystery book ever written, Kate always got to be the detective.

By the time they were in junior high, Kate often joined the guys in the weekly neighborhood tag football games held on the lawn of the Mott College Library. When they reached high school, Mike, who was one year older than Kate, noticed that the tomboy had grown up. He realized that he enjoyed Kate's company as a girl, much more than when she was one of the guys. From then on, the two became almost inseparable.

Mike and Kate spent many hours talking about everything, especially their futures. Mike always talked about being a cop while Kate was never quite sure about where her true ambitions would lead her.

Kate used to dream that Mike and she would be detectives. They would be partners on the police force, as well as, partners at home. At some point in her fantasy, they would start their own private investigation agency. But over time, Kate learned to her disappointment that boys didn't want their girlfriends to have jobs traditionally reserved for men. And the average citizen, as well as most of the cops, didn't want women on the police force, never mind as detectives. Eventually, Kate set aside her investigative ambitions and chose an accepted female occupation – nursing.

After Mike graduated from high school, he got a job on the assembly line at a General Motors plant and started putting some money away for the future. The next summer, after Kate's high school graduation, they were married in a beautiful ceremony at the Woodside Church, right across the street from the Mott Campus lawn where they had spent so many afternoons during their childhood.

That fall, Kate entered the School of Nursing at Temple,

and Mike joined the Marines to fulfill his military obligation on his timetable rather than waiting to be drafted.

During the second year of the three-year nursing program at Temple, Kate met Mike in Hawaii for his two-week R & R. Nine months later, she gave birth to the twins, a girl named Shelby and a boy named Shane. After her maternity leave, she returned to finish her last year of studies. By the following fall, Kate was working in the operating room at Temple.

Mike was away during most of that period, and Kate spent her time divided between home and work. She was fortunate that she could rely on her parents to help her care for the children because it eliminated the need, as well as the expense, for baby-sitters or a day-care center. Her parents were happy to help her in any way they could.

When Mike returned home after his discharge from the marines, he joined the Flint Police Department. He was partnered with Brian Goss, another long-time resident of the east-side neighborhood. Brian was two years older than Mike and had mentored him during their formative years, especially when it came to playing football.

Mike had a high regard for police work and he was good at it. He was also becoming accustomed to the responsibilities of being a family man. After years of being in the service and away from his family for long periods of time, Mike was finally settling into a routine home life. Although there were times when the horrors of Vietnam pushed their way from the deep, dark recesses of his subconscious mind to the forefront, often causing violent night terrors accompanied by times of depression, Kate, his best friend, was always there for him. For the most part, things were good and this was the happiest time of his life.

Life was good for Kate, too. Her family was together and they were financially secure. Her good fortune afforded her the opportunity to complete the last step in her educational goal: the eighteen-month nurse anesthesia program at Temple. She started the anesthesia classes shortly after Mike began his police career.

Mike was very supportive of Kate's educational endeavors, and he rather enjoyed caring for the twins in her absence. He even took over some of her household chores to give her time to study. She had only four months of clinical requirements left to complete when Mike was killed.

Mike's death was devastating for Kate. She had never suffered any major trauma in her life. She started to withdraw, feeling that the only safe place for her was deep within herself.

Mike had been her best friend all of her life. Even when he was in the service, she knew that he was there for her. Now he was gone, really gone. She was sure that she could never be strong enough to survive such a loss, and she began to think that it didn't matter anyway because she felt that she had no future without Mike.

Kate's parents made every effort to pull her out of the darkness with their unconditional love and attention. With their support, she tried to charge ahead with life as had always been her custom, but everyday was like marching through mud up to her knees, zapping her strength to the point of mental and physical exhaustion. Eventually, she came to realize that she had to deal with Mike's death but more importantly, she had to deal with life. Shane and Shelby had lost their father and they needed their mother now more than ever.

Kate needed to finish the last few months of her anesthesia training and study for her board exams. She had to run her household and pay the bills with less money than before. Every day was a struggle but she knew she had to find the strength to go on. Thank God for her parents, who kept her from drowning in self-pity and depression. John and Mary knew that Kate could make it, and that she would be not only all right but also stronger than ever, even though Kate didn't know that for herself at the time.

Now, just over a year after Mike's death, Kate was beginning to feel back on track again. She could think about Mike without tears. She could recall the past without the hollow sadness that had been her constant companion since that fatal bullet made her a widow.

"Yes, life is getting better. Not good yet, but getting better everyday," Kate thought as a smile spread across her face. She figured that she would work one more year on third-shift and then by the following fall, when the twins would be in school for a whole day, she would have enough seniority to switch to days. Then she could get back on a regular sleeping schedule and a routine family life with her children.

Kate parked in the lot reserved for the third-shift employees and used the emergency room entrance into the hospital. She liked using that entrance because the ER status gave her a clue as to how busy her night might be because the activity in the OR was often a reflection of the activity in the ER.

"Hi, Katie," Dr. Thomas Dunbar drawled as she walked by the open door of the ER employee lounge.

Dr. Dunbar, an excellent ER physician, was the most eligible and desirable bachelor at the hospital, in his own mind. He wasn't particularly handsome but he was quite tall, had a good build, and was always impeccably groomed and dressed. A southern gentleman from a fine family that had long ago lost their wealth, Dr. Dunbar played the role of the graciously mannered, southern aristocrat to the hilt.

"Hello, Dr. Dunbar. And it's Kate, not Katie, remember?" she said with feigned annoyance.

Kate had known Dr. Dunbar for about five years, ever since she started nursing school. She respected him as a physician and considered him a friend, although their relationship had always been a casual, professional one that was contained within the hospital walls.

Dr. Dunbar had quite a reputation as a ladies man, especially when it came to dating the student nurses. He had dated several of Kate's classmates before the time that he came flirting up to her in the hope of scoring a date. Kate made it quite clear that she was married and adamant that she was not interested in his seductive advances.

He was impressed with Kate's stand and he respected her wishes. Yet, he found her to be so attractive and charming that he wanted to get to know her better. That was when, as a pretext to capture her attention and obtain her friendship, he began asking Kate for advice on which nurses he should ask out. Once in a while, she offered an opinion or suggestion but most of the time, they just exchanged friendly banter.

Dr. Dunbar continued, "Well now, I know that your name is Kate but that sounds so strong and independent, and Katie sounds so cute and vulnerable, just like you."

"Only in your distorted imagination. I am not some helpless little damsel in distress so don't even try to use that line on me," Kate said to him, hand on hip, before turning to walk out of the ER to the elevator lobby.

Kate took the elevator to the tenth floor where she went into the anesthesia locker room/lounge. She put on her white, starched scrub dress, changed into her OR shoes, and covered her hair with a paper hat.

Each of the female anesthetists was issued six white, wraparound scrub dresses that had one button at the neck and one at each side of the waist. The dresses came almost to Kate's ankles when they were issued but she shortened them, as did all of the nurse anesthetists, to above her knees before she sent them to the laundry to be starched and pressed.

Those scrub dresses brought delight to most of the male staff members but especially, to a certain thoracic surgeon who would hold the back, bottom edge of the dress while the anesthetist walked away, causing the whole back of her dress to open, exposing her panties. The last time, "Tricky Dicky", as he was affectionately known, pulled that prank, the anesthetist was ready for him. When her dress popped open, everyone could see a picture of him taped to her butt. He acted thoroughly embarrassed but it would take more than that to humiliate him. Actually, most were sure that he was secretly pleased by the stunt.

"Oh Kate, are you in there?" Rae called from the anesthesia lounge/locker area to the bathroom area. The male anesthetists changed into scrubs in the doctors' locker room but the women had to change in the coed anesthesia lounge so they were relegated to the bathroom.

"Yes. I'm here. I'll be out in a second," Kate called back.

Rae Ellen Gilbert, the second-shift CRNA, was one of the friendliest, most upbeat people in the whole hospital. She had a quick wit and a sharp tongue when the occasion called for it, and she always had a story to tell that helped to keep things lively.

Rae had been six months ahead of Kate in the anesthesia program at Temple so they had had some classes together. Kate had always liked Rae and admired her work and her stamina. Like Kate, Rae was married and had two children when she started anesthesia school. And like Kate, Rae was without a husband by the time she finished the program. The difference was that Rae's marriage ended in divorce. Kate wasn't sure if it was the pressure of the program or a sign of the times, but eighty-percent of the married students who entered the anesthesia program ended up divorced within one year after graduation.

Kate entered the lounge area to find Rae changing her clothes.

"What are you doing? Anyone could walk in here and see you in your underwear," Kate gasped.

"Lucky them," Rae said with causal indifference.

"How was your evening?" Kate asked as she filled her pockets with pens, paper, scissors, and other supplies that she might need on hand.

"Good. We were busy earlier but we finished in enough time for me to clean, stock, and check everything so it looks like you might have an easy night," Rae reported.

"That would be nice."

"Hey, did you hear the latest about 'Ole Tricky Dicky'?" Rae asked, eager to repeat her most recent story.

"No. What now?" Kate said with some reservation.

"It seems that Dr. Richards was checking on one of his patients in the ICU. He had the curtain pulled around the bed so he could perform an examination, and when he bent over to listen to the patient's breath sounds, he bumped butts with the nurse caring for the patient in the next bed. Never one to pass up a chance for a good feel, he grabbed her butt through the curtain. Imagine his surprise when he pulled the curtain back and saw the patient's wife, not a nurse."

"Oh, my God. You're kidding me!" Kate exclaimed in disbelief.

"No, I'm not," Rae said as she crossed her heart and raised her hand. "It really happened and he didn't even miss a beat. He just made some comment about close quarters and went on his way. The nurse from ICU who told me the story said that the patient's wife wanted to know who that nice doctor was. Can you believe that?"

Kate and Rae both laughed.

"Okay, Kate. I'm out of here. Have a good night," Rae said on her way out the door.

Kate enjoyed Rae's sense of humor because it always put her in a good mood. She smiled and made a mental note that when she finally had more personal time, she would like to renew the personal friendship with Rae that had begun when they were students.

Kate checked the mirror in the lounge to make sure that all of her hair was covered before she headed out to the OR. She had grown accustomed to the demands and responsibilities of the night schedule, and she had devised a routine that worked well for her. First, she would check with the night charge nurse, Margaret "Maggie" MacGregor, RN, for the case status. What Kate did next would be determined by what cases were in progress, scheduled, or pending. Kate would either relieve the anesthetist sitting on any case in progress, prepare for any scheduled or pending case, or check the anesthesia stock and equipment in each OR and make any changes necessary to ensure that the anesthesia equipment in each OR was patient ready.

After leaving the anesthesia lounge, Kate spotted Maggie and Armstrong "Army" Sargent, the third-shift surgical tech, sitting in the OR office drinking coffee.

"Hi, you guys! Looks like maybe we're gonna have a little quiet time tonight," Kate said as she entered the office.

Army Sargent, an excellent scrub tech who was initially trained as a medic and then a surgical scrub tech in the Army, was sitting on a chair that was tipped back and leaning against the wall. Kate thought the chair looked quite feeble under Army's large frame, but he didn't seem too concerned.

Army was the out-of-doors type, stood about 6 feet 5 inches, and looked gruff and tough. Actually, he was gentle, kind, and generally, soft-spoken. It was reassuring having him on the third-shift team, especially when it came to lifting and moving patients. Also, because the OR suite is often deserted at night, Army's presence gave Kate a feeling of security.

Kate had never been concerned about her safety at the hospital until one night shortly before she went into anesthesia. She was the RN covering the third-shift. She was sitting in the OR office where she could see down both corridors. At the end of each corridor was a limited use stairwell door. On the outside of the tenth floor door was a large sign with big, bold, red letters that read "STERILE AREA—NO ADMITTANCE," but the warning sign didn't stop everyone. That night out of the darkness from the end of the A corridor, Kate spied a man stumbling up the hall toward her. He appeared to be intoxicated, was having difficulty walking, and was obviously irritated about something because he was yelling and cursing at some imaginary person.

Kate called security and was thankful for their immediate response. The security officer had been responding to a similar complaint on the ninth floor when he learned that, in an effort to evade capture, the intruder decided to hide out on the tenth floor. When the officer arrived Kate was pleased to see that he wasn't one of the typical Temple security officers, who more closely resembled her late grandfather than a security force to be reckoned with. The guard was able to subdue and remove the guy from the OR suite without further incident.

Kate found the whole situation very unsettling and never took her safety in the hospital for granted again.

Army stood and stretched. "We can only hope that it will stay quiet for a while. Now if you two lovely ladies can carry on for a time without me, I'm going down to Labor & Delivery (L&D) for a few minutes. Joey's working tonight and, well, if she gets to know me better maybe I can interest her in having dinner with me some time instead of just breakfast dates in the hospital cafeteria." Army winked at them as he left.

Joey Ford, one of the third-shift RNs on L&D, usually accompanied the emergency C-Sections patients to the OR. Most of the third-shift hospital staff know that Army and Joey have been dating for weeks, even though they pretend that they are just "good friends" in an effort to discourage the gossip that often runs rampant in the hospital.

The hospital employee community is a microcosm of the city that it serves, especially on third-shift. Fellow employees are neighbors who become friends and learn to rely on each other if they are lucky. Getting stuck working with someone who is difficult can be intolerable, and a staff member with quarrelsome attitude doesn't last long because the others ostracize him. Everyone knows that cooperation and collaboration among the staff members on the third-shift can be a matter of life and death.

Kate is lucky. The members of the third-shift OR team compliment each other well, each with his or her abundant strong points and minor weaknesses that mesh well to create an effective, professional team. Yet, as close as they are at work, they seldom socialize together off duty.

Maggie had been a good friend to Kate over the last year, listening while Kate struggled to maintain a sense of professionalism at the hospital when she felt as if her whole life was going to hell in a hand-basket. Now it was Kate's turn to be the understanding confidant. Lately, Maggie had been preoccupied with something or someone and she seemed to be working up the courage to discuss it with Kate, dropping hints here and there.

Maggie rarely talked about herself so Kate knew very little about her. The only relative she had ever mentioned was an aunt who lived in Florida. Maggie moved to Flint from Florida about 18 months ago and lives alone in a small house about two blocks from the hospital. About six or eight weeks ago, she started dating some mystery man. Finally, she let her guard down and slowly and deliberately started telling Kate about him. Soon she was rambling on and on like a high school freshman who was dating the most popular senior in the school. At the same time, she remained coy and reluctant to reveal anything about his identity.

Kate listened for about 20 minutes before she apologized and excused herself. She promised to continue their conversation after her rounds were finished, but for now she had to go check the code box and the anesthesia equipment in the operating rooms. Even though Rae reported that she had done everything, Kate felt more comfortable if she double-checked things herself.

Kate checked the code box that contained all of the equipment and supplies necessary to establish and maintain a patient's airway in an emergency, including a laryngoscope and blades, endotracheal tubes, and airways. She always kept two sizes of tubes ready for use, one sized for an adult female and one for an adult male.

After that she went to each of the twelve operating rooms to check the anesthesia machines. These machines are what the anesthetist uses to deliver oxygen and anesthetic gases to the patients during surgery. They support the monitors and contain all of the supplies and medications that may be required to maintain the patient's vital functions while under anesthesia. Attached to the machine is a ventilator, a mechanism to assist or control the patient's breathing. The anesthetist monitors the patient's vital signs while administering the anesthetic gases and medications required to safely induce and maintain the patient in such a state that he is asleep, with muscles relaxed, while all vital functions remain either intact or under the control of the anesthetist. In short, the gas machine is the lifeline between the anesthetist and the patient.

About 15 minutes after Kate left the office, she heard Maggie calling her name.

"Maggie, I'm here in OR 7. What's up?"

"No case, if that's what you mean. I'm going off the floor to run a few errands. I'll be back in about a half-hour. Would you listen for the phone?"

The phone line that was used to schedule cases could only be accessed in the surgery office so someone always had to be available to answer it. Kate said she would listen for the phone while she continued making rounds. She completed her chores and eventually made her way back to the office.

By 1 a.m., both Maggie and Army had returned to the surgery office. It was apparent that Maggie didn't want to continue the earlier conversation with Army present so nothing more was said about "Mr. Wonderful".

"Anything happening down on labor and delivery?" Kate asked Army.

"They only have two patients and both are in early labor so it's pretty quiet down there," Army answered.

"What about you, Maggie? See anything interesting on your travels?" Kate quizzed.

"Not really. I stopped by ER where one of the X-ray techs was taking a portable film of a nondisplaced fracture that Dr. Dunbar had just casted. ER has just routine stuff and nothing for us."

"Good. Nothing expected from L&D or ER. Listen you guys, I feel like I'm starting to get a headache so as long as it's quiet, I'm going to take some aspirin and lie down in the anesthesia lounge for a few minutes. I'll see you later," Kate said as she left the office.

Maggie headed for the nurses' lounge to read, knowing that if the phone rang, she could hear it from there. Army went to the doctors' lounge to watch TV. Third-shift in the operating room was always unpredictable but usually busy, so everyone took advantage of this quiet break.

A couple of hours later Maggie decided to go to the cafeteria. Army brought his dinner so he didn't want to go.

Besides, he seemed engrossed in some movie on the lounge TV. He assured Maggie that he would answer the phone and notify her of any emergencies. She picked up the code box and headed to the anesthesia lounge.

Kate awoke with a start when Maggie knocked on the anesthesia lounge door. "Who is it?" Kate said. Her sleepy voice cracked.

"It's just me, Kate," Maggie said while opening the door. "I didn't know if you were sleeping or not. I'm going down to the cafeteria and I thought you might want to go, too."

"Yeah, sure. Give me a second. Boy, I really crashed. What time is it?" Kate asked as she tried to shake off the remnants of her nap.

"It's about a quarter after three or so."

Kate straightened her uniform and her hair. "Why don't you tell Army that we're leaving the floor so he'll know to answer the phone? And I'll get the code box."

Kate had to take her emergency airway equipment with her when she left the floor because she was the only anesthetist in the hospital and had to be prepared to respond to a code situation at all times.

"I already spoke with Army and here's your box so let's go."

"Shall we take the stairs?" Kate was always touting the benefits of physical activity.

"Are you kidding? The stairs?" Maggie whined, knowing that Kate would persuade her to use the stairs. She always did. That's one debate that Kate always won. The elevator-or-stairs question was rhetorical, as far as, Kate was concerned.

"Come on. You know exercise is good for you. We'll take the stairs down and the elevator back up, okay?" Kate said with the tone and authority of an exercise coach.

As always, Maggie reluctantly agreed and the two headed for the stairwell in the back corner of the rotunda. The light on the stairs is generally poor but especially at night, because there's no sunlight to shine through the windows located on the landing of each floor. The shadowy environment didn't seem to matter to most because the stairway was seldom used anyway, partly due to the inconvenient location, but mostly because of the close proximity of the elevators. Although the stairs went to the basement, Kate and Maggie planned to exit on the first floor where the cafeteria is located.

Halfway down the stairwell, Kate and Maggie heard a commotion with voices echoing up to them. They picked up their pace until they were running. Kate's code beeper sounded as they raced down the stairs toward the sound. She was being summoned to a code located on the basement floor of the rotunda stairwell.

"Anesthesia's here. What's happening?" Kate called out in an authoritative voice, loud enough to be heard above the cacophony of the small crowd gathering at the foot of the stairs. Before anyone responded, she spotted a woman's body lying on the basement floor. Kate recognized the patient as MJ Iverson, a third-shift X-ray tech.

MJ took most of the portable X-rays at night so she spent a fair amount of time in ER and OR. She was good at her job and she rather enjoyed traveling throughout the hospital.

MJ was a tall, willowy beauty with a porcelain complexion and huge blue eyes. Unable to see her own natural beauty, she covered much of it up with too much make-up. But then, she seemed to do everything to excess. Her hairdo was so dramatic, it would be better suited for a formal evening. Her uniforms were too short, too tight, and way too low cut in the front.

She was friendly enough to most and too friendly to many, especially the male employees. Most of the men enjoyed her company and casual flirting while the women usually just tolerated her.

By the time Kate and Maggie reached the basement floor, Dr. Dunbar and other ER employees were preparing to place MJ on a backboard so they could lift her onto a cart. A respiratory therapist was delivering oxygen via a mask and ambu-bag while an intern stabilized her head and neck. Dr. Dunbar was administering external cardiac resuscitation, as best he could, while the cart holding MJ was moved from the small confines of the stairwell floor down the short hall to the emergency room.

Once the cart was moved into an ER cubicle with its wheels locked, Kate used a laryngoscope to look down MJ's throat to view her vocal cords. She placed an endotracheal tube between MJ's cords and removed the scope. She put 10 cc of air in the small cuff at the far end of the tube to help keep it in the proper position in the trachea. She secured the outside end of the tube to MJ's face with tape while the respiratory therapist began to administer oxygen via the tube with an ambu-bag. During the intubation process, other members of the code team connected a monitor, started intravenous lines, and prepared other emergency supplies and drugs, as the cardio-pulmonary resuscitation (CPR) continued.

Code situations may appear as a state of confusion but each participant is performing his function as part of the well-organized team. All code team members have routine shift responsibilities in the hospital which usually are not concerned with split second, life and death matters. Yet, they know that at any minute, they may be called upon to use their special skills and knowledge in a critical situation. When that happens, their emergency mode takes over and these professionals respond to each patient, young or old, rich or poor, stranger or friend, in the same manner and with the same desire to preserve and maintain life for all. However, after the crisis, when the reality of each individual patient reaches the team member on an emotional level, the same dedicated professionals sometimes find it difficult to hide their emotions.

This code seemed to last forever before Dr. Dunbar finally called it quits. He looked at the clock to note the exact time and pronounced MJ dead. The group that participated in the resuscitation effort gathered in silence in the ER coffee room to complete the medical records of the event. Soon they began to wonder out loud to each other.

"How could this have happened?" "What exactly did happen?" "How could MJ have fallen over the guardrail?" "Did she jump?" "Was she pushed?" No one seemed to have any suggestions or maybe they were just reluctant to make any speculations.

Word of the mishap quickly spread throughout the hospital. The gossip and rumors traveled just as fast, including many titillating comments about MJ's reputation as a party-girl. She never made it a secret that she clearly preferred bachelor doctors and wanted to find a doctor husband. But in spite of that fact, she was always available to party with any man that she found interesting.

Kate and Maggie cancelled their plans to go to the cafeteria. Neither had an appetite any more. They had just lost one of their own. Maggie returned to the OR without Kate who had to finish her paper work. After Maggie left, Dr. Dunbar approached Kate appearing to have something on his mind. He remained silent when other ER personnel entered the lounge.

Realizing that he was not going to have an opportunity for a private word with Kate, Dr. Dunbar eventually touched Kate's shoulder and leaned close to her as he whispered, "Please call me later."

He then turned and left the room before she could respond. His request surprised her but she considered it for only a moment before her thoughts returned to finishing her report. When her paper work was done, she headed for the tenth floor deep in thought.

MJ's death was very tragic, to say the least, and it was devastating to participate in the code of a colleague, especially an unsuccessful one. In addition to being distracted by MJ's death, Kate couldn't stop wondering about how MJ fell.

Kate knew that her friends often described her behavior about some things as obsessive-compulsive, particularly her insistence for a logical sense of order. As a small child, she realized that if she could organize her thoughts about any subject into a logical sequence, she could easily learn and retain all of the information. When something didn't make sense to her, she would spend hours contemplating all of the angles until she could organize it. Only then could she understand it and commit it to memory.

Another part of Kate's desire for answers was her intense curiosity, or as some fondly described it, "her nosey attitude." Mary Cavanaugh often tells the story that Kate's first word wasn't "Mama" or "Dada" but rather "Why?" That's when the questions started and they haven't stopped yet.

Also, she had always had a powerful intuition. Sometimes she knew when things were going to happen. She didn't know how she knew, she just knew. And she learned a long time ago to trust her instincts.

Kate sensed her need for logic, her curiosity, and her intuition kicking into overdrive and she felt compelled to get to the facts of MJ's fall. It was as though destiny had thrust her into the middle of this tragedy to force her to find a reason to explain the irrational acts of an apparently rational person. Whether Kate was consciously aware of it at the time or not, she was about to embark on an adventure that would forever change her life.

Kate's first instinct was to call Brian Goss. Besides being a close friend, Brian was a detective, not an amateur sleuth like Kate, but a real detective with the Flint Police Department. Kate and Brian had grown up in the same neighborhood and it seemed like she had known him forever. Because Brian had been Mike's partner on the police force, as well as an old friend, he too, had been devastated by the tragedy of Mike's death. Brian and Kate formed a special bond while grieving and offering each other emotional support. Brian became somewhat of a "big brother protector" to Kate.

The phone rang three times before Brian answered, "Goss."

"Hi, Brian. This is Kate. I'm really sorry to call you. I mean, I'm really sorry to wake you up. It's ...(Kate looked at her watch). Oh my God, Brian. I am so sorry! It's 5 a.m. I don't know what I was thinking. I just needed to talk to you. There was a terrible accident at the hospital tonight. Well, maybe it wasn't an accident, I don't know. I'm sorry. Go back to sleep. I'll call you later."

"Wait a minute. What are you talking about? What

accident? Kate, what's going on?" Brian sputtered as he tried to wake up and understand Kate's message.

"Brian, listen. I'm sorry I called you because I'm at work and I really can't talk right now. I promise I'll try to phone you later today after I get home from work. I'll explain everything then. In the mean time, if you go down to the station before I talk to you, check to see if an accident report was filed tonight about a woman named Mary Jo Iverson who fell to her death at Temple."

"Someone fell in the hospital and died?"

"Yes, Mary Jo Iverson, an X-ray tech. She fell down the stairwell and died."

"Kate, are you are alright? You sound ... I don't know ... rattled."

"I'm upset. That's why I called. I wasn't really thinking straight or I wouldn't have called at this hour. I'll be fine. Really. I have to get back to work. I'll talk to you later. Bye."

Kate was a little embarrassed when she hung up. She was sure she must have sounded slightly crazed. If she expected anyone to help her with her inquiries, she knew that she had better smarten-up and think before she acts. Otherwise, she would end up looking like some kind of an airhead.

Kate stopped by the X-ray department on her way back to the OR. She wanted to talk to the staff there and get their take on the events of the night. She learned that MJ's attitude had been very upbeat lately and that she had been in a particularly good mood when she signed out for a break just before her death. It quickly became obvious that everyone thought it was an accident. No one mentioned anything about an intentional fall or suicide.

Maggie and Army were in the OR office when Kate exited the elevator onto the tenth floor. Maggie was describing her version of the demise of MJ Iverson when Kate joined them. Maggie and Army had seen many emergencies but neither was part of the code team, so they didn't routinely observe the drama of a code situation.

To observe a code in progress can be overwhelming even

to a seasoned hospital employee. To see the code of a coworker should be especially devastating, but Maggie seemed more fascinated than distressed and was gratuitously embellishing the story with graphic details.

"I'm surprised by your attitude, Maggie. I'm very disturbed by this whole incident but you seem to be describing MJ's death like you're retelling your favorite scene in a horror movie," Kate scolded.

"Come on, Kate. Don't take it so personally. It's not like she was your best friend or anything. It's not even like you liked her very much. Or did you?" Maggie eyed Kate quizzically.

"I really didn't know her that well. I only had contact with her when she came up here to take films during surgery. Oh, and she would take X-rays of the patients after intubations for tube placement. She was okay but it doesn't make any difference whether I liked her or not. She was one of the team. She was one of us," Kate explained.

"Yeah, well, she never acted like much of a team player. Even Army was disgusted with the way she would throw herself at him, especially in front of Joey. MJ knew very well that Army was trying to get something going with Joey and she did everything she could to upset everybody," Maggie said defensively.

"Is that right, Army?" Kate asked.

"Yeah, she tried to get me interested in her or, at least, that's how she acted. I think that she was a harmless flirt but mostly, she was just a pain in the butt. I don't think Joey ever really paid too much attention to her actions, that is as long as I didn't pay too much attention to MJ," Army explained.

"Maybe she was a flirt. That's not such a big deal. It's just sad that she died right here in our hospital where our business is saving lives." She paused, then asked, "So, what do you guys think happened tonight?"

Silence. They dropped the subject and quietly filed out of the office to finish their duties before the first-shift employees arrived.

When the day crew began to filter into the OR area, Kate

located Leslie Morgan, the chief anesthetist, to give a quick report. She told her about the code during the night and that she really didn't know any of the specifics about the fall itself. She wasn't in the mood for any more MJ talk so she left, as quickly as she could, to avoid any grilling from her colleagues. But the quickest feet in the world couldn't out run the thought of MJ's death or the vision of her lifeless body lying crumpled at the bottom of the stairwell.

Chapter Two

Friday Morning, October 22, 1976

When Kate arrived home, the twins were sitting with Mary at the kitchen table eating cereal. Kate greeted everyone and kissed Shane and Shelby on their foreheads as she walked by them on the way to her room. She had a quick shower, put her bathrobe on, and returned to the kitchen. Even though she missed her dinner at the hospital, Kate still wasn't hungry and decided not to eat.

"Grandma is taking you guys to school today so that Mommy can get some sleep, but I'll pick you up at lunch time and we'll go to Kewpee's for lunch. Then if you aren't too tired, we'll go to the police station and see Uncle Brian. Okay? How does that sound?"

Kewpee's was known as *the place* in downtown Flint for hamburgers and French fries. The restaurant was housed in a charming castle-like building that was once the soda shop for the Vernor's Ginger Ale bottling plant. The always smiling and very vocal Kewpee employees were as colorful as the surroundings, which combined to create a welcome, friendly atmosphere for one of the city's favorite gathering places.

Shane and Shelby were pleased with their Mom's suggestion for their afternoon lunch adventure, especially the chance to get a Vernor's ice cream float. Plus, they were excited about visiting the station to see Uncle Brian.

"Okay, I'll see you later. Thanks for taking the kids to school for me, Mom."

Kate again kissed each of her children, gave her mom a hug, and started to leave the kitchen when her mother stopped her. Kate's words sounded normal but her affect was flat and distant.

"Kate, is everything alright?" Mary asked in that voice of motherly concern.

Kate sighed deeply. "Yes, Mother. I'm just tired. It was a very ... ah... stressful night."

Kate looked at her children and back to her mother, giving a not-in-front-of-the-kids look. "I'll talk about things with you later, but right now I'm just beat. I really need to get some sleep."

"Sure, honey. I understand. You get some rest and we'll talk later," Mary said as Kate left the room.

Mary had immediately noticed that Kate was distracted. She recognized that forlorn expression with the far-away look in Kate's eyes that she'd seen so often after Mike's death. Kate had had a very difficult battle with herself to keep moving forward at that time, and Mary feared she might be slipping back a little.

Mary pushed the negative thoughts aside and made a concentrated effort to convince herself that Kate was only tired, just like she said. At the same time, she resolved to offer to keep the children with her more often over the next several weeks in an effort to give Kate a chance to rest.

Kate used the phone in her bedroom to call the station. She left a message for Brian saying she would be stopping by that afternoon to explain what had happened the night before. After she hung up, she turned the ringer off so that it wouldn't disturb her sleep.

Kate pulled the drapes and climbed into bed. She was exhausted. She hadn't realized just how tense she had been until she felt herself begin to relax as she stretched out between the crisp, cool, cotton sheets. She fell asleep quickly, albeit a fitful sleep with dreams full of dark images that needed saving but were beyond her reach.

About three hours later when Kate awoke at 10:30 a.m., she

still felt tired and was groggy. She rolled out of bed and headed for the kitchen. She fixed a bowl of cereal, and as she put the milk away, she pulled out a can of Coke. Try as she may, Kate could not develop a taste for coffee. She tried it with sugar. She tried it with cream. She tried it with chocolate. She tried it with all of them. She tried it with none of them. Finally, she decided to hell with it. Why should she bother? She would drink Coke. Pop for breakfast, lunch, dinner, and all points in between. She loved the taste of Coke, especially ice cold, straight from a glass bottle. That was the best, as all Coke connoisseurs know. But today she wouldn't be that fussy, she thought as she popped the top on a can of Coke for her first caffeine shot of the day.

Kate dressed as she did most days, in jeans, a sweatshirt, and running shoes. She brushed her long, straight, sun-streaked blonde hair into a ponytail. Her make-up routine was simple, a bit of pale blue eyeliner, mascara, and pink lipstick. She scrutinized her image in the mirror. At 5 feet 2 inches and 107 pounds, she was often described as pretty or cute, never gorgeous or beautiful. But at 25 years old, she could still pass for a teenager. As an adolescent, she resented looking younger than her age but now she rather enjoyed it.

Kate did a bit of housekeeping until it was time to pick up the kids. She parked down the street from the school and started walking up the sidewalk. She stopped when she saw Shelby and Shane running to meet her, waving their most recent artistic creations, and bubbling over with excitement as they told of their latest adventures at school.

As twins, Shane and Shelby shared a special bond and were as close as siblings could be. When they told their stories, their narration came across as one story told by two because they often finished each other's sentences. Kate helped each of the children into the back bucket seats of her car and fastened their safety belts. As they made the short trip from the school to the downtown area, the children continued chattering. Within minutes, Kate was parked in the Kewpee's parking lot and the kids were clamoring to get out.

Lunch was consumed at breakneck speed, partially

because of their voracious appetites, but mostly to get the ice cream float for dessert.

When finished eating, the trio walked hand in hand to the police station just a block down the street. The afternoon temperatures were mild and the trees along the street were bursting with beautiful autumn colors.

Kate waited by the front desk for Brian, and the children visited with the office staff. Everyone had liked and respected Mike and enjoyed it when he would bring the children to visit the station. After his death, Mike's extended police family often included Kate and the children in their social activities and always welcomed them with genuine fondness.

Brian greeted Kate with a hug and a kiss on the cheek. Before he escorted her to a conference room, he motioned to the desk sergeant to keep an eye on the kids for a few minutes. He had some papers in his hand that had "Mary Jo Iverson" written on them.

Brian began, "We got a call about 4:30 a.m. to report that Mary Jo Iverson, a female employee at Temple, apparently climbed over a stair-railing and jumped or fell to her death. An autopsy has been ordered and our detectives will be investigating. That's all I know right now, except that Greg Martin and I might get the case."

"That would be great if you get this assignment because then maybe we could work together. You know, unofficially, of course," Kate said nonchalantly, trying to hide her excitement at the thought of assisting with the investigation.

"Well, we'll have to see about that," Brian hedged.

"Come on, Brian. I know the rules and I've never stepped out of line when we've collaborated before, right?" Kate implored.

"Yeah, but you've never helped with a case like this before. You only gave me medical information and explanations."

"Brian, I only want you to share information with me so that I can try to come to some conclusion on my own as to what happened to MJ. I promise not to get into anyone's way.

Besides, I'll be telling you everything that I find out using my hospital connections," Kate pleaded.

"You know that it's not up to me. Greg's my partner and he has a say in what happens. Besides, we don't have the assignment yet."

"I know that. Just support me if the question comes up."

"Okay, we'll see, but for now, what can you tell me about MJ that I don't already know?"

"She is... MJ is... I mean, was an X-ray tech on the third-shift. I've known her causally for about the last six months or so. She had a reputation of being sort of a party-girl and made no secret of the fact that she wanted to marry a doctor. She was always upbeat, almost bubbly. When some of the nurses took offense because of her too short uniforms, her caked-on makeup, and her continual flirting, she seemed oblivious. Personally, I thought she was a team player and easy to work with. The stories about her party habits were just rumors, as far as, I know. I never saw her act down or depressed and would be completely surprised if she committed suicide. I think her colleagues in the X-ray department feel the same way. The circumstances surrounding the death are suspicious, but I'd like to believe the fall was some kind of an accident."

"Okay, that's a start. Did you see MJ last night?" Brian asked, jotting down notes.

"No, I don't think so," Kate answered after a brief pause.

"Did you notice anything unusual last night?"

"Not that I can recall right off hand, but I'll think about it."

"The detectives will be conducting interviews with the hospital employees today so someone will probably be talking to you. I'll keep in touch with you too, in case you come up with something."

"Thanks, Brian. And talk to Greg for me, will you please? I want to help. Please give me a chance," Kate said, placing her hands together in front of her chest as if she were praying.

Kate stood to leave. "I'd better get the kids and go home.

You have to go back to work and I need to get some things done before work tonight."

Brian and Kate walked back to squad room arm in arm as they chatted about how much the twins have grown. Brian looked at Kate, who was smiling when she said, "Not to change the subject or anything, but how's your love life these days?"

"Always the romantic, aren't you Kate? Well, sorry to disappoint you, but it is the same today as every other day lately. Nonexistent! I don't have the time, besides I haven't met a suitable lady that makes it feel right. You can understand that, can't you?"

"Yes, I understand that all too well, but you have been saying that for a long time. If that nurse, you know the one that I was telling you about that I work with, ever becomes, should I say 'available,' I'd like to try to set you two up on a blind date. What do you think?"

"We'll see," Brian mused, rolling his eyes.

After a few minutes more of visiting, Brian again promised to keep in touch. Kate and the twins said all of their good-byes and walked back to their car at the restaurant.

It took a huge effort on Kate's part to keep the mood light in an attempt to protect her children from the gritty realities of life that were playing out before her eyes. Her intuition kept telling her that MJ's death was drawing her into a perilous position. The thought of putting herself in harm's way put a knot in her stomach. As intrigued and excited as she was to investigate, she knew that her first and foremost obligation was for the protection, well being, and best interests of her children.

At home, Kate had two calls to make. First, she called her parents to arrange for the children to have dinner and sleep over, because the next day, Saturday, they wouldn't have school. Next, she called the pathology department at Temple to speak with Dr. James Park.

Dr. Park is the chief pathologist and the county medical examiner. He worked with Kate on a project of hers from nursing school, and they have remained friends ever since.

Today, luck was with Kate. Dr. Park was in his office and available to take her call. She explained to him that she had been on duty and had responded to the MJ Iverson code. She told him she had concerns about the questionable circumstances surrounding the death, especially as to how they may relate to her and her third-shift working assignment. She asked for a report on the physical findings from MJ's autopsy.

Dr. Park told Kate that the postmortem exam was scheduled for the next morning and that he would be glad to assist her. He had no qualms about discussing the Iverson case with Kate because as a respondent to the code of MJ Iverson, Kate already had legal access to MJ's chart and records.

She gave him her home phone number so he could contact her during his daytime office hours in case she missed him in the morning after her night shift.

Kate spent the next couple of hours playing with the twins until her mother arrived. She smiled when she saw Mary skip down the sidewalk with Shelby on one hand and Shane on the other. The children used their free hand to carry their little overnight cases.

Kate's lack of sleep was catching up to her, and she knew that she would be useless tonight if she didn't get some rest. She turned the radio on and changed it from station to station until she heard some soft music. She set her alarm for 10 p.m. and had no difficulty falling asleep.

Friday night at Temple was almost always busy and from the look of things when Kate walked in, tonight would be no different. Patients were crowded everywhere when she walked through the ER to the elevator lobby. Dr. Dunbar caught up to her just as she entered the elevator. He put his hand up and held the door to stop it from closing.

"Kate, will you meet me for coffee sometime tonight?" Dr. Dunbar spoke with urgency and sincerity, and with no sense of his usual sarcasm.

"Uh, sure, if I can. It really depends on how busy we are in the OR tonight. I'll call you."

Kate continued up to the tenth floor. No one was in the

office so she assumed they were busy in the OR. She quickly changed into her scrub clothes, covered her hair, put on a mask, and went to OR 7.

OR 7 is the largest operating room in close proximity to the OR offices, lounges, and supply rooms and therefore, was most often used on the late shifts because of the convenient location.

Rae was at the head of the OR table finishing her charting in preparation for Kate to relieve her. The patient on the table was a 30 year-old male who had been in a car accident. He had no fractures or head injury but had sustained a lacerated liver. The surgeon, Dr. Mark Dwyer, and his assistant, a first-year surgical resident, Dr. Nick Lecorts, had completed the repair on the liver and were checking for any other internal trauma before closing. After giving report to Kate, Rae was finished with her shift, and the patient's care was transferred to Kate.

Rae's usually upbeat mood was subdued. She stood by while Kate monitored and recorded the patient's vital signs, reviewed the chart and anesthesia record, checked the anesthesia equipment and supplies at hand, and noted the surgeon's progress. Rae knew that all of those steps were necessary for Kate to acclimate herself to the status of the anesthesia and surgical situation. Kate addressed the surgeon to announce that she had relieved Rae as the anesthetist and gave him a status report on the patient. Once Kate had settled in at the head of the table, Rae began whispering in her ear about MJ's accident. Kate listened as she kept vigil over the patient.

"I couldn't believe it when I heard about MJ. We went partying together a few times. She was always fun, you know, ready for a good time. Some say accident, others say suicide. What do you think?"

"I find it really hard to believe that it was a suicide," Kate whispered. Dr. Dwyer shot her one of his "be quiet" looks over the top of his half-glasses.

Rae also saw Dr. Dwyer's silent reprimand. She waved to Kate and turned to leave the OR. Once she was out of Dr. Dwyer's sight, she pulled her mask down and with exaggeration, mouthed the words "I'll talk to you later" before she exited the OR suite.

Army was at the scrub sink and soon would be gowning and gloving to relieve the second-shift scrub tech. Maggie was already taking report from the RN on the case.

Dr. Dwyer, an excellent trauma surgeon and teacher, explained his methods and techniques to the resident while he finished the exploration. Dr. Lecorts watched intently as the master worked and was pleased when Dr. Dwyer allowed him to close the incision.

Maggie, Army, and Kate had yet to have an opportunity to discuss the events of the night before. Normally, they would have talked about it in the OR during the case but not with Dr. Dwyer there. All conversation is his OR had better be related to the case at hand.

It was 1:30 a.m. by the time the case was finished and Kate and Maggie transported the patient to his room. Kate stayed to give report to the RN receiving the patient. Maggie returned to the OR to help Army finish cleaning OR 7. Next, they went to the workroom to clean and package the instruments that had been used during the case. When Kate got back to the OR, she cleaned, stocked, and readied OR 7. Although no other cases were scheduled, there was a C-section pending.

By 2:30 a.m., the OR was quiet and Kate's chores were done, but Maggie and Army were still busy in the instrument room. Kate took this opportunity to call Dr. Dunbar in ER, who agreed to meet her in the cafeteria in ten minutes. She fetched the code box and told Maggie that she was leaving the floor for thirty minutes.

Kate took the elevator to the first floor. It had only been one night since MJ's deadly fall and Kate wasn't ready to use the back stairwell, especially since she was alone. She saw Dr. Dunbar sitting in the dining room section reserved for the physicians where she joined him. He stood as Kate approached and helped her with her chair.

"Always the gentleman," Kate thought.

"Hi, Dr. Dunbar," Kate said.

"Hi, Kate. And please call me Tom."

Dr. Dunbar seemed atypically nervous and was having difficulty initiating the conversation. Kate sat quietly and waited for him to make the first move because she really had no clue what the meeting was about. He finally started talking to the table, unable to face Kate.

"I wanted to talk to you to explain some things," Dr. Dunbar stammered. "I know that you think that I'm some kind of an arrogant asshole."

Kate started to object but he held his hand up and continued to talk. Obviously, he didn't want to be interrupted so Kate sat back in her chair and let him finish.

Now Dunbar faced her. "And to some extent, you might be right. I know I act like a jerk sometimes but I'm harmless. Really," he sighed almost to himself. He paused as if gathering strength. "I want to talk to you about MJ. I can't believe what happened."

"What did happen? Do you know?" Kate quietly asked.

"All I know is that one of our nurses, you know, Becky Wilt?" Kate shook her head yes. "Well, Becky was going up to the cafeteria. She opened the door to the stairwell just as MJ landed. Becky was startled and screamed in horror. She yelled down the hall toward ER for help before she checked MJ. Becky said she didn't hear MJ scream or make any noise at all. The only sound she heard was MJ's body hitting the cement floor. MJ's eyes were closed and she wasn't breathing. She landed mostly on her back so Becky did a quick assessment, being careful not to move her head or neck. She could see a pool of blood forming on the floor under MJ's head. MJ's carotid pulse was weak and irregular, and then it stopped. The ER crew arrived almost immediately. We started CPR and moved her to the ER. You know the rest. We couldn't get her started. We just couldn't get her started," he repeated, shaking his head and looking away.

He blinked back a tear and continued. "I expect the post to show that she died from the fall but I can't figure out how or why she fell. If she had slipped or tripped, she would have fallen only one flight to the next landing. But to have gone down the middle, she would have to have gone over the safety rail. I don't understand how anyone could accidentally fall over that rail. I also don't believe that anyone could have forced her over the rail even if they had wanted to. She would have hollered her head off and given one hell of a fight. Which brings us to the last option, that she jumped. I just don't believe it. I can't believe it."

He paused again. Tears again welled up in his eyes and his voice cracked. "Kate, I'm telling you all of this because I don't have anyone else I can talk to about MJ who will understand. You may not even understand but I have to talk to someone. We've known each other for a long time now. You've always been honest and straightforward with me. I need a friend right now."

Dr. Dunbar was quiet. Kate looked down at the table, trying to absorb everything he had said and wishing she had a Coke to sip on. He sat back in his chair and slammed his fist onto the table causing her to jump. A few people looked up but no one said anything.

He regained his composure and continued. "MJ and I had been dating for the last month and I really liked her a lot. Her little flirty act was just as pretentious as my sarcasm and smooth lines. We both used an attitude as a protector, an insulator against rejection. When we got beyond the surface junk, we found that we had a lot in common and we enjoyed each other's company. I was even trying to sever ties with my other women friends which I had never done for any other woman."

"That might be a monumental task, given your reputation," Kate thought.

Dr. Dunbar looked sad and lonely. "On the night she died, MJ and I had plans to meet at 3:30 a.m. on the tenth floor landing of the back stairs. It was kind of a special place for us. That was where we first ran into each other, literally." He was talking more rapidly as if he had to hurry and finish his thoughts while he was still composed. "She must have gone there early. She knew I was coming. She knew how I felt. She wouldn't have jumped. None of this makes any sense."

Kate began to realize the depth of his anguish and felt ashamed for not being more sympathetic to his confession from the beginning. It also occurred to her that if MJ had made it to her rendezvous point for her meeting with Dunbar, then she was literally within feet of where Kate was sleeping in the anesthesia lounge when she went over the safety railing in the stairwell. "Had I been sleeping so soundly that I couldn't hear a call for help?" She wondered.

"Oh, Dr. Dunbar. Tom. I am so very sorry for your loss. This has got to be so difficult for you and to have responded to her code on top of everything else."

Kate touched the backs of his hands with her hands for a moment as she silently communicated her support and understanding for him. While they were sitting quietly, Kate saw Maggie approaching. She quickly jumped up and went to meet Maggie in an effort to distract her long enough to allow the teary-eyed Dr. Dunbar a graceful exit.

"Hi, Kate. What's going on with Dunbar?" Maggie asked, watching his rather abrupt exit.

"Oh, nothing," Kate said casually. "We were just having coffee but he had to get back to ER. It's always something, you know."

Kate changed the subject. "Any word about the C-section patient?"

"Yes. Joey called and said that the patient delivered so the section won't be necessary."

"Good for her. Vaginal delivery is always better for the patient." Kate checked her watch. "I was just getting ready to go back up stairs. Are you staying down here to eat or getting something to take back up with you? We haven't had a chance to talk much about last night, and I'm interested in what you think."

"I'm not sure. I want to check the food before I decide. Why don't you go back and I'll see you when I get there, a half-hour at the most. We can talk then."

When Kate got back to the OR, Army told her that he had just scheduled a trauma case. She rechecked the anesthesia setup in OR 7 before she went down to the ER to get a history and physical report from the patient and to talk to any relatives that might be present.

Kate saw Dunbar and Maggie standing by the desk talking when she entered the ER. Assuming that Kate was there to interview the trauma patient scheduled for surgery, he directed her toward cubicle No. 2. Kate started to talk to Maggie about the scheduled surgical case, but Maggie interrupted her by nodding her head and holding up her hand as if to say, "Don't worry, I have things under control."

Kate took Maggie's hint and proceeded to cubicle No. 2. She pulled the curtain aside and entered the small patient area where she practically ran into the surgical resident, Dr. Lecorts, who had just finished examining the patient's laceration.

"So, we meet again. Actually, I guess we've never really met. I'm Nick Lecorts and you are...?" he said as he reached to shake her hand. When he realized that his gloved covered hand was bloody, he apologized and quickly lowered it.

Kate smiled at the slightly embarrassed doctor. "Kate McKenna, nurse anesthetist. Nice to meet you, Dr. Lecorts," Kate replied, purposely addressing him by his title since a patient was present.

This was the first time that she actually looked at Dr. Lecorts. At 6 feet 2 inches, he was a foot taller than Kate and drop-dead gorgeous. He had lot of very dark brown hair, a slightly olive complexion, a charming smile that accentuated his dimples, and beautiful dark brown eyes that twinkled when he smiled.

When Kate felt herself staring at him, she quickly turned her attention back to the patient. She noticed an elderly lady with a bloody bandage on her right hand and arm. Dr. Lecorts excused himself while Kate spoke with the patient.

"Mrs. Hutcheson, my name is Kate McKenna. I'm a nurse anesthetist and I will be giving you your anesthesia tonight. I have a few questions for you, and then I'll explain everything that's going to happen regarding your anesthesia. When I'm finished, I'd be happy to answer any questions you may have."

Kate finished her pre-anesthesia assessment, provided Mrs. Hutcheson with information and reassurance, and excused herself when she left the cubicle.

Kate saw Dr. Lecorts at the ER desk with the patient's chart. He filled her in on all of the pertinent information on Mrs. Hutcheson's chart and explained the proposed surgical plan. She completed the anesthesia care plan that was attached to the history and physical form where Dr. Lecorts had made his notes, complete with his signature at the bottom of the page.

The physician's signature declared that he had performed a history and physical examination on the patient prior to surgery. It also served as the doctor's order, requesting that the nurse anesthetist on duty provide the anesthesia.

Kate finished her pre-operative charting and waited for the ER staff to finish the patient's OR preparation. When everything was ready, Kate helped to transport Mrs. Hutcheson to the operating room.

Dr. Lecorts scrubbed on the case with the attending surgeon, Dr. Andy Barlow, one of the younger physicians on staff. Dr. Barlow allowed conversation in the OR because the patient was asleep. Finally, they had an opportunity to talk about MJ but no one in the room seemed to have any new information about the death, aside from gossip. The subject quickly changed to the upcoming presidential election between Michigan native Gerald Ford and Southerner Jimmy Carter. Because Flint is a union town, the majority of the voters are Democrats. The OR debate for the evening was whether the constituents would follow the Democrat tradition or support their native son.

The case went well and Mrs. Hutcheson's tendons were repaired. Kate took her patient to the surgical unit on the eleventh floor, gave report to the nurse on duty, and returned to the OR by 6:45 a.m.

It was 7:30 a.m. by the time she finished her work and reported off duty. She decided to stop by Dr. Park's office to see if, by chance, he had arrived yet. Even though it was Saturday, she knew that he would be coming in sometime that morning to do the post-mortem exam on MJ.

Dr. Park was sitting behind his desk with his reading glasses perched on the end of his nose as he reviewed the stacks of reports on his desk. When Kate knocked on the door, he looked up and over his glasses.

"Well, come right on in here young lady," he said in his soft southern accent. "I was just going over the Iverson chart. I understand that Miss Iverson worked here. Did you know her?"

"I knew her but not well, only here at the hospital. She was one of the regular third-shift crewmembers so we often worked on the same cases. Like I mentioned before, I responded to her code and I find the circumstances surrounding her death very suspicious. I'd like to have more information to help me answer some of the lingering questions I have about this whole incident. I hope you have some news you can share with me."

"I don't mind telling you what I know."

Kate smiled graciously and he continued.

"The post is scheduled for 8 a.m. From the brief preliminary exam that I made just after she was admitted, I can tell you that she broke her neck and has a depressed skull fracture with massive trauma to the brain and the brain stem. That was undoubtedly the cause of death, or at least, the most apparent one. She also had multiple bruises, contusions, and lacerations. She probably sustained internal injuries and other fractures, as well."

"Do you have any results from the blood screen?"

"Yes, just a minute," he said as he flipped through some papers. "Nothing. No alcohol, no barbiturates, no tranquilizers, no amphetamines, no marijuana. Let's see, no uppers, no downers, no hallucinogens, no street drugs, no nothing."

"Well, that's good to know because to me that makes suicide even less likely. I want to find answers but I'm really hoping that it wasn't a suicide. I guess I don't want to carry any guilt because of some suicidal sign that I should have seen but didn't. Boy, that sounds self-serving. What I really mean is that a homicide is a terrible thing, but suicide seems even more pathetic. MJ's death would be easier to accept if it was the result of some kind of a terrible accident."

Kate continued, "I did talk to a couple of her coworkers, but none of them could offer any explanation as to what might have happened. It was a routine night, nothing special. MJ signed out for a break at 2:50 a.m. and never came back. The next they knew down in X-ray was that she was dead."

"Do you have any more questions?" he asked.

"Let me see, not that I can think of just now. Thanks for your help. I really appreciate it a lot," Kate said. "We had a busy night last night so I'm on my way home to get some sleep. Talk to you later and thanks again."

Dr. Park waved and turned his attention back to the papers on his desk. He had a few more minutes before he had to go down to the morgue to begin the post on MJ.

Chapter Three

Saturday Morning, October 23, 1976

Kate hurried home, had a quick shower, ate a bowl of cereal, and was asleep within two minutes of closing her eyes. She had had an irregular sleeping schedule for such a long time that she had trained herself to shut her mind off and fall asleep quickly, which worked quite effectively on most occasions. The problem she had now was that she couldn't stay asleep. Often she awoke after only an hour or so, and then she couldn't get back to sleep. Most of the time she walked through life in some stage of sleep deprivation. This morning, however, she had no difficulty sleeping until noon.

When she awoke, she felt well rested and better than she had in days. Determined to put thoughts of the hospital business aside, at least for the day, she concentrated on spending the afternoon with her children doing "Mom" stuff. She went to her parents' house for lunch and to pick up the twins.

She had a special afternoon planned for the kids. She took them to the store to buy their Holloween costumes. They had a great time trying on all of the different masks and costumes, changing their voices and personalities with each new character. After scrutinizing ever costume in the entire store, they finally made their choices. Both decided that they wanted to be a character from their favorite TV show, "Sesame Street." Shelby chose "Big Bird" and Shane chose "Cookie Monster."

Sunday Morning, October 24, 1976

Kate took the children to Sunday school and afterward they went to her parents' home for dinner. Kate told her mother the basic facts about the tragedy at the hospital that had caused her distress on Friday morning.

Mary already knew about MJ's death because she had read about it in the paper. And she had already figured out that that must have been what had caused Kate's edginess when she got home from work. Mary was pleased that Kate had confided her feelings to her rather than suppressing them as she often did. Mary decided that everything with Kate was all right and that she could relax her guard a little over Kate's emotional well being.

Kate asked Mary if she would mind watching the children for several hours that afternoon because she wanted to attend the memorial service for MJ that had been planned at the hospital chapel for 2 p.m. Of course, Mary agreed.

Kate, still dressed in her church clothes, left her parents' house and headed straight for the hospital. It felt strange for her to be going to the hospital all dressed up. But her clothes were just another factor contributing to her general discomfort. She hadn't talked to any of her colleagues about the memorial service so she had no idea who would be there or what to expect.

The hospital chapel is quite small with only enough seating for about thirty people. Most of the seats were filled. There were no doctors present aside from Dr. Dunbar and Dr. Arden Scott, the chief of staff. She saw a couple of department heads, a few from administration, and a small representation from both the X-ray department and the general third-shift staff. None of MJ's family was present. Someone mentioned that they had planned to have their own private service after the medical examiner's office released the body for burial.

The hospital chaplain, a minister from one of the neighborhood churches, made the only comments during the service. From what he said, Kate assumed that he didn't know

MJ. She guessed he talked to MJ's supervisor to gather the bit of personal information that was included in his remarks.

It was a sad ceremony. Sad because she died so young, sad because of the shared assumption that she had caused her own death, but most especially sad, because during the service not one individual acknowledged having a personal relationship or friendship with MJ.

Kate left immediately at the conclusion of the service. She was not in the mood to talk to anyone. She drove around town for a while trying to clear her mind and adjust her attitude before she returned to her parents' home. Tomorrow was a school day and she had things to do.

Kate spent a quiet evening with the twins and took time to read two nighttime stories.

After the kids were in bed, she had housework and laundry to do. When 10 p.m. rolled around, instead of winding down, she started to get a second wind. She found enough chores to keep her busy until about 2 a.m. She showered, went to bed, and finally fell asleep about 3. She tossed and turned all night.

Monday Morning, October 25, 1976

When Kate's alarm sounded, she answered the phone before she was awake enough to realize that it was her alarm clock ringing, not the phone. She groaned as she got out of bed and crossed the room to silence the obnoxious noise.

Kate had moved the clock from her bedside table to the dresser years ago after she turned the alarm off in her sleep one morning causing her to miss an appointment. She couldn't take the chance of sleeping through another alarm, especially now that her sleeping schedule was so inconsistent.

She was still tired but she forced herself to wake up. She splashed her face with cold water before she looked at herself in the bathroom mirror. She saw a very haggard person looking back at her.

"Oh, Kate. You really need to start taking better care of yourself. You look awful!" she chided herself out loud.

"Shane! Shelby!" she called in a melodic tone. "It's time to get up and get ready for school."

Kate was lucky. The kids always woke up in a good mood and got going without protest. They began their morning routine and Kate headed to the kitchen to fix their breakfast. After the table was set with cereal, toast, and juice, Kate opened a can of Coke for herself. While the children ate, she finished getting ready.

After dropping the kids off at school, she stopped by to visit her parents who were having after-breakfast coffee.

"Hi, you two. How are you this morning?" Kate asked with a pseudo-cheery tone. She got a Coke from the refrigerator and joined them at the kitchen table.

"I'm good," Mary said.

"Me, too," John chimed in.

"And you, young lady. In spite of the sunny tone of your greeting, I can tell by the dark circles under your eyes that you aren't so good," Mary said.

"Well, I guess there's no fooling you," Kate said, stating the obvious.

"That's right. Moms always know."

"I knew that there was no way of getting past you. I had a look in the mirror this morning so I know how bad I look."

"Oh, Kate. I didn't mean to say that you looked bad. I just..."

Kate interrupted her. "I know what you meant, Mom. You're right. It's okay. You didn't hurt my feelings. I'm not upset. Really."

Kate reached for her mother's hand and gave it a squeeze.

"My problem is that I'm just really, really tired. That's one of the reasons why I stopped by. I have a few calls to make and errands to run this morning, and then I'd like to try to get some good sound sleep. I'd really appreciate it if you would pick the kids up from school."

"Don't give it a second thought, honey. I'd be glad to pick them up," John said, patting Kate's shoulder.

"Thanks, Daddy. I'd like to sleep during the day and pick

them up by suppertime. That way we can spend the evening together. Will that work for you?"

"Sounds good," John answered as he poured himself another cup of coffee.

"Would you like something to eat?" Mary asked with almost a pleading tone.

"Thanks, Mom, yes. I'd really like a bowl of oatmeal with brown sugar and cinnamon toast."

Mary was delighted. "Good, good. I'll fix it right away."

Kate ate her breakfast and visited with her parents a while longer before she returned home to make her phone calls. She dialed the number to the police station.

"Brian Goss."

"Hi, Brian. This is Kate. How are you this morning?"

"Not bad yet but it's starting to get busy already."

"Oh, okay. I'll get to the point. I just wondered if you had any news that you can share with me."

"Just a little. The case was assigned to Greg Martin and me. I don't know how well you know him but he is one of the good guys."

"I don't really know him at all. He's from the east-side so I recognize him when I see him. I know he's been your partner for a while, but we've never actually been introduced. It's good to hear that you respect his work but I wouldn't expect anything less from a partner of yours."

"Flattery won't work, Kate."

"That wasn't flattery, Brian, that's the truth. Anyway, I picked up a little information from a couple of doctors and some of MJ's coworkers. We'll have to get together soon. I'll call you later when you have more time."

"Okay. Thanks, Kate. Bye."

Kate called Dr. Park. He wasn't in his office so she left a message with his secretary saying that she would be stopping by his office to review MJ's autopsy report first thing Tuesday morning when she got off duty.

It was only 10:30 a.m., but Kate felt that she could easily fall asleep. She pulled the drapes in her room, turned off the ringer on her phone, disrobed, and eased under the covers. She closed her eyes, took a few deep relaxing breaths, and gently drifted off to sleep, very much like one of her patients under anesthesia.

Kate opened one eye and peered at her clock to check the time, 5:30 p.m. "Seven straight hours of sleep. Must be some kind of a record," she thought. She sat up and stretched.

After a shower, Kate felt totally renewed. She dressed and went to her parents' house, where she ate supper before returning home with the children. During dinner, John and Mary both commented on how much better Kate looked and wasn't it amazing what a few hours of sleep could do for a person.

Kate and the twins played board games for about an hour before it was time for the children to bathe and get ready for bed. After story time, it was lights out.

Mary arrived at 9:30 p.m., and Kate was off to the hospital. She felt good and was optimistic that tonight would be a good night. She arrived early so she could stop in the ER to talk with Dr. Dunbar for a few minutes before her shift. They walked together to the elevator lobby for a little privacy. He seemed to be in a little better mood but was still upset. They had only a few minutes to chat before the elevator came. During that brief time, they made tentative plans to talk later.

Dr. Dunbar was on his way back to the ER when Maggie stopped him. "Tom, I tried to call you all weekend."

"I wasn't answering the phone. I guess I needed some down time. What did you want?"

"I was concerned about you. You've been putting in a lot of hours lately. You need to take better care of yourself. You look really tired. You should have let me come over and cook for you. I'll bet you haven't had a decent meal in days. See, you need me to take care of you," Maggie said.

Maggie was moving closer and closer to Dr. Dunbar while she talked until their faces were inches apart. He was looking at everything around but her, trying to tune her out. Finally, when he could no longer ignore her because she was literally in his face, he took a hold of both of her arms and gently backed her up. His voice was stern.

"Maggie, I told you several weeks ago that we wouldn't be seeing each other anymore. Things haven't changed."

"I know what you said about breaking up, but I'm sure you didn't really mean it. After all that we've been through together, I know how much we mean to each other. Tom, I love you and I know you love and need me, too. We need to be alone and talk this through."

Maggie continued but Tom wasn't listening. He was distracted by his own thoughts. How could he possibly think about Maggie when MJ was the only one on his mind?

"Tom? Tom!" Maggie insisted loudly, when she noticed that he wasn't hearing a word she said.

Dr. Dunbar pulled his thoughts back to the present. "What?" He spit the word out with annoyance.

"I said, 'I think that we need to talk this through,' don't you agree?"

"Yes. We obviously need to talk about this."

"All right. Good. I know that you have to get back to ER and I have to get upstairs. I'll call you in a little while so we can set something up for later tonight. Okay, Tom?" Maggie asked.

Maggie waited for his answer but he just walked away.

Maggie ignored his irritation. She was smiling, pleased with herself that she'd finally gotten through to him. She knew that he had been distracted lately by that little slut MJ, but all of that didn't matter any more because she was very much out of the picture. Now things could go back to the way they were. She loved Tom so much and she knew that he loved her, too.

The OR had been very busy all weekend, all day Monday, and most of that evening, but by the time Maggie, Army, and Kate started their shift, it was quiet. Kate hoped that things would stay that way for a while because she wanted to do a little more information gathering, especially since she learned that MJ was probably very near her on the tenth floor when she fell.

Rae joined the third-shift staff that had gathered in the OR office. She said the rumor mill was working overtime about MJ's private life. She heard that MJ was seeing a single doctor in what was being described as "a relationship with good potential," whatever that means. She also heard that MJ's wonderful relationship had already gone sour, and she threw herself down the stairs to stop the pain of a broken heart.

"Well, enough of that business for tonight. I'm out of here. Kate, all of the ORs are cleaned and stocked and so is the code box. Have a good night," Rae said as she left the office.

As soon as Rae stepped on the elevator, Maggie stood to address Army and Kate. "I can't imagine that you actually believe that some man, a doctor no less, would ever be interested in MJ for anything more than a piece of ass. Isn't that what she is, correction was, famous for? And I don't understand all of this sympathy for that clumsy piece of trash. She couldn't even walk down a flight of stairs without falling over the guardrail, for God's sake. I am not the least bit interested in that little slut and if you are going to continue talking about her, then I'm going to find something else to do." Maggie stomped out of the room.

From her name one might assume that Maggie was Scottish but from her looks, the guess would be Irish. She has red curly hair, fiery green eyes, and her complexion is fair and freckled. Usually, she was quite attractive but during her tirade, her face was so distorted that Kate could hardly recognize her.

Kate and Army looked at each. Dumbfounded, they said in unison, "What was that all about?"

"I don't understand her outburst at all. Something has to be going on with her that probably doesn't even have anything to do with the hospital or work, never mind with MJ. I'll give her fifteen minutes or so, and then I'll try to find her. Maybe she needs someone to talk to for a change instead of always being the good listener. She was there for me so many times, I'd like to help her if I can," Kate said sympathetically. She headed out to check the ORs.

"Women, I just don't get them," Army said to himself, shaking his head.

After she left the office, Maggie went to the workroom where she called Dr. Dunbar. "Tom, everything's quiet for now. Can you meet me at our place on 10 at 1 a.m.?" Maggie cooed into the phone.

Tom didn't try to hide his irritation. "Yes, I'll meet you. You're right, we need to talk. I'll see you in OR 5 at 1."

"All right, Tom. I'll see you then," Maggie said, oblivious to the tone of Tom's comments. "I love you," Maggie said. Tom had already hung up the phone.

By the time Kate caught up with Maggie in the instrument room, her whole attitude had changed. Maggie was singing as she stowed the instrument and drape bundles. Kate never mentioned Maggie's earlier behavior but rather just reported that she was on her way to finish her room checks and to put a set up in OR 7.

Maggie told Kate that she was going to finish her assignments so everything would be done for the night because she wanted to use the quiet time to review a journal in the hospital library.

Kate left the instrument room bewildered. Trying to figure out these strange mood changes of Maggie was becoming more and more difficult. "Maybe some things are just beyond explanation," Kate thought to herself as she headed for OR 7.

Kate thought about Maggie while she worked. Eventually, she convinced herself that maybe Maggie hadn't really been acting that strange. After all, everyone was on edge lately. Kate thought that she was probably acting just as weird. She was evaluating her own behavior when her heard a knock at the door. She turned toward the door expecting to see Maggie and was surprised to see Dr. Lecorts.

"Hello, Kate McKenna, C-R-N-A," Nick said, emphasizing each letter of her title. "How are you this fine evening?"

"I'm well, sir, and how are you?" Kate answered with an air of pseudo-formality.

"Good, thank you. I had a few minutes so I thought I'd come by to visit you, but it looks like you're busy right now. What are you doing?"

"I'm opening and preparing the anesthesia supplies in this room so everything is ready for a patient. We call it 'setting up the room' or making the room 'patient ready'. I always keep one OR set up because I don't want to get caught unprepared if some doctor decides to bring a patient straight to the OR without scheduling first. I'm the only anesthetist in the hospital on third-shift and there's no one else here that can do my work. I have to be ready. How did you find me?"

"Just took an educated guess."

Kate eyed him suspiciously. "Really?"

"Actually, I knocked on the anesthesia lounge door and when I didn't get an answer, I looked in the surgery office. When I didn't see you there, I came to OR 7 and here you are working you little fingers to the bone. So, are you any good at you job?"

"Most people think so. I'm always learning more but I think that I'm pretty good and getting better all of the time."

"I don't want you to jump to any conclusions or let it go to your head, but I have been asking around about you."

"You what?" Kate shot back at him, a little sharper than she had intended.

"Calm down. I was asking about the expertise of the anesthesia staff because I have an interest in anesthesia. I was especially curious about the nurse anesthetists because we didn't have nurse anesthetists in Saskatchewan where I went to medical school. Only the doctors gave anesthesia. I was wondering about your medical background and training. Plus, if I am going to be a great surgeon someday then I need to know about anesthesia, too. Right?"

"You have got a good point there. The better the surgeon understands the anesthesia process, the easier it is for me to do my job, and for him to do his. So, what can I do for you?"

"That's a loaded question?"

His response surprised Kate. She became flustered and started to blush. "I meant, why are you here? May I help you with something?"

"I certainly hope so. I'm sure that I'll be really hungry

when I get finished with my shift in the morning and I'll need a good nourishing breakfast. I've eaten in the hospital cafeteria too many times and I'm ready for a change. I was wondering if you could recommend a good place?"

Kate replied with naïve directness and without the slightest inkling that Nick was about to suggest a breakfast date. "I don't often eat breakfast out but when I do, I usually go to the Big Boy over on Dort Highway."

"That sounds good but I don't know where Dort Highway is. I'm going to need some directions."

Kate looked at him with disbelief. "Surely he's kidding," she thought.

Nick continued, "And it would be nice to have some company."

Kate smiled but said nothing. It finally dawned on her that not only was he flirting with her, but he was also asking for a date.

"So would you join me?"

Kate explained that she had to go home and get her children off to school, but she could meet him at 9 a.m. Nick agreed and the plan was set.

She drew a little map for him with the directions to the restaurant. When she handed it to him their hands touched. She was surprised at the intense sensation she felt from such a brief contact. She wondered if Nick was aware of the spark that she felt.

Nick started to leave when he stopped and made one more comment. "I really do have some anesthesia questions that I would like answered. I was wondering if you would give me some good common sense knowledge about anesthesia?"

"Kind of like 'Anesthesia 101' or 'All You Ever Wanted to Know About Anesthesia and Never Got a Chance to Ask,'" Kate said with a hearty laugh.

"That's exactly right," Nick said, laughing along with Kate. "Maybe we could talk about it at breakfast?"

"Sounds good to me. I'll see you later."

Nick left and Kate finished her work. She felt exhilarated

but yet, she had a small, nagging reservation. She had not been attracted to, never mind dated, any man since Mike's death so she needed a little self-convincing and reassuring that this interest in Nick would be proper. She began making mental lists of the pros and cons of having a breakfast with him. After several minutes of careful deliberation, she was confident that she had made the right decision.

"Yes," she told herself, "having breakfast with Nick will be okay."

Kate was replaying the last few minutes in her mind when she went to the office to check on Maggie. Army had gone to visit with Joey, leaving Kate and Maggie alone on the floor. Kate wanted to keep the conversation light to prevent a repeat performance of Maggie's earlier outburst so she decided to ask Maggie about her "boyfriend."

The distraction worked. Maggie was happy to talk about the love of her life but she still wouldn't reveal his identity. She told Kate that he had been very busy the past few weeks so she hadn't seen as much of him as she had wanted to. But things were going to change because she knew that she was a priority in his life. He told Maggie that he'd been so concerned about her spending time alone, waiting for him, that he actually considered ending their relationship for her sake. But she told him absolutely not. She knew that they were such a special couple that a little inconvenience from a busy schedule should never be a deterrent to their relationship.

Maggie talked for a long time about how she cooked for him, gave him massages, bought him clothes, and was knitting a sweater for him. Everything she did was for him. She gave him everything he wanted or needed, or that she thought that he wanted or needed.

Maggie sounded like she was committed to him, almost to the point of obsession. That thought left Kate with an uneasy feeling that she immediately tried to dismiss. Kate wondered if he felt the same way about her, and if he appreciated everything she did for him. She hoped so for Maggie's sake.

Maggie appreciated that Kate had listened to her carry on

about her wonderful man and her extraordinary relationship. She sat back and looked at Kate with sympathy.

"Poor Kate," she thought. "Here I am going on and on about my life and I haven't ask you a thing about how you are doing," Maggie said sweetly and sincerely.

Kate was thankful that she could talk to Maggie and avoided any reference to MJ. Mostly, she talked about her weekend with the children and the fun things that they had done. She casually mentioned that she had finally met someone who made her look twice. She had known him by sight for while, but she finally talked to him. He invited her to have breakfast with him. She wasn't sure that she was ready to start dating again, but he was interesting and he made her laugh. Kate purposely refrained from mentioning Nick's name because she was reluctant to make claims of any kind of a relationship when none actually existed.

Maggie eyed her suspiciously but made no comment about Kate's revelation. She was curious about the identity of Kate's new attraction but since Kate hadn't pressed her for a name when she talked about her lover, Maggie felt that she should grant Kate the same courtesy. She changed the subject.

"I've finished all of my room rounds and assignments. I'd like to call a friend in Florida at 1 a.m. She works until midnight and we always have a hard time reaching each other. We made plans to talk tonight if I wasn't busy. Army will probable stay down on L&D for a while so do you think you could answer the phone from about 5 to 1 a.m. until I get back from the first floor pay phone?" She checked her watch. "It's about 12:30 right now."

"Sure. That gives me time to run down to ER for a second. I'll be back shortly and then I'll be in the anesthesia lounge."

"Okay, I'll stop by before I leave the floor to make sure that you're back," Maggie said.

Kate left the office, grabbed the code box, and walked across the rotunda and around to the back stairs. She hadn't used those stairs since the night MJ died. She knew that she had to eventually and she decided that now was the time. From the first step, she felt so uncomfortable that she ran all the way to the basement. She spotted Dr. Dunbar in the ER sitting at the desk working on a patient's chart. She chatted with him while he charted. She decided against telling him about Maggie's outburst. It wouldn't do any good and would probably just make him feel worse than he already did. She was ready to leave when his tone changed. He said he had some good news for her.

"Someone has been asking me about you," he said coyly.

"And who might that be?" Kate asked.

"Oh, just a lowly surgical resident by the name of Nick Lecorts."

"So, you're the one he was talking to. He came up to the OR a little while ago for a visit. He seems like a nice guy."

"I bet you wouldn't give him a hard time if he called you Katie."

"Yes, I would," she snapped. Then she backed down and softened her tone. "I mean no, I probably wouldn't." She felt a little embarrassed but didn't understand why she should. "I didn't really give you a hard time, did I? I was kidding you just as much as you were kidding me," Kate said in her own defense.

By this time, they were both laughing. It felt good. Kate checked her watch, noting that it was time to get back up stairs. When she started to leave, he gave her a quick hug. She excused herself, saying that they should contact each other later. On the trip back to the tenth floor, she noticed that she could smell Dunbar's cologne on her lab coat. "He always wears too much of that stuff," she thought.

Kate had just walked into the anesthesia lounge when Maggie appeared at the door. Maggie gave her the strangest look and said, "You smell like Dr. Dunbar."

"Yeah, I guess I do," replied Kate. "I just saw him down in the ER and he gave me a hug. He always wears too much cologne. Some of it must have rubbed off."

Maggie turned and left without a word. She stopped after a few steps and forced a smile for Kate's benefit. "Please answer the phone if it rings. I'll be leaving soon."

Kate agreed. She settled onto the couch and replayed

the last few minutes. She was certain that she had just seen a flicker of something in Maggie's behavior, something curious, something not normal, but just exactly what that something was, Kate couldn't explain. She was beginning to question her instincts. So many strange things had been happening lately it was hard to say just what normal really is any more.

Maggie was furious. She stomped back to the workroom. Her mind went into overdrive and her thoughts were darting about and slamming into each other, causing minor explosions with each collision.

"That back-stabbing little bitch. I knew something was up with those two. I saw them down in the cafeteria holding hands. She tried to distract me so I wouldn't notice, but I did. I just knew she was talking about him earlier in the office when she was telling me about the new guy in her life who made her look twice and invited her to breakfast. She must think I'm the biggest idiot in the world. All that time, pretending to be my friend, when all she really wanted was my man," Maggie thought. She had an obscene image of Tom and Kate together.

Maggie felt herself losing control and she tried to calm down. Her chest was heaving rapidly and she started to hyperventilate. She began to feel faint so she sat on a nearby stool and dropped her head down to her knees. She took slow, deep breaths and concentrated on clearing her thinking. She didn't want Kate to be the "bad guy" because she had been her best friend, maybe her only friend, for the past year, and for Maggie, finding a friend was difficult.

"Let me think. Let me just slow down and think. Things aren't really adding up here. Kate has always been open and honest with me. It never seemed like she was trying to hide anything from me, in fact, just the opposite."

She tried another approach to resolve to her dilemma. "Kate doesn't know who my boyfriend is so she couldn't know that she was hurting me. She is my friend. She is my best friend and is not trying to betray me. Yes. That's the truth," Maggie said to herself in a calm, quiet, advising tone.

"He is the one who's not my friend, that sorry son-of-a-bitch. First he couldn't see me because of that little whore MJ, but I eliminated that problem. Now he thinks that I am going to hang around and wait on him hand and foot while he goes after my very best friend in the whole world. Well, he's crazy. He's out of his goddamn mind if he thinks I'm going to stand still for any more of his bullshit," Maggie said a little louder.

She regained her composure. Her appearance and attitude had again changed. She was calm and her breathing was slow, deep, and regular. She had an air of determination and resolve. She knew what had to be done.

Maggie had already made the arrangements for Dr. Dunbar in the OR for their meeting. When they were seeing each other regularly, they sometimes met in OR 5 and that is what she had planned for him tonight.

OR 5 is a large room at the far end of the A corridor, away from the offices and lounges. The room has a surgical procedure-viewing platform that can't be seen from the little windows in the double doors between the corridor and the room.

Maggie had prepared their spot on the platform as usual, with blankets and pillows to make a little love nest for them. Most of the time their meetings in OR 5 were quick liaisons, but on one occasion when both the ER and OR were quiet, they had more time to explore their desires and develop their fantasies.

Tonight, the meeting would be different. Dr. Dunbar had forced Maggie's hand. The romantic rendezvous that she had planned for him would never take place. Things had changed. Maggie decided that Dr. Dunbar would be spending his eternity with his beloved MJ. She had to hurry to finish the rest of the preparations for his surprise before 1 a.m., when he would arrive for their meeting.

Dr. Dunbar signed out of the ER at 12:55 a.m. He walked up to the first floor and passed the empty business offices that lined the A corridor until he came to the staircase at the end of the hall. He climbed the stairs to the tenth floor. This route made it highly unlikely that anyone would see him or know his destination. He arrived at OR 5 at exactly 1 a.m.

He would have preferred to meet with Maggie somewhere other than in the hospital and most especially, in any place other than where they had been intimate. But she was so persistent and so unreasonable that he needed to explain to her once and for all that he was just not interested in having any type of a relationship with her. He wanted her out of his life. She was acting so possessive that he didn't even want her for a friend. He would try again for the easy let down but if she didn't get the point, he would have to be direct and rude. He needed this chapter in his life to be over. He resented spending any time thinking about that bitch right now. She was crowding his space. He should be able to let his mind concentrate on his feelings for MJ and to deal with his grief for her without Maggie's interference.

When he stepped into OR 5, all of the lights were out. He could see somewhat with the help of the narrow beams of moonlight streaming through the OR windows. As his eyes adjusted to the dim light, he noticed Maggie's outline up on the observation platform where she waited for him.

She was trying to conceal her anger by taking deep breaths to relax. When she saw Dr. Dunbar, she said nonchalantly, "Hi, Tom. I'm glad you could make it. It's nice to see that you are so punctual. I guess we have some talking to do."

Her little act fooled him and he let down his guard. He thought maybe, she finally knew what he had been trying to tell her for weeks. Maybe, she finally understood that it was over between them.

"Hi, Maggie." He walked toward her on the platform. He climbed the six steps up to where he could see Maggie more clearly. She was seated on the blankets she had placed on the floor of the platform. He sat down on the floor facing her before he began to speak.

"I was hesitant to meet you tonight, but I'm glad we have this chance to be alone. We really do need to talk. Do you understand what I've been trying to tell you these past few weeks? We had a few weeks together that were nice, but now it's over."

"I know that's what you have been saying, but I didn't believe you. I couldn't believe you really meant that you didn't want to be with me. We've been through so much together. We were so committed to each other."

He realized that she was irrational and out of touch with reality. He tried to be calm, but she was trying his patience. The more she said, the angrier he got.

"I don't know what you're talking about. We had dinner a couple of times. We went to your place a couple of times. We had a few quickies in the hospital. That's it. We haven't been through anything together, and I never said that you were anything more to me than a friend," Tom reiterated for the umpteenth time.

Maggie responded in a sickeningly sweet voice. "Tom, I know that you never said you love me, but it would have come to that if it hadn't been for that little slut MJ. She's the one that came between us."

He gazed at her in disbelief. Then his eyes narrowed as he spit out the words to his next question. "What are you talking about?"

Maggie ignored his question. "I knew that you had been seeing her these past few weeks. You wanted to spend time with her instead of me. But I figured if she was out of the way that you would come to your senses and realize that I'm the one you love."

"You goddamn crazy bitch, what have you done?" Tom yelled at her.

His piercing eyes stared hatred at her. He wanted to hit her. He had to get away.

Dr. Dunbar turned away from her and started to leave the platform. When he did, she plunged the needle on the syringe she was holding into the base his neck and injected its' contents. He turned toward her, surprised by the assault.

"What the hell do you think you're doing?" he mumbled.

Dr. Dunbar's words trailed off. He stumbled when he tried to take a step. She grabbed his arm preventing a fall and eased him down onto the blankets.

"Like I said," Maggie continued sarcastically. "I figured that if MJ was out of the way, you would come back to me, but oh no, you couldn't do that. You had to go after Kate, my very best friend in the whole world. You wanted to leave me alone with no lover, no best friend."

Maggie kept talking while she uncovered her supplies. Everything she needed was ready.

"I suppose you're curious about what happened to MJ. Since you're such as captive audience, so to speak, and you're so interested, I'll tell you," Maggie said with caustic sweetness. "I knew the two of you had been meeting on the rotunda stairwell on the tenth floor. You know, your special place on ten. I followed you up the stairs one night. I thought you were coming up to see me. I almost called to you, but then I realized that you were on your way to see her. There she was, waiting for you on the tenth floor landing. Anyway, I was in ER Friday night when I overheard you tell her to meet you on 10 at 3:30 a.m. You are such an insensitive bastard. You used almost the exact words to her that you had once written to me.

"It was fate that brought your plan to meet MJ to my attention. Like a dutiful lover, I saved every note that you ever gave me. I immediately went to my locker to check them and sure enough, there was one that said 'Meet me at our place on 10 at 3.'

"Perfect, I thought. All I had to do was slip the note to MJ, which I did when I stopped by the X-ray department. It was so easy. I just said, 'Oh, it looks like you dropped something.' She picked up the note that I had planted on the floor and read it with a smile since she obviously recognized your handwriting. She was so thankful to me for finding the note and kept telling me so. What a stupid bitch! All I could think of was how much I was going to enjoy getting rid of her.

"Of course, I was the one who met her. After she got her little shot of succinylcholine, it was simple to push her over the railing. She deserved it, you know, interfering with my life like that. She was using her perverted sexual favors to lure you away from me, and I was determined to stop her. And I did stop her, didn't I?"

Maggie continued her monologue as she worked fast and furious to complete her plan. She knew that the initial dose of succinylcholine she had given would be wearing off within minutes so she had to quickly complete the task at hand.

Succinylcholine is a muscle relaxant that paralyzes but does nothing to render the "patient" unconscious so he could hear and understand everything she was saying. As the fervor of her tirade intensified, the pitch of her voice increased. When she realized that she was screaming at him, she made an effort to control her tone, lest she get caught.

After putting gloves on, she placed an IV catheter in his left hand, to which she connected an IV tubing that she had prepared earlier. She opened the clamp on the tubing and the fluid started dripping into his vein. She explained to him that the IV fluid contained sodium pentothal. She told him that he would soon be going to sleep forever.

"You should be happy," she told him. "Now you can be with your beloved slut, MJ, forever."

Dr. Dunbar became unconscious. Maggie taped the IV catheter more securely and put his fingers on the tape. Next, she put his hands all over the IV bottles and tubing to make sure that his fingerprints would be found. She positioned him lying on his side with his right hand on the IV tubing clamp. She removed the blankets, pillows, and everything else that could show that she had been there.

She checked his vitals. He had stopped breathing and his pulse was weak and thready. She leaned down to kiss him on the forehead but decided against it.

"Bye, Tom," she whispered. She left the room.

Maggie checked the time, it was 1:30 a.m. "Only thirty minutes to erase that mess from my life. It's time to start over," Maggie thought. She put the linen down the laundry shoot and returned the pillows to the linen storage area. She placed the papers and boxes that had contained the IV tubing and solutions, the medication vials, and the gloves she had used in a plastic bag in her locker. While in the nurses' lounge, she washed her hands and arms, and changed into a clean scrub dress. She wouldn't want people to think that she smelled like Dr. Dunbar, now would she?

Maggie went to the OR office to finish some paperwork. She had been seated at the desk for only a few minutes when the phone rang. Kate came to the door of the anesthesia lounge to answer the call but saw that Maggie had returned.

The call was from pediatrics. They had a 10 year-old boy with a "hot" appendix that needed to be scheduled immediately, Maggie announced after hanging up the phone.

Kate headed to OR 7 to set it up for a pediatric patient. Maggie called L&D to tell Army to get back up to the OR to set-up for the case.

The OR team spent the next couple of hours preparing for, completing, and cleaning up after the appendectomy before retiring to their respective lounges to wait the arrival of the day-shift crews.

While alone, Maggie retrieved the bag of trash from her locker and added it to the trash from the appendectomy case. She was pleased she'd covered her tracks so well, but causing deception and erasing clues had become her forte. She could easily write a highly impressive and convincing single-spaced, two-page resume on her experiences with covert activities. She gloated to herself that she was so much smarter than anybody around there, or as a matter of fact, anywhere.

About 2 a.m., the list of patients waiting in ER to see a doctor was getting longer and longer. Two physicians were on duty but one of them, Dr. Dunbar, had taken a break around 1 a.m. and never returned to the ER. At the direction of the other doctor, the ward clerk began looking for him. She called the operator to have him paged. She also called the cafeteria, the laboratory, the library, and various doctors' lounges and call rooms throughout the hospital but no one had seen him, and he never answered his page. The ER staff, more perturbed than worried by Dunbar's absence, continued with their work.

Chapter Four

Tuesday Morning, October 26, 1976

By 7 a.m., Kate hadn't received another call from Tom so she figured that ER had gotten busy or maybe he was just talked out. She was impatient to get home. She reported off duty and headed straight for her car until she remembered she was supposed to stop by Dr. Park's office. She retraced her steps back to the hospital and headed to the pathology department, where she turned down the hall to his office.

He wasn't in but he left her a copy of the preliminary autopsy report on MJ with his secretary. She thanked the secretary, folded the report, and put it into her purse. Again, she headed for home.

Kate felt happy, vibrant, and not the least bit tired. She was getting excited about her date. She turned on the radio and sang at the top of her lungs along with the new hit "Dancing Queen" by ABBA, while she drove.

On the short walk from the garage to the backdoor, Kate felt the October chill. Thc funny thing was that she couldn't remember any coolness on her walk from the hospital to her car. She must have been too occupied with thoughts of Nick to notice. The idea of enjoying the company of a good-looking, eligible man seemed surreal. She tried to get a grip on her emotions and imagination. She reassured herself that she was being realistic with both feet planted firmly on the ground. No floating on clouds for her, not this early in the morning anyway.

Maggie started the two-block walk to her small bungalow. She was feeling better than she had in more than a month, during which time she briefly, very, very briefly, thought that she might be getting sick again. Now she knew for sure that she had been wrong because when she was sick, she was never, never happy, and today she was happy, very happy.

"Boy, am I glad that everything is okay because I am not in the mood to start taking those goddamned pills again," Maggie said to herself as she recalled the regime of tranquilizers, antidepressants, and antipsychotics that her physician in Florida prescribed for her manic/depressive schizophrenia.

Maggie was home in less than ten minutes. She showered and went to bed. As she was lying in bed trying to sleep, she began to think about Tom. She vowed to never think about him again. He was gone, erased from her life. She would never again look back to any of that unhappiness. Onward and upward, that's where she was headed.

Her thoughts changed to Kate, her very best friend in the whole world. She recalled a time when Kate offered to introduce her to a friend who worked at the police department. Maybe the time was right for her to take Kate up on her offer. Kate would introduce her to the man who would, without a doubt, be the one true love of her life.

She felt vitalized by the thought of finally having a life that would be "happily ever after." Sure that she wouldn't fall asleep with so many wonderful thoughts filling her mind, Maggie decided to take a sleeping pill. She went into her bathroom, removed a make-up case from under the sink, and opened it. She began sorting through the case. It was filled with prescription drugs of all kinds from at least ten different physicians, some from Florida and some from Michigan.

She finally selected a bottle labeled "Seconal." She poured two of the capsules into her hand and recapped the bottle. She threw the bottle back into the case and put it back under the sink. She went to the kitchen and opened a beer. She swallowed the two pills and downed the beer. She watched TV for a while until she started to feel drowsy. She turned the TV off, took her phone off the hook, and went to her bedroom.

Well, that should do the trick," Maggie sighed as she yawned and stretched. She removed her robe, hung it over her bedroom door, and slid her nude body between the sheets. Her thoughts quickly became fuzzy and she drifted off to sleep.

The OR staff gathered around the office to receive the daily report and case assignments. The group split up into twelve teams, one for each operating room. Each team, consisting of one RN and one ORT, gathered the supplies, instruments, and other equipment that would be used for the cases scheduled in their OR.

Having finished "pulling their cases", Faith, RN and Paula, ORT, the team assigned to OR 5, quickly headed down the A corridor to set up. Their first case was a bowel resection with one of the slowest surgeons on staff. It often took so long for him to close the patient's incision at the end of the procedure that everyone was sure that the inside had already healed before the skin was closed.

Faith and Paula knew that they would probably be spending the whole day in the OR with no chance for a break. They wanted to set up the room, as quickly as they could, so that they could get a break and have a smoke before the case started. They entered the room and flipped on the lights. One by one, they opened the sterile bundles of drapes, gowns, instruments, and supplies that they had placed on the flat top tables positioned around the room.

While Paula continued opening packages, Faith started checking the ancillary equipment in the room. She noticed that one of the IV poles was missing.

"Why is it that every time I'm in a hurry, someone pinches some of my equipment?" Faith complained.

"What's missing?" Paula asked.

"One of the IV poles. I'll have to go find one," Faith said. She started out of the room.

"Hey, wait!" Paula called, when she spied the pole. "It's up on the observation platform."

Faith turned back into the room. "What the hell is that

pole doing up there?" she said. She headed toward the platform stairs.

Faith stopped short on the third stair. She grabbed the handrail, did a double take, and screamed at the top of her lungs. Paula dropped the handful of suture packets that she had begun to open and looked at Faith who continued screaming as she tried to back down the stairs. Not known for being particularly graceful under the best circumstances, Faith fell on the floor at the bottom of the stairs. She stopped screaming, picked herself up, and cautiously started back up the stairs. At the top, she took a closer look at Dr. Dunbar. She checked for a pulse. There was none.

A crowd had begun to gather around the entrance of OR 5. Faith sent Paula to the office to notify the head nurse and any available doctor while she ushered the crowd away from the doorway. She closed the door and stood guard until the head nurse, Shannon Hill and Dr. Andy Barlow, came down to the room.

Dr. Barlow checked Dr. Dunbar's condition. He was dead. Shannon called the hospital operator and told her to notify the hospital administration, the chief of staff, the police, the hospital security, and the medical examiner that Dr. Thomas Dunbar was found dead in one of the operating room. Next, she called the entire OR staff to the office and told them that an accident had occurred in OR 5 that had resulted in a death. The crowd began to mumble.

"Please, I must have your attention and your confidence. To stop any speculation, I will tell you that the person that died was Dr. Thomas Dunbar, one of our ER doctors," Shannon said.

A slight gasp broke the silence.

"I can also assure you that Dr. Dunbar's death appears to have been an accident and none of you need be in fear for your safety."

Shannon told the staff that the OR schedule would be adjusted to include the cases from Room 5 and no cancellations would take place. The discretion and cooperation of all of the staff was requested, and they were told to avoid any discussion that might disturb the patients. The staff was also advised to cooperate with the hospital administration and the Flint Police Department as they conducted an investigation. The staff was told that at 3 p.m. they should reconvene at the OR office to be updated.

The police dispatched Detectives Brian Goss and Greg Martin to Temple Memorial Hospital in response to a report that another Temple employee was found dead inside the hospital. When they arrived on the tenth floor, they were directed to the doctor's locker room to change into scrub clothes. They were escorted to OR 5 by Shannon and Mr. Clare Eggleston, the hospital president, who had arrived in the OR office shortly after he was notified of Dr. Dunbar's death.

The investigation would begin with interviews of the team that had been assigned to OR 5 because they were the ones who had found the body. Detective Martin conducted the interviews with Faith and Paula, while Detective Goss went back to the doctors' locker room to assist the rest of the members of the crime team in locating the appropriate OR attire. Dr. Jim Park had already changed into scrubs so he gave Brian a hand with the rest of the police team, most of whom he knew from his work as the county medical examiner.

"Hi, Dr. Park," Brian said as he reached out to shake Dr. Park hand. "How are you?"

"I've been better," Dr. Park replied. "This death is very disturbing."

"Yeah, I know what you mean. It kind of looks like it might be a suicide."

"Well, we'll see," Dr. Park said as they all headed down to OR 5.

"Good morning, Mother. Hi, my little sweeties. How is everyone this morning?" Kate asked, grinning from ear to ear, hugging her mother, and kissing each child on the top of the head.

Kate pulled a chair back from the kitchen table and joined them while the children ate their toast and cereal. She poured herself a glass of orange juice but declined her mother's offer for anything to eat.

"You certainly are cheery this morning. It must have been a good night at the hospital."

"Not too bad actually. Did an appendix on a kid that went very well."

"Do you have any plans for today?" Mary asked.

"I have an appointment at 9 a.m. I'll go after I drop the kids off at school. I'm not sure how long it will take. I also have to try to reach Brian and Dr. Park."

Mary figured that Kate wanted to talk to Brian and Dr. Park about the death at the hospital. She didn't like the idea that Kate was insinuating herself into a situation that didn't seem to be any of her business but she had learned a long time ago that Kate had a mind of her own, and her curiosity always got the best of her. If Kate thought that she could make a positive difference in someone's life then she would dedicate the time and effort it took to make it happen.

"Sounds like you may not have a chance to get any sleep this morning. Why don't I pick the twins up from school and keep them until supper? That way you'll have a chance to sleep. If you like, I'll cook supper for all of us so you can eat before you leave with the children," Mary suggested.

"Mom, that sounds great," Kate said, pleased with her mother's offer.

Directing her attention to the twins, Kate said, "You two little munchkins finish up here and then go brush your teeth while I go have a shower."

Kate finished her juice, slid her chair back from the table, and left the room.

Once in her room, she took her clothes off and stood nude in front of the full length mirror on the back of her closet door. She had always considered herself the athletic type. In high school, she played field hockey, softball, and ran track but she hadn't been as active lately. In fact, the only real exercise she got these days, aside from all of the walking at work, was when she went biking with the twins. They got bicycles last spring and she tried to go biking with them at least once a week.

She studied her image in the mirror turning from side to side. She thought that she still looked pretty good in spite of a few faint stretch marks on her tummy. As she struck a seductive pose, she laughed out loud at herself.

In the bathroom, she washed her face and brushed her teeth before her shower. That was her routine. She always used a special soap on her face and she hating having bad breath when everything else was clean so she had to do things in that order. Her friends claimed that habit was another sign of her obsessive/compulsive behavior but she regarded her actions as regimented.

Kate decided not to wash her hair so she fastened it up with a barrette and put on a floppy shower cap. She started toward the shower but stopped. She opened the cupboard under the sink and removed a toiletry gift set. She took the soap from the box and entered the shower. The hot water felt good on her skin. She worked up a lather with the perfumed soap that she had been saving.

"Saving for what? A special occasion? This *was* a special occasion," she thought.

Out of the shower, she used the lotion and powder that came with the soap. She brushed her hair into a ponytail that she braided. She used her blue eyeliner, mascara, and pink lipstick. She dressed in a T-shirt and jeans with a pullover sweater and running shoes. She checked herself in the mirror again and nodded her head with approval at her reflection.

Kate dropped the kids off in front of their school and watched them with pride as they made their way up the sidewalk to the front door. She loved them so much. Just watching them made her feel blessed.

While she drove, Kate sang, "I'd Really Love to See You Tonight" along with England Dan and John Ford Cooley on the radio. The morning was cool but the sun was shining, the leaves were changing beautiful shades of red and gold. What a beautiful day!

She entered the restaurant and glanced around but she didn't see Nick. She started to panic. Her mouth went dry, her heart pounded, and she immediately regretted that she had accepted his invitation. She checked her watch. It was 8:53 a.m.

"Oh, my God. I'm too early," she thought.

She panicked. She didn't want to appear too enthusiastic, or worse yet, desperate. She wanted to retreat. She felt stupid. She decided to go back out to her car and wait ten minutes before she came back in, when she saw Nick coming out of the men's room.

Nick spotted Kate immediately and motioned her over to a booth where he had apparently been sitting before her arrival. He stood until she was seated then he sat down across the table from her.

They both started to speak at once and both stopped as if on cue. Nick said, "Ladies first."

"I see you have some coffee already. Have you been waiting long?"

"No, not really, maybe about fifteen minutes. I didn't order any food, just coffee. Are you hungry?"

"Yes, I like some raisin bran cereal with skim milk, whole wheat toast, and a Coke, please."

Nick was looking down at the menu as Kate rattled off her order and looked up with surprise at her response.

"A Coke?" he questioned.

"I know. A lot of people think it's weird that I have Coke for breakfast but, try as I may, I cannot acquire a taste for coffee or tea so I drink Coke to get me going, especially after working the night-shift."

They talked casually about the hospital while they ate. They continued talking after the dishes were cleared. Nick continued sipping on his coffee. Kate had finished her Coke long ago. Their conversation took a personal turn when Nick looked directly at Kate and bluntly asked her to "tell me all about yourself."

Kate began her story.

"I was born at Temple Memorial Hospital and raised in an

east-side Flint neighborhood, the East Village. My parents are from Flint and have lived here all of their lives. After my dad graduated from high school, he took a job with General Motors where he worked until he retired last year. My mother is, as she had always been with the exception of a two-year stint as a secretary, a full time homemaker. I am an only child, born after my mother had two miscarriages. I was raised in a loving, caring home, where the income was just a little more than what was needed so I had all of the basics and some of the extras. I had a very happy, healthy childhood.

"I met my husband, Mike, when we were just children but I never considered him anything more than a friend until my junior year in high school. Mike was a senior that year. One day he took a different look at me and saw a young lady instead of his neighborhood tomboy buddy. That's when we started dating.

"Mike graduated from high school and started working at one of the GM plants. The next year, after my graduation, we were married. I started nursing school that fall and Mike joined the Marines. After my second year of school, the twins were born. I started back to school, as soon as I could, and I finished about the same time as Mike's discharge from the Marines. He joined the Flint Police Department when he returned home. I worked in the operating room at Temple for a while before I started the nurse anesthesia program there. I was near the end of my anesthesia training when Mike was killed, shot by a passenger in a car he had pulled over. Since his death, all of my energy has been concentrated on my children, parents, home, education, and career."

Nick listened attentively. When she finished, he said, "What about you?"

"What do you mean?" Kate questioned.

"I mean, when is the 'personal you' going to be a priority in your life?"

"Well, I did put time in on my education and career but I haven't had much time for the personal me. After Mike died, I didn't do very well emotionally. I had never had to face any personal tragedy in my whole life unless you count when my cocker spaniel, Sugar, died.

"I've come a long way over the last year. Grew up a lot. Took charge of my life. Learned independence. Not independence really, I've always been independent but I learned how to be on my own. You know, accepting the responsibility for my children and taking care of them and myself. Being there for them when they need me, like someone was always there for me. I'm doing well these days and I guess I've begun to think about the personal me. I'm here, aren't I?"

"So you are," Nick said, smiling warmly.

"Now it's your turn. Tell me about yourself, Dr. Lecorts."

"That's Nick."

"Yes. Nick."

The waitress came by, filled Nick's coffee cup, and brought Kate a fresh glass of Coke. Nick started telling his story.

"My grandfather, Nickoli Lekortsokov, was born in Kiev, the capital city of the Ukraine. When he came to Canada in the early 1900s, his name was officially changed to Nick Lecorts by the immigration services as was frequently done to accommodate language translation difficulties. He met and married a Ukrainian girl named Anne Pakulak, who had immigrated about the same time that he had. They moved to Saskatchewan where they bought a quarter section of farmland. That's 160 acres. They built a two-room log home where they raised ten children before they retired from farming and moved to a small house in town.

"My father was the third child but the first son. He was named Orest after his grandfather. He carried on the family tradition as a farmer and bought a quarter section of land adjacent to his parents' land. Originally, he built a small log cabin for his bride, my mother, Olga. Later, he built a larger house that eventually had electricity, although it never did have running water.

"My parents had six children and I, being the oldest son, was named for my grandfather, Nickoli. I was also the first to declare that I wanted a life away from the farm. My desire to go to the university met with a variety of reactions but no opposition. My family was always very supportive psychologically but not much financially because no one had any extra money. Most of my extended family had barely enough means for their own survival, yet they always lent whatever support they could afford. My family has been my personal cheering section and I love them all very dearly.

"After pre-med school, which I finished in three years rather than the customary four, I was running very low on funds. I took a year off from my studies and worked in the gold mine at Yellowknife in the Northwest Territories. The following year, I entered medical school at the University of Saskatchewan in Saskatoon, where I can say with all modesty that I was an excellent student and junior intern.

"After graduation from medical school, I accepted a rotating internship at Temple. The hospital has a very successful recruiting program with the University of Saskatchewan. Previous participants in the Temple intern/resident program gave high recommendations so I felt quite confident in my plan to come to Michigan. I finished my internship and started a residency in general surgery last July. That brings my story up to the present."

"Really, that's all of it? There's no 'significant other' along the way? I find that hard to believe."

Nick seemed a little embarrassed by her compliment.

"I left that part out because I didn't want to bore you. But since you asked, I did have two relationships in undergrad school that lasted about six months each. I really didn't put much time or effort into them because I didn't have the time or money to spare.

"In medical school, I had a serious relationship for two years with a girl named Carolyn. She was a classmate and we had planned to open a rural family practice together. But a year before graduation, she was critically injured in car accident. She sustained a severe closed head injury and was in a coma for months. She eventually woke-up but with significant mental and physical disabilities. She didn't even know me when I would visit her. She needs long term managed health care and is living in a nursing home in Saskatchewan. For a long time after that, I was emotionally unavailable and I just put my personal life on hold to concentrate on my medical career. Recently, I decided to pay more attention to the business of finding a lifetime partner. I've wanted to start dating again for some time and I've had a few dates since coming to Flint, but I haven't met anyone who even remotely piqued my interest for a second date. Until now, that is."

Kate smiled. Now it was her turn to be mildly embarrassed.

"What a nice thing to say," she said graciously.

"It's true, Kate. I've thoroughly enjoyed this time with you. I hope that we can see each other again soon. But for now, I've got to get going."

"Before we leave, there is one more thing I'd like to ask you about," Kate said.

"Sure, what is it?"

"Did you know MJ Iverson and what, if anything, do you know about her death?"

"That's two questions."

"I know but it's only one subject."

"Okay. I didn't know MJ by name but I'd seen her around the hospital. And I don't have any first hand knowledge about her death. All I know is the hospital gossip. I heard that she fell or jumped over the safety stair rail and died on impact with the basement floor. Was she a friend of yours?"

"Not exactly, just a coworker really."

Kate glanced at her watch and was surprised to see the time. "It's almost eleven. I have to go, too. I've got to work tonight and I need to get some sleep before then."

Nick and Kate left the restaurant together. He walked her to her car and helped her with the door. He made some flattering comments about her little sports car and how it seemed to fit her personality. He promised to call her sometime in the next couple of days, but both were sure that they would see each other at the hospital before then. They spent hours talking but hadn't mentioned anything about anesthesia. He reminded her that he was serious when he said he wanted some anesthesia facts.

"It wasn't just a 'pick-up line,'" he said. He made her promise to set up another date so she could bring him up to speed on her anesthesia techniques.

Kate was home and in bed within twenty minutes but she couldn't sleep. Too much caffeine and too many thoughts about Nick kept her mind churning. She got out of bed and cleaned the house, did a couple loads of laundry, made a shopping list, went through her mail, and paid her bills. Now, she was physically tired and very sleepy. She turned the ringer on her bedroom phone off, climbed back into bed, and fell asleep quickly and soundly, anticipating sweet dreams.

Chapter Five

Tuesday Afternoon, October 26, 1976

Greg Martin was back in his office at the police station going over some of the findings of Dr. Dunbar's death with Brian Goss. In his preliminary report, Dr. Park suggested that suicide was highly probable. Dr. Dunbar was an ER physician who was skilled at starting IV's. Being right-handed, he could have easily started an IV in his left hand. Plus, there was an obvious lack of any other apparent cause of death. The autopsy and toxicology screens should give the definitive answer.

The team covering the crime scene took the IV tubing and bottle to the police lab to be checked for fingerprints and drugs. Nothing besides the used IV equipment in the OR seemed amiss. The room was dusted for fingerprints, but as expected, no prints were found since everything in the operating rooms, including all of the furniture and even the walls, is wiped down every day at the end of the scheduled surgeries.

The two sets of prints found on the stair railing that led to the observation platform in OR 5 were later identified as those of Dr. Dunbar and Faith, the RN who found his body.

The initial determination of the time of death was somewhere between 12:50 a.m., when he left the ER and 7:20 a.m., when his body was discovered. The detectives determined that the employees on duty in the operating room during that time were Maggie, Army, and Kate.

"Brian, why don't you contact Kate this afternoon and tell her about Dr. Dunbar's death in case she hasn't already heard about it. Find out if she knows anything about it or heard or saw anything out of the ordinary last night."

"Okay. Actually, I was hoping I could be the one to break the news to her. Maybe it won't be as upsetting coming from me," Brian said as he was leaving Greg's office.

Greg continued, "While you're talking to Kate, I'm going to try to contact the other employees, Armstrong Sargent and Margaret MacGregor."

Both detectives left the station about the same time.

Army spent the night and part of the next day with Joey so he didn't return home until the following afternoon. He was only home for about five minutes when a car pulled into his driveway.

Greg Martin introduced himself. He told Army about Dr. Dunbar and some of the circumstances surrounding his death. Army was asked to give an account of the previous night, as best he could remember, which he did. Greg advised Army that he would be questioned again and that he should try to recall any other details that might be helpful to the investigation.

After Greg left, Army immediately called Joey and told her what had just happened. He told her that the events over the last few days had him concerned. He was particularly worried about her safety. He made arrangements to pick her up for work at 10:30 p.m. that night because he didn't want her alone in her car or in the parking lot at the hospital.

Maggie awoke to the sound of someone pounding on her front door. She climbed out of bed and put on her robe that was lying on the floor where she had dropped it earlier that morning. She stopped at the living room window on her way to the front door and peeked out between the drawn drapes to see who was at the door. She spied some man that she didn't recognize. Still half-asleep and slightly cautious, she cracked open the door, leaving the guard chain in place.

"Yes, sir?" Maggie said through the small opening.

"Are you Margaret MacGregor?"

"Yes, I am. Who are you and what do you want?" Maggie questioned him.

"My name is Detective Greg Martin. I'm with the Flint Police Department," he said, holding up his badge and identification. "There was an accident at Temple last night and we are interviewing staff members who were on duty at the time. May I came in and talk to you for a few minutes?"

"Just a second," Maggie said. She shut the door to release the security chain. She checked her image in the wall mirror by the front door, arranged her hair a little, and straightened her robe before she reopened the door.

"There now. Come right on in and have a seat. Can I get you anything?" Maggie said as she directed the detective to the couch.

"No, thanks. I'm fine," he said. He sat down and took out his note pad.

Maggie listened intently as he described the events surrounding the discovery of Dr. Dunbar's body in the OR suite. She showed what she thought would be the appropriate amount of surprise and distress. He continued by asking about her night at the hospital.

She said she couldn't recall anything out of the ordinary but she would think about it. She said that they had done an appendectomy on a child about 2 a.m., she thought, but the record could be checked. Greg told her that she would be questioned again. He thanked her for her cooperation and left.

Kate awoke around 4 p.m. feeling refreshed. She had a number of calls that she wanted to make before going to her parents' for dinner and she felt pressured to get started. She wasn't particularly hungry so she just popped the top on a Coke and got her list of phone numbers.

Kate was ready to dial Dr. Park's office when she remembered she had put her copy of the preliminary report of MJ's autopsy in her purse without even glancing at it.

She got her purse and removed the report. She unfolded it slowly and deliberately as she walked to the kitchen table. She smoothed the report out on the table very carefully with both hands, almost ceremoniously, as if out of respect for MJ. She took a deep breath and began to read.

Externally, it was noted that MJ had a severe depressed skull fracture with lacerations. It was apparent that her neck was fractured. Multiple smaller lacerations, abrasions, and contusions were noted on practically all areas of her body but especially on her limbs. She didn't appear to have any defensive wounds on her hands, fingers, or anywhere that might indicate that she had tried to defend herself against an attacker. No tissue was found under her fingernails. There was no apparent trauma that indicated the use of any type of a weapon. She didn't have any ligature marks on her neck, wrists, or ankles.

The internal examination revealed that she was a previously healthy young woman, normally developed, with no acute or chronic illnesses. She was not pregnant. Her brain and brain stem showed massive trauma that was determined to be the cause of death.

The serum toxicology report was included with the autopsy report. It was negative for any sign of drugs or alcohol. The tissue toxicology report was pending.

The clothing that MJ had been wearing at the time of her death showed no obvious signs that she had been dragged across the floor prior to her fall. There was no apparent evidence of foul play nor was there any direct evidence that would support the theory of suicide. The summation at the bottom of the report was simply stated.

"Death due to massive trauma to the head and neck, resultant from a fall."

"No one has any answers as to the 'how' or 'why' MJ fell to her death," Kate said to herself.

She sat in silence for what seemed like a long time, trying to digest everything the report had revealed, as well as, everything it didn't say. She was deep in thought when the ringing phone jolted her back to the present. She answered after three rings. It was Brian.

"Hi, Brian. I'm glad you called. I wanted to talk to you. I

was just getting ready to start calling around because I wasn't sure where you would be at this time of the day."

"Kate, what are you doing?"

"I just finished reading the results of MJ's autopsy report."

"Are the kids home?" Brian said with unusual directness.

"Why? What's up? You sound... I don't know... formal. Brian, what's going on?"

"Kate, there have been some new developments. I'd like to fill you in on them but not over the phone. Can you meet me somewhere so we can talk?"

"New developments, what kind of new developments? New developments in MJ's case?"

"Not exactly. Something happened at the hospital last night, but I don't want to get into it on the phone."

"Okay. Why don't you come over here? The kids are at my parents'. I'll put on a pot of coffee. It'll be done by the time you get here."

"Sounds good. I'll be there in about fifteen minutes."

She put the coffee on and hurriedly brushed her teeth, washed her face, brushed her hair, and got dressed. She was just finishing the Coke that she had started earlier when the doorbell rang.

She opened the front door and greeted Brian with a quick hug. He came in, headed for the kitchen, and seated himself at the table as if he were at home. He had spent so many hours in that kitchen at one time that it did indeed feel very much like home. Kate poured him a big mug of black coffee and she opened herself another can of pop before she sat down.

Brian wanted to start with the autopsy report. She showed it to him and explained some details he didn't understand. None of the basic information was new to him but he did appreciate some of her explanations. Now it was his turn to share what he had learned.

"When the investigators were going through MJ's clothing for any clues they, of course, checked her pockets. In one of the pockets of her uniform, they found a hand-written note that said, 'MEET ME AT OUR PLACE ON 10 AT 3.' They showed it to some of the people who had been working with MJ that night but no one claimed to have written it. However, one of the X-ray techs from the second-shift thought she recognized the handwriting as that of one of the ER doctors named Dr. Tom Dunbar. When ER employees were shown the note, they agreed."

Kate nodded. "Yeah. Dr. Dunbar told me that he had been dating MJ for a few weeks before her death. It probably was his handwriting. Actually, Dr. Dunbar's relationship with MJ was one of the reasons I wanted to talk to you today."

"Do you know him?"

"Yes. I've known him for about five years, ever since I was a student nurse. Over the years, we developed a casual, platonic relationship. He used to date some of my classmates from nursing school.

Brian sat quietly and looked at Kate as though he was studying her. She noticed his peculiar expression. She decided he must be trying to lay the blame of MJ's death on Dr. Dunbar and was trying to figure out how to tell her that without hurting her feelings.

"Oh my God, Brian. You don't suspect that he had anything to do with MJ's death, do you? Because if you do, you're wrong."

"What makes you so sure about that?" Brian countered.

She told him about her conversations with Dr. Dunbar over the last week, including the fact that MJ was supposed to meet him on the tenth floor landing the night of her fall. She explained how he had been devastated by MJ's death and how baffled he was by the circumstances of the fall.

She reminded Brian that she had always been an excellent judge of character and that she was absolutely certain that Dr. Dunbar's confession to her about MJ was true and sincere.

She continued, "Dr. Dunbar told me he had planned to meet MJ on the tenth floor landing in the rotunda stairwell at 3:30 a.m., but before he even had a chance to leave ER to go meet her, she had already fallen to her death. I was there during the code. He tried everything to save her but there was just too much trauma. I talked with him later. He was a wreck," Kate concluded.

"Greg and I did consider that Dr. Dunbar may have had some information about the death of Miss Iverson that might help our investigation. Of course, we weren't certain of anything because we didn't know for sure if he was the one that wrote the note, although it looks like he probably did. We were going to talk to him but we didn't get a chance."

"Well, try again," Kate encouraged. "I know that he would be very cooperative. MJ's death is as big a mystery to him as it is to the rest of us. In fact, I'll call him this very minute. Maybe he can come over here right now or we could all go down to the station and include Greg in our conversation," Kate insisted.

Brian sighed and quietly looked down and away. She looked at him with an increasing feeling of apprehension.

Cautiously, she asked, "What is it, Brian?"

He took a deep breath as he reached for Kate's hands but she snatched her hands away from him.

"What? What is it?" she pleaded. Her eyes filled with tears. Her heart started to pound until she could hear it in her head.

"What aren't you telling me? Say it, Brian. Just say it," Kate screamed.

"Kate, calm down," Brian ordered. He took her trembling hands in his. "It's important that you listen to me carefully and calmly. I have some unhappy news for you but you need to pay close attention to what I say. Okay? Can you do that for me?" Brian said kindly but firmly.

Kate let out a long sigh. She realized that she had been holding her breath in anticipation of Brian's news. She felt like she might cry but she didn't want to. She tried to relax by taking deep breaths and letting them out very slowly. After a moment, she looked at Brian and gave him a nod as if to say, "Okay, I'm ready."

Brian looked Kate straight in the eyes as he began to reveal the shocking discovery of the first-shift OR staff. Sometime during the night shift, Dr. Dunbar had apparently gone to one of the operating rooms far from the OR office and committed suicide.

Brian told Kate that his visit to her today was actually official business. He was there to take an initial statement from Kate as a possible witness to Dr. Dunbar's death since she had been working in the operating room suite at the apparent time of death. He told her that Greg was interviewing Mr. Sargent and Ms. MacGregor.

Kate stared at him in disbelief, trying to absorb the meaning of his words. All of the events of the last week were running through her mind at the same time and everything was becoming jumbled. Her mind was whirling. She started to feel dizzy and distant. When Brian spoke her name, for a split second, she thought that it was Mike's voice. Startled back to reality but suddenly emotionally exhausted, she started to cry.

Brian put his arm around Kate. Her shoulders heaved with her sobs. After a few minutes, she tried to regain her composure and excused herself as she headed for her bathroom.

She ran cold water into her hands and splashed it onto her face a few times until the diaphragmatic spasms, remnants of her sobbing, subsided and her breathing got back to normal. After a few more minutes, she felt calm enough to return to Brian. She knew she had to let him finish telling her what he knew, and she had to add whatever information she could to that.

Kate glanced at her reflection in the mirror over the sink. Her eyes were red and puffy, and her whole face looked flushed. She brushed back a few wisps of hair that had fallen into her face and returned to the kitchen.

"Brian, I'm really sorry for such a childish display. I'm very upset about what's been happening at the hospital and on top of everything, I had flashes of Mike just then. I guess it was all too much for me. I'm better now. I think we should finish this. What else do you have to tell me?"

"Let me see," Brian said, trying to decide where to pick up his story. "Dr. Dunbar was found in one of the operating rooms at the end of the A corridor. He was on an observation platform."

"That would be Room 5," Kate interjected.

Brian acknowledged her comment and continued.

"The nurses in the room didn't even see him at first but they noticed an IV pole with an IV bottle hanging on it that was out of place. Apparently, the pole shouldn't have been on the platform. When they went to retrieve it, they found his body. He was lying on the floor with a needle in his left arm that was hooked up to an empty IV bottle labeled D5W. We suspect that it contained some kind of drug but we don't know which one yet. When we find out what drug or drugs were in the solution, I would like you to tell me what you can about them."

"Sure, Brian. I can do that. You know I'll do anything to help. Now what? Where do we go from here?" Kate asked in a professional tone.

"An autopsy for Dr. Dunbar is scheduled for this afternoon. We can discuss the results when we get."

Kate nodded and Brian continued, "You will have to give another statement to Greg but for now, I would like to know if you saw or heard anything last night."

"Let's see," Kate said with her brow furrowed in concentration. She tried to clear her mind of all of the irrelevant information that she had been bombarded with during the last few days. She needed to translate her jumbled recollection about the night before into a clear, concise account.

"As I recall, it was a pretty routine night. I entered the hospital through the ER as I usually do and I saw Dr. Dunbar working there. I spoke with him briefly before I went up to the OR. I told him that if things were quiet, I would try to come back to the ER later. As it turned out, the OR was quiet.

"I took report from Rae Gilbert, the second-shift CRNA, while I changed into my scrub dress. After Rae left, I went from the anesthesia lounge to the OR office to visit with Army and Maggie, the rest of the third-shift crew."

"That would be Margaret MacGregor, RN and Armstrong Sergeant, ORT," Brian confirmed from his notes.

"That's right. We sat and talked for a little while then we all went different ways to do our night duties. While I was setting up OR 7, Dr. Nick Lecorts, a surgical resident came to the OR to visit with me."

Kate paused very briefly and showed just a faint smile before she continued. Brian noticed the fleeting change in her demeanor but didn't comment.

Kate continued, "About 12:30 a.m., when my work was done, I went down to the ER for a few minutes to talk with Dr. Dunbar but he was busy so I went back to the operating room. His mood seemed okay. He was concentrating on his work. I remember that he gave me a hug before I left the ER. That was the first time that he had ever done anything like that but I really didn't think much about it at the time. I think we agreed to contact each other later if we wanted to talk again that night. He never called me so that was the last time that I talked to him," Kate said solemnly.

"I went back to the anesthesia lounge until about 1:45 a.m., when a call came in that we were getting a pediatric patient for an appendectomy. We did the case, cleaned things up, and went to our respective lounges until the first-shift staff started coming about 6:30 a.m. I reported off duty and left the hospital. That's it. I can't think of anything else right off hand."

"Okay. That's good for now but Greg and I will be talking to you again so if you remember anything, you can tell us then."

Brian was getting ready to leave when he stopped and turned to Kate with one last question.

"I want to talk as friends for a minute. I have one more question for you of a personal, or rather, friendly nature. When you spoke of the visit from..." Brian started flipping through his notes, stopped, and read, "...Dr. Nick Lecorts, I thought I saw a very subtle change in your expression. Was that just my imagination?"

Kate could feel herself blushing and she felt slightly like she had been caught doing something wrong. She wondered, "If I tell Brian about my interest in Nick, will he accuse me of being disloyal to Mike's memory?"

Kate decided that would not be the case so she told Brian about her breakfast date with Nick that morning and how much she enjoyed having the company of a man again. She explained that she was planning on seeing him again and that she would like it very much if he would join them sometime because she would like Brian's impression of Nick.

Far from being upset, Brian was pleased that Kate had finally decided to get back to having some kind of a social life, especially because she's still young and has two beautiful children who could use a dad. He was also flattered that his approval of her choice in men mattered to her but then he had thought of Kate like a little sister for a long time.

Kate waved good-bye as Brian pulled out of the driveway. She stood with her hand on the doorknob for a while after she closed the door. What an emotional roller coaster she was on—the lowest low that comes when a friend dies and the highest high when the prospect of a new love looms on the horizon.

When the time came for her to go to her parents' house for dinner, she still wasn't hungry even though she hadn't eaten all day. She put her jacket on and walked down the block to the Cavanaugh's home.

She let herself in through the back door. She could smell dinner cooking. "Roast beef," she thought. Even though it smelled delicious, it still didn't stimulate her appetite. Her mother was in the kitchen and she could hear her father and the twins playing games in the living room. Kate took the opportunity while they were alone to tell Mary about Dr. Dunbar's apparent suicide.

Mary was worried by this new set of circumstances and voiced her concerns to Kate about her safety. Kate assured her mother that she was perfectly safe at the hospital and that she was coping with the tragedies in stride, physically and emotionally.

Kate knew that if she didn't eat something tonight, her mother would be even more concerned so she managed to eat a bit. The food in her stomach made her feel tired. Or maybe she felt that way because she'd had only four to five hours of sleep. During the visit with her parents, she could hardly keep her eyes open.

By 7 p.m., Kate, the children, and her mother went back to Kate's house where she promptly went to bed. Mary got the children ready for bed and read them their story.

At 10 p.m., Mary woke Kate so she could get ready for work. By 10:40, Kate left the house and was on her way to the hospital.

She entered the ER with the same trepidation she felt the first time she used the back stairs after MJ's death. She added this circumstance to the long list of occurrences of the last week that she knew would leave her life forever changed.

Tuesday Night, October 26, 1976

One by one, as Kate, Maggie, and Army arrived on the tenth floor for duty, they were escorted to the empty recovery room by the hospital president, Mr. Clare Eggleston. Soon, the Rev. Bill Blackwell and Detective Greg Martin joined them.

Mr. Eggleston explained to the OR staff members that they had been relieved of their duties for the night. Instead of their OR assignment, they would be having meetings with representatives from the hospital administration, the clergy, and the police department to discuss the deaths of their colleagues and any personal repercussions they may have suffered from the losses.

Each of the OR workers was paired with one of the representatives with whom they talked for about an hour in three small private meetings. At the end of the hour, they switched pairings and had further discussions. When those groups finished, Mr. Eggleston made arrangements with the cafeteria to send some sandwiches for them to the recovery room.

After a brief break to eat and freshen up, they once again switched pairings and continued their meetings. Finally, they met as group to discuss the two nights that the deaths occurred in an effort to stimulate any further recollections. When no more information was forth coming, the meetings were concluded. The hospital employees were thanked for their time and excused with pay for the remainder of the shift.

Army wanted to go to L&D to visit Joey. He thanked everyone for the opportunity to talk about his personal concerns and for the chance to have a little down time before he had to face work again. He said good-bye and left. Down on L&D, Army had an opportunity to describe the meetings to Joey because she was having a quiet night with only one patient to care for. When finished, Army went to one of the empty labor rooms to sleep until Joey's shift was over. Then he would give her a ride home.

The committee members also left the recovery room area, leaving Kate and Maggie alone. They hadn't talked about the deaths privately and this seemed like the perfect time to get their feelings out. Kate didn't detect any of the animosity toward MJ from Maggie that she had noticed in the past. Rather, Maggie seemed genuinely concerned and saddened to the degree that was appropriate for the circumstances. She had only nice things to say about both MJ and Dr. Dunbar. At some subconscious level, Kate felt relieved to hear the change in Maggie's sentiment.

Kate and Maggie finally covered every aspect of the deaths. They also had a good, personal heart to heart talk and they freely poured out their inner most feelings to each other. They felt closer than ever after their soul-cleansing experience of friend leaning on friend. Kate was certain that they had finally started to purge the black cloud of doom and gloom that had occupied their minds for the past few days, allowing a glimmer of hope and a ray of sunshine to enter.

"I really believe that Dr. Dunbar and MJ must have been having some kind of a romantic relationship that went awry," Maggie proposed. "MJ must have jumped to her death when she realized that Dr. Dunbar wasn't the Prince Charming that she had imagined. And when he found out that his blatant insincerity had caused a death, he killed himself. How tragic!"

Maggie didn't have the story quite right and Kate could have confirmed or countered some of Maggie's proposed theory. But Kate didn't want to repeat any confidential information. And as much as Kate liked Maggie, she was still uncertain about which thoughts or ideas might antagonize Maggie or inflame her temper. She thought it best to just listen and interject as little as possible to Maggie's theories. Their friendship was developing into something very special but not to the point where Kate could get a good reading on Maggie's thoughts. Kate didn't want to say anything that would spoil the mood.

While Kate had been sizing up Maggie, Maggie was in turn trying to get a read on Kate. Kate's comments and demeanor during their private talk had convinced Maggie that Dr. Dunbar was not the man that Kate had fondly referred to in one of their earlier conversations. Yet she needed reassurance so Maggie decided to ask Kate about her "new friend."

"The other night you started to tell me about this new guy in your life that made you sit up and take notice. Are you ready to divulge his identity?" Maggie said lightly.

Kate was relieved that the conversation had taken an upbeat change. Again, she blushed at the thought of Nick and she reasoned that was a good sign so she decided it was a "tell-all time."

"Do you remember that surgical resident, Nick Lecorts?" Kate asked cautiously.

"Kind of hard to forget a good-looker like that," Maggie replied with a grin on her face.

"Well, he took me out to breakfast and we had the nicest visit. It was so good to just sit and talk."

"Yeah, right. Just sit and talk, like with a good friend," Maggie goaded her.

"We did just sit and talk. And I flirted but just a little. Boy, did that feel good. To feel attractive to someone and to be attracted by someone, it's just been so long. I feel young again."

"Oh, like you're so old!" Maggie said. They both laughed out loud.

"Thanks, Maggie. It feels good to laugh. I've been so depressed lately because of the... you know, those things that we aren't going to talk about for a while. So enough about me already, what about you and yours?"

"My story isn't as rosy, I'm afraid. That guy that I thought the sun rose and set on, turned out to be a creep, a married creep at that so I sent him packing. I even dumped his half knitted sweater that I was working on," Maggie declared with pride.

"Gee Maggie, I'm sorry."

"It's okay, really. I've come to terms with it and I feel lucky that I found out now before I invested any more time and emotions in him," Maggie stated very matter-of-factly.

Kate's eyes flashed as though a light bulb had just gone off in her head. She grinned widely. "Listen, I've got a great idea. Remember that cop I was telling you about? My friend, the one that was Mike's partner?"

"Oh no," Maggie said as she held her hand up to stop Kate from continuing. "This is scary because it sounds like you're getting that 'let me fix up my poor old single friend' tone in your voice."

"Come on, just let me finish. We talked about him before so it's not like I'm dropping a big surprise on you. His name is Brian Goss. He's a detective with the Flint Police. He's one of my best friends and you're one of my best friends and neither of you is attached right now. The timing couldn't be better. But that's only half of my brilliant idea."

"You mean there's more?"

"Yes. I thought it would be perfect to have my two best friends chaperone me when I go on first night date with Nick."

"Are you serious? You want someone tagging along on a date with your new heartthrob?" Maggie asked with disbelief.

"I think it would be great. And I know the perfect place where we could go. This Saturday is the ER's big charity Halloween party at the interns' quarters. You know, the one where everyone dresses in hospital garb."

Maggie nodded in recognition. Kate continued.

"I know that Dr. Dunbar was on the planning committee for the party. When I was having my private conference with Mr. Eggleston, I asked him directly if the party was going to be cancelled. He assured me that the party would be held because it was a charity function. Instead of canceling out of respect for Dr. Dunbar, they decided to dedicate the party to him and rename the charity in his honor, the 'Dr. Dunbar Safe Haven'."

"That's quite an honor."

"Yes, I thought so, too. Anyway, about the party. I could go with Nick and you could go with Brian and we could all go together. It would be a lot of fun. What do you think?"

"Never mind what I think, what do you think the guys will say?" Maggie said still skeptical.

"Don't you worry. If you agree, I'll take care of all of the details. Just leave everything to me," Kate said with an air of confidence.

"Okay. There comes a point in every woman's life when she has to put her fate in the hands of a trusted friend. And so my friend, I'm at your mercy," Maggie said.

"Oh great! This is just great! It will be so much fun." Kate was jumping up and clapping her hands like a little kid. She was pleased with her suggestion and excited at the prospect of getting her best friends together. Finally, something to feel good about at work and at home.

It was about 5 a.m. Kate and Maggie decided to call it a night. They gave each other a quick hug before they headed out to the parking lot.

Chapter Six

Wednesday Morning, October 27, 1976

Kate was tired. She drove straight home from the hospital. It was about 5:15 a.m. when she woke her mother to tell her that she got off work early. She wanted to go to bed right away if Mary would take the children to school. Mary agreed.

Kate had a quick shower and put on a nightshirt. She was a little hungry so she had a bowl of cereal before she went to bed. By 7:30 a.m., when Mary woke the children, Kate was asleep. Mary warned the twins that their mother was already home and sleeping so they must be very quiet when they're getting ready for school. The children were washed, dressed, fed, and on their way to school by 8:45 a.m. Mary watched them enter the school before she drove away.

Maggie headed straight home, happier than she had been in a long time. This time she was really happy, not the false feeling she had when she was with that lying Dunbar. She'd thought that she could count on Kate to be her friend and now she knew that she had been right. She'd waited her whole life for a friend like Kate who could point her in the right direction and guide her along the way without being judgmental or displaying a superior attitude.

Maggie showered, decided against breakfast, opened a beer, popped a couple of Seconals, climbed into bed, and started reading on the marked page of her latest romance novel. She hadn't read much by the time she finished her beer because she couldn't concentrate. She was busy mentally writing a novel of her own where she was the heroine. In her story, she had already suffered all of the trials and tribulations and now she was almost to the point where she would live happily ever after, much like her real life.

"Thank you God, for my friend Kate," Maggie whispered before she closed her eyes and drifted off to sleep.

Kate awoke with a start when she heard the phone ringing. She checked the time and it was already 11 a.m.

"Hello," Kate said.

"Hi, Kate. Did you have a good sleep?" Mary asked.

"Yeah, Mom, I did. Thanks to you."

"Good, I'm glad. I just called to see if you are going to be able to pick the children up from school."

"Yes, I plan to. I got six hours of solid, deep sleep so I feel pretty good. Thanks for the call. I'll talk to you later."

"Okay, honey. I love you."

"Love you, too, Mom. Bye."

Kate got ready for the day and left the house to get the kids from school. On the ride home from school, it was decided that lunch would be soup and sandwiches and the afternoon activities would include a bike riding adventure. While the children ate lunch, Kate made a few phone calls.

She called Brian at the station first because she thought the chance of getting him on the phone was better than locating Nick.

"Brian Goss."

"Hi Brian, it's Kate."

"How's it going? I understand you had a pretty powerful session last night."

"I'm good and you're right. The meetings were intense at some points but on the whole, I thought they were productive. We finally had a chance to get everything out. What did Greg think?"

"He was pleased with everyone's cooperation. But I need to tell you something, confidentially, of course. I know that the others are your coworkers and friends but you can't discuss our conversations with them. Some people, like hospital employees with police records; employees who might have a grudge against the hospital or other workers; employees who were on duty during the deaths; and those who were in contact with the deceased or working on the tenth floor, are going to be the subjects of further, in-depth investigations."

"Why Brian? What's going on?"

"With both deaths, some signs could point to suicide but other things don't add up so both are being investigated as homicides. That's all I can tell you right now."

"Do you think I need to be afraid of going to work?"

"No, not at all. You've got to know that I'd tell you if I had even the slightest inkling that you might be in any danger."

"Yeah, I know that. And as far as anyone looking into my background, I don't have any problem with that. My life is pretty much an open book. Now, can I change the subject a bit?"

"Sure. What's on your mind?"

"Okay, here goes. But first I want you to keep an open mind and let me finish my proposal without you butting in."

"That sounds a little ominous," Brian said cautiously.

"No, it's not at all. Really," Kate said in her most convincing voice. "Just hear me out."

She cleared her throat and began speaking. "Maggie MacGregor, the third-shift RN, and I are both going to the hospital's Halloween party this Saturday. It's a charity affair for a battered women's shelter. Dr. Dunbar worked on the party committee for several years. This year, the party is being dedicated to his honor. It's a dress-up party but everyone usually wears hospital garb. It's a lot of fun and it's for a good cause. Anyway, would you like to accompany Maggie to the party and double date with Dr. Nick Lecorts and me?"

"Oh Kate, my friend the match-maker. I'm not sure about the timing here with the open investigation and all," Brian said obviously reluctant.

"Come on, Brian. Just think about it," Kate said in a pathetic, whiny voice.

"If I agree to this, you are going to owe me big time," Brian warned.

"Well, maybe you'll have so much fun, the arrangement will be payment enough."

"Always the optimist. So, do I have to give you an answer right now?" Brian wondered.

"If you can because there are plans to be made. Maggie knows what I'm up to and now you know but I haven't talked to Nick yet."

"Okay, you talked me into it. I'll go."

"Oh good!" exclaimed Kate. "I'll give you Maggie's phone number so you can call her ahead of time to make your transportation arrangements. Now, all I have to do is to convince Nick that he should go with us. Geez, I hope he doesn't have to work. Well, if Nick can't come with us then just the three of us will go together. I think it would be nice if we all met at my house before we go to the party. What do you think?"

"Sounds good to me. You just be the little social director and let me know when to be where. I have to go for now but I'll talk to you later."

"Okay. Thanks Brian. Bye," Kate said. She hung up the phone, very pleased with herself.

After Brian put the phone down, he made a note in his date book in the space for Saturday, October 30, "Maggie – Halloween Party – Kate's house first."

The phone rang almost immediately after Kate placed the receiver on the cradle.

"Hello."

"Hi, Kate. It's me, Brian, again."

"Oh no. You haven't had second thoughts already, have you?"

"No, nothing like that. I forgot to mention that Greg wanted me to ask you if you would be willing to give us a little inservice on some of the drugs that are used for anesthesia. It would be at your convenience, of course, but as soon as possible."

"Coincidentally, Nick asked me for the same kind of

information just the other day. How about if the four of us get together? I think evenings will work best for Nick but I'll check with him to make sure."

"Ask him about tonight if that will work for you. Do you need more time than that to get the information together?"

"Not at all. Tonight will be fine for me. I'll ask Nick if he can join us. If he can't then I'll meet with you and Greg anyway," Kate suggested.

"Good. Get back to me, as soon as you can, and let me know what time will work the best," Brian requested.

"Okay. Bye."

Kate called the hospital and asked the operator to page Dr. Lecorts and ask him to call Kate McKenna at home. The phone rang within ten minutes.

"Hello."

"Hello, yourself. How are you today?" Nick asked.

"Good. How about you?"

"I'm fine."

"That's an understatement," Kate thought.

Nick continued, "I didn't get a page from you last night so I guess that you were busy. Eh?"

"I was busy but not in the OR. Army, Maggie, and I were sequestered in meetings until 5 a.m. with Mr. Eggleston, Rev. Blackwell, and Detective Greg Martin to discuss the deaths of MJ and Dr. Dunbar. Then we were excused for the rest of our shift so I went home and went right to bed. My mother got the kids off to school and I slept until about 11 a.m.," Kate explained.

"How was the meeting?" Nick asked.

"Not too bad, kind of cathartic in a way. I finally said everything I needed to say. And it was good to know that everyone was as interested in our emotional well being as they were in discussing the facts of the investigation. When we finished, I felt like a weight had been lifted from my mind. Does that make sense?"

"Yes, I know exactly what you mean."

"Good. Sounds like we're on the same wavelength here.

Anyway, after the meeting, Maggie and I stayed and talked for a little while. I told her about you."

"What does that mean?"

"I mean, I told her that we had breakfast the other morning and that I was interested in seeing you again."

"Is that so?" Nick replied in a smooth even tone when he actually felt like slapping his leg and yelling, "Way to go Lecorts."

"Yes, I would. In fact, I would like it very much if you would go to the hospital's Halloween party with me on Saturday."

"I've heard about that party. It's a charity event, right?"

"Right!"

"I think that sounds like fun. I'd be happy to go with you."

"Oh good," she said with relief, "because I've already talked to Maggie MacGregor and Brian Goss, an old friend of mine who's with the Flint Police, about double dating with us the night of the party."

"That sounds like a good plan."

"Okay, that's all set, now one more little thing. Remember when you said that you wanted some anesthesia information?"

"Yes."

"Well, it seems that a couple of the detectives want some of the same information so I'm going to talk to them this evening. If you're free, you're welcome to join us," Kate offered.

"I'll check and let you know."

"Okay, I have to go for now but I'll talk to you later. You call me or I'll call you. Whatever works."

"Okay. Nice talking to you. Bye."

"Bye," Kate said. She smiled just because.

The children were getting fidgety because they wanted to get started on their bike ride so Kate hurried and finished her last call. She called Dr. Park. Again, she was unable to connect with him but his secretary gave her the information she needed. Dr. Dunbar had been injected with sodium pentothal. Kate winced because she knew that it was highly likely that the drug that caused his death came from the anesthesia pharmacy stock. For the benefit of the twins, she put all thoughts about everything except them aside and devoted her entire attention to the bicycle trip.

It was a beautiful day, crisp and cool but sunny with not much wind. The leaves on most of the trees in the neighborhood had turned to a beautiful golden yellow with half still clinging to the trees. The rest were strewn about the yards, sidewalks, and streets. Everything glowed as if covered with sunshine, including the faces of Kate and her children.

The trio rode their bikes over to the park and then down by the creek that curved around through the neighborhood until at last they arrived at the picnic area of the golf course. They stopped for a rest and a snack of lemonade, crackers, cheese, and pickled bologna before heading for home.

They arrived back at the house in time for Kate to answer the ringing phone. It was Brian asking Kate to meet with Greg and him at the station at 6 p.m.

"I have a few more details to attend to before I can be sure. I'll call you right back."

She called her mother to see if she could watch the children. When that was done, she paged Nick to check on whether or not he would be able to attend the meeting. With everything arranged, Kate called Brian. He was on another line so she left a message for him confirming the meeting time and place. She also requested to have a chalkboard available.

Kate promised the children Sloppy Joes for dinner. She gathered the ingredients to make sure she had everything she needed before she went to take a shower. She had Shelby and Shane sit in front of the TV and made them promise not to get into anything for fifteen minutes while she took a shower.

They were well behaved and always eager to please their mother. They showed cooperation, caring, and kindness toward one another and rarely displayed any sign of competitiveness between them. Kate's request was a challenge to them as a unit, not against each other, and they accepted the responsibility with delight.

Kate quickly showered and dressed for the meeting. The water was refreshing and she hoped it would be stimulating enough to make up for the fact that she wouldn't be getting any sleep this evening before work. She had been gone only fifteen minutes when she returned to the living room. When the children saw her, they jumped up to greet her, pleased with themselves that they had behaved so well. Kate was pleased, too. Seeing the joy in their faces made everything in life seem worthwhile. Kate made their dinner and sat with them while they ate. They mostly talked about Halloween and their school party on Friday. After they finished their dinner, Mary arrived so Kate could go to the meeting.

Kate kissed the kids, hugged her mother, and left.

She saw Nick in the police parking lot and they walked into the station together. They got a few looks and approving nods while they waited at the desk for Brian to appear. Obviously, Brian had already told some of them that Kate was dating again. When Brian appeared, Kate introduced him to Nick. He escorted them a conference room where Greg Martin joined them.

"I really appreciate you taking the time to come here to share your anesthesia know-how with us," Greg began.

Nick and Greg shook hands when Brian introduced them.

"Alright young lady, I'm going to turn things over to you. Brian said that all you needed for your explanation was a chalkboard. Here's some chalk to get you started." Greg handed Kate two sticks of yellow chalk.

She walked up to the chalkboard at ease with her lecturing task. She had given the same lecture to critical care and recovery room nurses many times.

"First, let me explain that while one of you has a medical background, the others don't, and none of you has a background in anesthesia so I'm going to give you the same information that I give to educated, non-anesthesia people. If at any point, I use a word or give an explanation that you don't understand, please stop me. I've found that if one person doesn't understand something then probably somebody else doesn't understand it either. And it's easier to explain as I go rather than trying to go back to the subject later.

"Okay. Let's get started." Kate drew some figures on the chalkboard while she talked. "I'm limiting my comments to adult general anesthesia, one type of anesthesia used during surgery. This is what is generally referred to as 'going to sleep.' Personally, I don't use that phrase because too many people equate 'going to sleep' or 'being put to sleep' with death. Like when an animal is 'put to sleep.' I just tell my patients that 'they will be sleeping' or that 'they are going to start to feel sleepy and the next thing they remember will be recovery room.'"

"Do you ever have patients that are afraid that they won't wake up," Brian wondered.

"Yes. And if their surgery is an elective procedure and they're still concerned after my explanation, I have them talk to their surgeon again for reassurance. If their surgery is urgent or an emergency and it would be life threatening to postpone it, I often promise them that they will wake-up. That usually helps to allay their fear and if for some reason they don't make it through the procedure, they don't know about my deception. That is the only time that I'm not one hundred percent honest with the patient.

"Okay. We need to get back to the subject at hand, adult general anesthesia. Picture general anesthesia as a triangle. On one point is 'sleep,' on another point is 'muscle relaxation,' and on the last point is 'pain relief.'

"Years ago when ether was used, one anesthetic agent or drug provided everything that was needed for a general anesthesia. But ether had its drawbacks, not the least of which was that it was explosive. So researchers, especially during the last thirty years, have been working to find other agents and drugs that could accomplish the same anesthesia results without the unwanted side effects.

"Over the years experience has shown that using IV drugs in combination with the newer inhaled agents and gases, provide a better anesthesia outcome and experience for the patient.

"The drug of choice for initiating sleep in an adult is sodium pentothal. You may have heard sodium pentothal referred to as 'truth serum' but with the doses that we use in anesthesia, the patients don't talk, they go to sleep. But sodium pentothal is rather short acting so either the pentothal must be repeated or other drugs must be given to keep the patient asleep.

"The choice of drugs for maintaining sleep is a combination of gases: oxygen; nitrous oxide, also known as laughing gas, the gas that some dentists use in their offices; and Ethrane, a new type of ether. The patient inhales the mixture though a mask or a breathing tube.

"Okay. So far, on the point of the triangle for sleep, we use sodium pentothal to initiate sleep, and Ethrane, nitrous oxide, and oxygen to maintain the sleep. Any questions yet?" They shook their heads no so Kate continued.

"On the second point, we need something for the muscle relaxation that's required for several reasons. The doctor frowns if the patient is moving while he is trying to do his surgery." A few chuckles. "And even though Ethrane has some muscle relaxing properties, they are not generally adequate for major surgery so a muscle relaxant drug is given to the patient via their IV. The doses of muscle relaxants used by the anesthetists may not just relax the muscles they can paralyze them. You may have heard of the curare-type muscle relaxants. You know, good old 'arrow poison?' That's what those drugs are like.

"Now that the patient is asleep and relaxed, the anesthetist needs to make sure that she has provided adequate pain control so sometimes IV narcotics are given in addition to the Ethrane and nitrous oxide. Now we have completed the anesthesia triangle.

"To keep things simple, remember sodium pentothal provides sleep. That's all. No muscle relaxation and no pain relief. The muscle relaxant drugs provide only muscle relaxation or paralysis, no sleep and no pain relief. And the narcotics are just for pain."

Greg spoke up. "You mean if someone is given a paralyzing dose of one of the muscle relaxants, he will become paralyzed but still awake, alert, and able to feel everything?"

"You've got it," Kate replied. "But keep in mind that we are very careful to make sure that that never happens."

Greg spoke up again. "Do you know what drug was found in Dr. Dunbar?"

"Yes, I got that information this afternoon. The serum toxicology report stated that they found a lethal dose of sodium pentothal. The only supplies of pentothal in the hospital are in the main pharmacy and in the anesthesia department pharmacy stock. Since Dr. Dunbar died on the tenth floor, it's a pretty safe bet that he got the drug from the anesthesia supply.

"Sodium pentothal is a barbiturate and is a controlled drug under the Harrison Narcotic Act but it has little value on the street. The patient doesn't get a high from it and it must be given very carefully IV. If it leaks into the surrounding tissues, it causes severe tissue damage. It's not kept in a locked cupboard like the narcotic drugs. It's stored in a powder form in the anesthesia workrooms. Plus, we keep a limited amount of the powder and sterile water mixture in syringes in the refrigerator. We have inventory accounting of sodium pentothal in the anesthesia department but it's not very rigid. Anyone who works in or around the OR knows how to get it. I'm sure that Dr. Dunbar had no trouble finding some."

Kate sighed. A wave of sorrow passed over her when she realized that she was in charge of the department when Dr. Dunbar got his lethal drug supply. "Did that make her somehow responsible for his death?" she wondered.

"What about the other drugs you mentioned, where are they kept?" Brian asked.

"Ethrane is packaged in bottles as a liquid and must be poured into a vaporizer on the gas machines to be used. The stock supply is kept in the workroom. The muscle relaxants are packaged in vials that are kept in the department's refrigerator. Neither the agents nor the muscle relaxants are controlled. And like I said before, the narcotics are kept in a locked cupboard."

Kate asked for more questions. When no one said anything, she said, "Well, I guess that's it. I hope you find this information helpful and if I can be of any further assistance, please let me know."

Kate shook Greg's hand and he left the room. The rest stayed for a few minutes to discuss the Halloween party.

"Brian, I can't thank you enough for agreeing to go on the blind date with Maggie," Kate said while she patted Brian's shoulder.

"My pleasure, Kate. Actually, I've seen Maggie before so I know that she's pretty easy to look at. It'll be fun to double date again," Brian said, making a reference to when they had double-dated before Mike died. Brian and Kate exchanged glances. If Nick picked up on the subtle exchange, he didn't respond.

Brian changed the subject a little when he went into his big brother mode and explained to Nick how much everyone cared for and looked after Kate's best interests so Nick's intentions toward her had better be honorable.

"Brian, lighten up a little bit. You're embarrassing me. We're just going to a party. It's not like we're making any commitment here," Kate complained.

"It's okay, Kate. It's reassuring to know you have such a good friend who obviously cares a great deal for you," Nick assured Kate.

Kate was pleased that Brian and Nick seemed to like each other.

Brian explained that he had some paper work to finish, said good bye, and headed for his office. Nick and Kate decided to go out for dinner. She convinced him that he would enjoy the atmosphere and food at Angelo's, the best and most charming coney island restaurant in the area. The patrons include everyone from street people to post-theater patrons in gowns and black ties. The most popular menu choice is Koegel hot dogs on buns with onions and coney sauce, and a side order of fries with gravy. Nick followed Kate's car when they drove to her house, where they stopped for a minute so Nick could meet Mary and the twins. Mary was immediately impressed with Nick's personality and manners. The thought of Kate keeping company with such a nice man with such a promising future was very reassuring to her, especially after the recent difficulties that Kate seemed to be having at work.

Shane and Shelby were very happy to meet Nick and were on their very best behavior including extending an invitation to visit again in the very near future. After a short visit, they continued on to Angelo's.

Kate ordered for both of them, the usual of course. To drink, Nick had coffee and Kate had water. Over dinner she described to him what she referred to as her "necessity for order," and explained how that personality trait often controlled her behavior. She further disclosed that she knew that she was being pulled into the murder mystery at the hospital and that caused great concern to her mother. But she assured him, just as she had assured Mary, that she would never do anything to jeopardize her safety. She was merely puzzle solving. Plus, Greg and Brian knew that she was gathering information and they had promised to watch over her.

She elaborated further. "Ever since I was a kid, I've felt challenged by a good 'whodunit.' At one time I even thought about becoming a detective. Mike and Brian always humored me by discussing their cases with me but I took those exercises seriously. I've always regarded my inquiring mind as sort of a hobby, a serious hobby. Over the years I've learned that I have very good intuitive instincts.

"A lot of people, in fact maybe most people, don't really put much faith in intuition. But sometimes I just know that things are going to happen before they happen. I know it sounds weird but I just get a feeling or premonition and I'm usually right."

Nick hinted that he understood what Kate was saying but not that he necessarily agreed with her comments.

"Kate, you know the detectives will figure out what happened at the hospital," Nick said.

"I know but I can't stop thinking about it. Like it or not, my mind has taken it on as a personal challenge. Do you think that makes me too weird?"

"Weird, maybe, but certainly not too weird."

Kate flashed him a look of disbelief mixed with disappointment until she realized from the big grin on his face that he was teasing her.

"Sorry, just my feeble attempt at casual humor. I couldn't help myself. You left yourself wide-open for that one. Anyway, back to the subject at hand. You can think about the mystery all you want but I hope you don't feel compelled to go sleuthing about. I don't want you to get hurt," Nick stated matter-of-factly.

"I don't want to get hurt either and I can't imagine that anyone would want to hurt me. I told you, I just doing a little information gathering," Kate reassured him.

"Well from what you said and from other things that I've heard, it looks like maybe the deaths were not caused by suicide. That leaves the choice of accidents or homicides. If accidents are ruled out then they were homicides. That would mean that somewhere out there is a murderer that seems to favor the area of the tenth floor at Temple. That makes me very uneasy. I don't want that person coming after you."

"Neither do I, believe me, neither do I," Kate insisted.

They finished their dinners and their discussion for the time being anyway. It was only 8 p.m. "Great," Kate thought. She had time to get at least an hour of sleep before going to work. Nick took her right home.

Chapter Seven

Wednesday Night, October 27, 1976

The Temple Hospital newsletter carried an announcement that a memorial service for Dr. Thomas Dunbar was to be held one hour before the Halloween party at the Interns' Quarters on Saturday, October 30, 1976, at 7 p.m. The remainder of the evening would be for partying and all of the proceeds collected for admission, food, and drinks would be donated to the Abused Women's and Children's Shelter in Dr. Dunbar's name.

Signs about the event were posted all over the hospital, the YMCA, the YWCA, the police and fire stations, and all city offices. Years ago the party was limited to hospital employees but when it became a fundraiser for the shelter, most city employees were invited.

The signs greeted Kate and everyone else when they entered the hospital for work on Wednesday night. They were reminders of all of the turmoil and sadness that was prevalent in the hospital these days but Kate hoped that in the OR things would be heading back to normal. Or at least as normal as third-shift in this city hospital operating room ever is.

When she reached the tenth floor, she realized her wish had come true. Two ORs had cases going and another patient was waiting in ICU for the next available OR. In OR 7, Dr. Andy Barlow was closing the shoulder area of a patient with a stab wound. In OR 10, Dr. Dwyer was performing an abdominal exploration of a patient with a gunshot wound (GSW). The patient waiting in ICU has a GSW to the thigh. It was going to be a long, busy night, just the kind everyone needs to get their minds back on the job.

The second-shift crew had already decided that the team working in OR 7 would stay and finish their case and the third-shift team would relieve the crew in OR 10. Everyone worked professionally and proficiently, albeit with none of the usual OR chatter. At first glance, everyone's actions appeared normal but with a second look, it became obvious that the comfort level among coworkers was damaged. Death had always been part of the hospital's condition but for patients not staff members. The secure feeling that had blanketed the staff for so long was starting to fray. Feelings of uncertainty permeated the hospital's spirit because too many unanswered questions remained. Sadness prevailed for the loss of life but most of the staff members also grieved for the loss of a way of life. It would take some time for a new exemplar to be developed, for a new routine to be implemented, and for a new normal to be defined.

The time flew by. By 6:15 a.m., all of the cases were finished and all of the cleaning and stocking was done. Kate, Maggie, and Army finally had a few minutes to sit and have a break. None had had time for lunch or even a bathroom break, as far as that goes. Yet, none were hungry, just thirsty. Maggie and Army had coffee. Kate had a Coke.

"Are you going to the party?" Kate asked, directing her remark to Army.

"Yes, Joey and I are going to the memorial and then we'll probably stay for most of the party. It depends on how long it lasts," Army answered.

"My guess would be quite a while. It will no doubt, be a very emotional gathering and after the memorial, people are going to want to let loose a bit," Maggie chimed in. "My friend here," nodding toward Kate, "has set me up with a blind date."

Kate protested. "Come on, Maggie. It's not really a blind date because you guys have met before, sort of. We'll just call it an arranged date between friends. You're my good friend and Brian is my good friend so it only made sense to get you two together."

Army looked from one woman to the other, trying to pick up on the details they were keeping to themselves. "Okay Maggie, so you are going with Kate's famous cop friend, Brian, and who might you be going with Miss Kate?"

Kate's face was beaming when she replied, "That would be my famous doctor friend, Nick Lecorts."

Army broke into a big grin while he eyed these two women on the verge of giggling like two high school freshman planning a date to the drive-in. "Good. Good. This is just what we need to lift the spirits around here. And finally, the rumor mill will have someone else to gossip about. Maybe now they will leave Joey and me alone."

Army rose to leave the office. "Speaking of Joey, I think I'll go see her for a few minutes. I'll give you ladies a chance to talk about what you're going to wear to the party." He slapped his hand against his forehead. "Oh, I forgot. It is supposed to be a hospital costume party. Are we still going to wear costumes?"

"As far as I know, some of the city employees might wear something from their regular uniform if not their whole uniform. The rest will be wearing hospital or medical garb. At least that's what I heard," Kate answered.

Maggie and Kate continued their conversation about the double date, letting their imaginations run wild with "what if this" and "what if that."

Maggie felt better than she had since before she found out about Dr. Dunbar and MJ. She would not allow herself to think about those losers. They were "personas non gratus," as far as she was concerned. She was so excited about the prospect of starting a new relationship with a great guy and sharing it all with her very best friend in the whole world.

All that Maggie had ever wanted was to have family and friends who loved her as much as she loved them. But it never happened that way despite all of her efforts. She gave her loved ones everything, her heart and soul, and all of her love. She gave so much of herself that there was almost nothing left. There was a time when she thought that she would completely disappear.

Not one of them had ever appreciated anything she did

for them. Rather, they all conspired against her. They lied to her. They deceived her. They fabricated stories about her. They tried to destroy her. They probably would have wiped her from the face of the earth if she hadn't stopped them. She did what she had to do to prevent her own demise. But that was all behind her now. All of that seemed like another lifetime ago. She was on her way to her new life with her new friends who would become her new family. She was convinced that she was the luckiest person in the whole world.

Kate and Maggie left the office to finish their assignments for the night before the morning crew arrived. The night had been so busy that Kate hadn't had a chance to talk to Nick. Before she left the hospital, she left a message with the operator for him saying that she would be sleeping in the morning but to call her around 2 p.m. if he got a chance.

Thursday Morning, October 28, 1976

Accidents had pretty much been ruled out. The detectives concluded that on the surface, both deaths appeared to be suicide but too many things didn't add up. Neither victim had given any indication or left any evidence of suicide. Besides, neither detective was ready to accept the idea of two suicides in the same building within a week's time. They considered that maybe they were dealing with one suicide and one homicide or perhaps two homicides. They just didn't have enough information for a definitive answer so the investigation was going forward on the assumptions that both deaths were possible homicides and the perpetrator was possibly a hospital employee.

Brian and Greg made a time-line chart from 24 hours before the first death to 24 hours following the last death, with emphasis on the whereabouts of the personnel who were on the tenth floor at the time of the deaths.

The detectives felt that the employees may have vital witness information and an immediate follow-up interview with each of the three third-shift OR employees was imperative.

Equally important was a thorough background check on each of the three. It was decided that Brian would proceed with the interviews and Greg would work on the background information.

Another team of detectives was checking into 10th floor laboratory personnel that were on duty during the time-line period but no leads were expected from that effort. The lab employees don't have knowledge or access to the OR.

Brian took this opportunity to tell Greg about the double date that Kate had arranged. "I told Kate that the timing wasn't really very good because of the investigation and everything else but she convinced me that it was just a party date with friends. You don't see any conflict, do you, Greg?"

"Well, it isn't like we expect anyone from the OR staff to be the bad guy but they are potential suspects just as they're potential witnesses. Just keep the social time separate from the interview time, all right? Don't talk about the case at all on the night of the party," warned Greg, "especially if you're drinking and I assume that you will be."

"I understand. That's good advice. I had thoughts along the same line. Greg, you've met Maggie and talked to her for a while. What do you think about her?"

"As far as what?"

"Come on, Greg. You know what I'm talking about. As a date."

"Well, she's not too bad to look at and she seems to have a level head from what I've seen. I think you should go for it. You've got nothing to lose, as far as I can tell."

"I'm glad you don't see any problem here because I need to call her and set up a 'get acquainted' date before the party this weekend."

Greg got started on his background checks and Brian decided to call Maggie. He checked his notebook and found her number. It rang four times before she answered.

"Hello," Maggie said with a sleepy voice.

"Hi, Maggie. This is Brian Goss. I had hoped I'd reach you before you fell asleep. I'm sorry I woke you."

"That's okay. I'm glad you called. I'm really looking forward to the party this weekend."

"Yeah, me too. I know this is really late notice but I'm calling to see if you're free to have an early dinner with me tonight. I thought it would be nice if we could get together before the party."

"That sounds like a good idea. Yes, I'd like to have dinner with you tonight. Since you don't know where I live, how about if I meet you at the Big Boy Restaurant on Dort Highway at 6 p.m."

"That'll be perfect. I'll see you then."

He replayed their conversation in his mind after he hung up. He knew he wasn't the sophisticated ladies man like some of his fellow officers but at least he tried to be honest with the women he dated.

Maggie was glad that Brian arranged to meet before the party date. And it was good to talk to him but she had quite a bit of drugs on board so she didn't want to think about anything right now except sleep. She closed her eyes and drifted back into her drug induced slumber.

At 1 p.m., Kate was in the kitchen fixing a bowl of cereal when the phone rang. It was Brian.

"Hi, Brian. What's up?"

"Greg and I have been going over our notes here and we need to talk to you again. Not about anesthesia stuff, your little talk pretty much answered all of our questions about the drug stuff. We made a time line chart of the events on the two nights of the deaths and we need you to note your movements and recollections on it. You know, witness kind of stuff."

"You need more details than what I gave to Greg the other morning?" Kate quizzed.

"Maybe the same stuff. I just want to go over it again and put it on our chart."

"What about 4 p.m. this afternoon? I could come down to the station."

"That would be great, Kate, because I'd really like to get

this interview stuff out of the way before the party. I know that you're busy. I really appreciate your cooperation."

"Okay. See you at 4 p.m. I've got to go for now before my cereal gets soggy."

She finished eating and got ready for the day. She had housework to do and she wanted to spend some time with her children. She called her mother to check on the twins. They had finished their lunch and were playing trains with their grandpa. Mary said she would bring them home within the hour.

At 2 p.m. on the dot, Nick called. Kate was happy to hear from him. Funny how a simple phone conversation could cause such exhilaration. It seemed like forever since she had a chance to talk to him even though it had been less than 24 hours. She told him about the busy night in the OR. She also mentioned Brian's phone call and the 4 p.m. meeting with him at the police station. She expected it to last about an hour.

"I'll be finished here at the hospital in about an hour. If you like, I'd be glad to come over and stay with Shane and Shelby while you go to your meeting. After that, we could all go out to dinner somewhere. How does that sound?" Nick offered.

"Thanks, Nick. That sounds great," Kate said.

She went into her room to change her clothes and do a little primping before his arrival. She had just finished in her room and was returning to the kitchen when she heard the door opening. It was Mary with the children. They were happy to be home and ran to meet her. As much as they loved their grandparents, Shelby and Shane much preferred the company of their mother.

"Shane and Shelby, I have a surprise for you," Kate began. "I have to go see Uncle Brian at the police station for just a little while this afternoon. Nick is coming over to spend the afternoon with us and he will stay with you while I'm gone."

"Yea!" they shouted as they danced around the room. She was so thankful that they liked Nick and welcomed him into their little world.

When Mary heard that Nick was joining Kate and the kids for dinner, she offered to cook for everyone and have it ready at 6:00. That sounded good to Kate and she was sure that Nick would appreciate a good home-cooked meal.

Before Mary had a chance to leave, Nick arrived. Mary and Kate took turns finishing each other's sentences extending the dinner invitation to Nick for that evening. He accepted the invitation with the condition that, not this weekend but the following one, he would be allowed to cook for all of them. He wanted to display his culinary skills by serving them a traditional Ukrainian dinner, like his mother used to cook for him.

After Mary left, the twins decided that the entertainment for the afternoon would be coloring, which pleased Kate. She preferred that they not be glued to the television, although she did encourage some programs, such as "The Waltons" and "The Little House on the Prairie."

Shane and Shelby gathered their favorite coloring books and a shoebox full of crayons, some old, some new. Shane selected a "Sesame Street" book and Shelby chose the "Every Holiday Coloring Book." The children announced a coloring contest with the boys against the girls so Kate would be coloring with Shelby and Nick would be paired with Shane. The twins explained the importance of keeping all of their strokes with the crayons within the lines. With that last instruction, the contest began.

When Shelby asked Kate why she was smiling all of the time, she explained that it was because she thought that the pictures were so pretty. She winked at Nick. She was smiling because she was happy. Amid and in spite of all of the tragedy at the hospital, she was happy. Happy that her surrogate big brother and one of her best friends might find happiness with each other. Happy that her children were healthy and well adjusted. Happy that her parents were still there for her with love and support. Happy that she had a successful career and a job she found challenging and thoroughly enjoyable. And happy that she had met a man who made her desires come out of hibernation. Her whole being felt like she was being swept down a rapid serendipitous river and she was becoming intoxicated by its caress. She hoped and prayed that the feelings were real.

After the pictures were finished, it was snack time. Kate poured each of the children a glass of milk to go with a plate of cookies and sliced apple. Nick passed on the food but did accept a cup of coffee. When Kate left for the police station, she left the children and Nick sitting in the kitchen eating their snack and discussing the merits of their coloring project. Each picture was declared a winner in one of the four categories of fastest, neatest, most colors used, and least colors used. Each work of art was given a gold star and a place of honor on the refrigerator door.

Kate was ushered into a conference room shortly after she arrived at the station. Both Brian and Greg were already in the room. When she entered, Greg stood to greet her and then excused himself, saying he had work to do. Brian offered her some coffee that she declined. She pulled a can of Coke from her purse. She made some crack about being a Girl Scout and always being prepared. Brian smiled but made no comment. Today, he would be all business.

Brian got right to the point, "What was your relationship to MJ Iverson?"

"I've known MJ for several years but only on a professional basis not a social one. I found her easy to work with and proficient in her job. She was a team player in her department and throughout the hospital, as far as I could tell. She had a 'happy go lucky' personality and was very friendly, especially to the men on staff. She was often described as a flirt and kept company with many different men, including married men, according to the hospital gossip. Although not usually accurate, most gossip contains some threads of truth."

Brian next wanted to know about Dr. Dunbar.

"He was an excellent ER physician. He was the one who developed the idea of having the Halloween Party as a benefit for abused women and children. He organized the party for the last several years. I've known him for about five years on a professional and casual social basis. I never dated him but some of my friends did. I considered him a friend. He used to ask for my opinion on which women he should ask out but those conversations were usually 'tongue in cheek.' We never really had a serious conversation on a personal level until after MJ's death, when he confided to me about his relationship with MJ and how important she had become to him. He was devastated by her death but I thought that he was coming to grips with the situation. He was sad but he was coping or so I thought. I was totally surprised to learn that he had taken his own life."

"Did Dr. Dunbar have the knowledge and expertise to take his life like that?" Brian asked.

"Yes, unfortunately for him, he absolutely did. Was there any evidence, anything, that might show that someone other than Dr. Dunbar had administered the drugs?" Kate asked.

Brian admitted, "The only fingerprints found on the syringes, tubing, and IV solution bottles were Dr. Dunbar's."

Next, Brian wanted to know about the people working in the OR the night of Dr. Dunbar's death. Kate explained that although she had met both Army and Maggie before she started working third-shift, she really got to know them quite well during the last year and a half.

"While in the service, Army served some time in Vietnam. He worked as a medic and a scrub tech in a field hospital. He could be described as a gentle giant but I have seen his temper flare a couple of times. It happened in response to someone in authority like a doctor, taking advantage of one of the regulars, usually one of the nurses. He's been dating the third-shift RN from Labor & Delivery, Joey Ford. She often comes to the OR for C-sections but not on the night of Dr. Dunbar's death. He's a good worker and a team player. I've never had any problems with him."

"What can you tell me about Margaret MacGregor?" Brian wanted to know.

"Brian, this all seems so formal. You know that she is my friend," complained Kate.

"Come on, Kate. Humor me. I'm trying to do my job here."

"Okay. Maggie was a good friend to me while I was in

mourning for Mike. She was an excellent listener when I needed one. She didn't press me for details that I wasn't ready to offer. She likes to listen to gossip or hospital stories but she keeps them pretty much to herself. We talk between us but we don't really gossip with others.

"Maggie never revealed too much about her personal life. She did tell me that she was from Florida originally. She said she was an orphan and had no family. She did mention an aunt once as her only relative. She's been on her own since she was a teenager and she put herself through school. She told me that she had been involved in a serious romantic relationship that had soured, which precipitated her move to Michigan. She never gave me any more details of her history than that.

"She broke up with someone recently but I don't know who he is. She didn't seem too upset about it. She eagerly accepted my idea about double dating to the Halloween Party. And I'm glad about it—two of my best friends are getting together."

Brian took notes but didn't give any indication that he had learned anything new. He showed Kate his time line chart and asked her to make notations of her movements, her colleague's movements, and any other memories during that time that she could chart. He asked her to initial each notation.

When Kate finished, Brian thanked her for her time and encouraged her to contact him if she thought of anything else that might be helpful.

"Kate, I'm sorry if this interview seemed cold. It's just that it's very important to get the facts straight. I really am looking forward to our date this Saturday," Brian said, walking her to the door.

"I understand, Brian. Really. I'll see you later."

Kate returned home to find Nick and the children finishing work on a puzzle. She complimented them on their fine work and then sent the children to wash-up for dinner. When they left the room, she started to tell Nick about her meeting but he put his finger to her lips to quiet her. He told her that she had plenty of time to tell him about the meeting but for now she needed time for herself, which included a nice evening with family and friends. He hugged her and kissed her lightly on lips. It was electric! She smiled. They were standing face to face, holding hands, when Shelby and Shane returned. The children didn't seem to notice the moment of intimacy.

Nick, Kate, and the children put their jackets on and headed to her parents' home for dinner. The twins decided that the boys should take care of the girls so Shane took his mother's hand and Shelby took Nick's. Shelby explained to them that when they go to Grandma's and Grandpa's, they always skipped. So if Nick didn't know how to skip, he had better learn. Nick surprised them all by not only skipping but by singing a little Ukrainian song to provide the beat. Kate was becoming more enamored by the minute.

John answered the door, greeted his daughter and grandchildren with hugs and kisses, and Nick with a firm handshake. Mary announced that dinner was about five minutes from being on the table and she hoped that they all brought hearty appetites. John invited everyone to make themselves at home. He excused himself to start a tape of music for dinner listening.

Mary served chicken stew with fresh baked biscuits. Before they started filling their plates, all joined hands while John said a few words of grace. Everything was delicious and everyone said so. For desert, she had baked an apple pie and she served each piece with a scoop of vanilla ice cream. Nick fit right in and Kate's parents smiled with approval. A successful evening. Kate's heart was singing and she was surprised that everyone couldn't hear it.

John and the children took Nick to the basement to show him the train set up. Kate and Mary cleaned the table and did the dishes. While in the kitchen, Mary had a chance to talk to Kate about her relationship with Nick. Kate tried to explain her feelings to Mary without seeming too emotional or melodramatic. She also told Mary about the plans for the weekend. Nick walked in on the conversation just as Mary was asking Kate what the kids would be doing for their Halloween celebration.

Kate explained that on Friday, they would be attending a classroom party in the afternoon and the neighborhood party would be held in the school gym that night. Then on Sunday, October 31st, she'd promised them that this year they could wear their costumes to some of the houses in their neighborhood, although she had yet to figure how she could take the children out trick-or-treating and pass out candy at the same time. Nick offered to stay at the house and pass out the candy so Kate could go with the children. How perfect. Everything was going so well that Kate was wondering what great thing would happen next.

Nick walked Kate and the kids back to her house and left so Kate could bathe the children and get them ready for bed. They said their prayers then she tucked them into bed. She pulled the rocking chair up between their beds so she could sit between them while she read a story. When finished, she kissed them on their foreheads and quietly left the room. It was 8:30 p.m. That left an hour and a half for sleep before her mother would come at 10 p.m.

Shortly after Kate left the police station, Brian left as well. He went to his apartment to get cleaned up a bit before his dinner date with Maggie. He arrived at the Big Boy parking lot at the same time as Maggie. He walked up to her car to greet her, opened her car door, and helped her out.

"Hi, Maggie. It's so nice to see you again. Since we haven't officially met, I am Brian Goss, at your service," Brian said as he made a little bow.

Normally, Maggie would have given him her hand to shake but he was still holding her hand from when he helped her out of her car. She was thoroughly impressed by his courtesy and pleased that he was much better looking then she had remembered. His blonde hair was as long as police regulations would allow and he had pale blue eyes that almost perfectly matched the shirt he was wearing. He still had a tan from the summer sun and could have easily passed as a California surfer.

"This is it," she thought with a smile. "This is the beginning of the rest of my life."

"Hi, Brian. It's very good to see you again. I feel like I know you already. Kate talks about you so often."

They walked into the restaurant together and were seated immediately. While they were waiting for their food, Brian started the conversation.

"Maggie, there's something that we need to talk about right up front."

"Sure, what is it?"

"I don't want the investigation that's going on at the hospital to get mixed up in our social life so I think it's important that we set some ground rules."

"Whatever you think is best. You're the investigator so I trust your judgement," Maggie said sincerely.

"Good, I'm glad you feel that way because there will come a time when you will have to be interviewed again but not today. When we're together socially, like this dinner, we should totally avoid that subject and talk about something more pleasant, like you and me."

"I totally agree. I'm rather tired of dealing with that tragedy, and everyone at the hospital is trying to get things back to normal."

They spent about an hour and a half eating dinner and getting to know one another. They also made arrangements for Brian to pick Maggie up at her house on Saturday for the party. When they left, Maggie went home and Brian went back to the station to finish a little work before calling it a night.

Even though Brian gave Maggie the little speech about keeping the investigation separate from their social lives, he knew that he couldn't follow that advice completely. There was no way he could ignore any pertinent personal information that Maggie might reveal about herself because Greg was doing a background check on her. Brian would automatically check Maggie's information against Greg's details.

Brian tried to recall exactly what Maggie had said about herself during dinner. The more he thought about it, the more he realized that he hadn't learned as much from her, as he already knew from his talks with Kate. Maggie only talked about the current events in her life. It occurred to him that every time he asked her a question about her past, she avoided giving an answer and asked him a question back instead. Her evasion had worked because he hadn't even noticed at the time. He had been much too charmed by her. Now he realized that she had been in total control of their conversation. He spoke at length about himself, his childhood, his job, his hopes, and his dreams but she revealed next to nothing about herself.

"How could that have happened?" he wondered. "Was Maggie shy when it came to talking about herself or was she trying to hide something? Was she trying to flatter him by keeping the conversation concentrated on him? Maybe he was just letting his imagination get the better of him or maybe his detective intuition was just kicking in. Whatever the case, he would think about it for a while before he said anything to Greg. He didn't want to make waves for no reason. He liked Maggie and he enjoyed her company. He was looking forward to going to the party and he didn't want to upset everyone's plans.

Thursday Night, October 28, 1976

Kate was hoping that the night would be quiet enough to give her a chance to regroup and reflect on the dramatic changes that were taking place in her life. When she left the elevator on the tenth floor, she spotted Rae in the surgery office. Rae motioned for her to come over and join the group that included some of the second-shift staff plus Maggie and Army. Kate noticed and made mention of the fact that Rae had already changed out of her scrubs. Rae said she had a date to keep so she was in a hurry to leave. Rae gave report to Kate saying that the night had been very quiet and everything was already done. She promised that, not only was everything done and double-checked, but also a fresh set up was in place in OR 7. As far as Rae knew, there were no cases pending. She wished Kate a good night and left.

Kate knew that with Rae leaving, she had to be prepared for a code so she immediately left the office to change her clothes. When she entered the anesthesia lounge the lights were off so she flipped the switch by the door. When the room lit up, there was Nick sitting on the couch, smiling from ear to ear. He had set a table with popcorn and Coke, complete with paper napkins and birthday cake candles, ingeniously held upright with a couple of surgical clamps. Kate was so surprised. He explained that they really hadn't had a chance to be together alone so he had planned that if the evening was quiet, they would have a little rendezvous. The other OR staff members were in on his little surprise and promised not to interfere unless there was an emergency. Still smiling from Nick's thoughtfulness, she went into the bathroom part of the lounge and changed into her scrubs. Before she came out, he dimmed the lights and turned the radio on to one of the Top Forty stations as the last touch to set the mood.

They spent almost two hours without interruption talking about everything from their childhoods, careers, aspirations, and families, to the more recent past, present and future events.

When Nick left, Kate went to make quick rounds of the ORs. Even though Rae checked and double-checked everything, she still felt it was her responsibility to check everything again. All was perfect, including the emergency set up in OR 7. She asked Maggie if she knew about any pending cases. There weren't any.

Maggie and Kate both ended up in the OR office where they starting discussing their budding relationships with Nick and Brian. Maggie began by telling Kate about her dinner date with Brian and again thanked her for her matchmaking.

"I had a great time with Brian today. It was just a simple dinner but it seemed so special. I think Brian had a good time, too, at least he acted like he did. He said he was looking forward to the party. Kate, I can't thank you enough for being my friend and caring enough about me to introduce me to the man of my dreams. I feel like that old saying was written just for me. You know the one that goes 'today is the first day of the rest of your life.' And, I owe it all to you. "

"I think you are giving me more credit than I deserve. You are a wonderful person, pretty, intelligent, and with a good personality. If your life is going well, it's because you've earned it. I'm really happy for you. And as far as you and Brian go, I knew that if I could ever get you two together, you would be good for each other. I've known Brian for a long time and if he looked like he was having a good time then he was having a good time. If anything, Brian is honest to a fault. So if he said it, then you can believe it. By the way, don't forget that I won't be working Friday night. I took the night off because I won't have time to get enough sleep during the day. When I pick the twins up after school, I'm going to take them to the cider mill. Then in the evening, the neighborhood is having a party at the school."

"Oh, that's right. I'd forgotten. That means I won't see you again until Brian and I come over to your house before the party on Saturday."

"That's right. Saturday, my house, you and Brian, Nick and me. We are going to have so much fun." Kate stood to leave the office. "But for now, I want to take advantage of this quiet time to get some rest so I'm going to lay down for a little while. Call me if you need me. I'll see you later."

Normally, when Kate tried to rest at the hospital, she didn't really fall asleep. It was more of a psuedo-sleep, a very light level of sleep, resting one's eyes and body but keeping the ears open listening for the phone or the code beeper. The body rests but the mind doesn't. The type of rest that usually helps chase fatigue away but can never be a substitute for the real thing. However, tonight was different. Kate fell soundly asleep within fifteen minutes of lying down. She knew she was tired but she wasn't aware of the degree of exhaustion that had engulfed her. The continuous bombardment of thoughts and feelings assaulting her senses had taken their toll. Her mind, spirit, and physical being were demanding a rest. She slept for four solid hours. She was awakened at 6:30 a.m., when the morning crew started arriving. She was somewhat embarrassed to be caught napping by her anesthesia colleagues from the first-shift, even though everyone knew that the anesthesia staff often tried to get catnaps while on the night-shift. It was an acceptable practice because some nights the anesthetist never got any break in the whole eight-hour shift.

Kate gave report which everyone had already guessed—a quiet night. She wished everyone a Happy Holloween, and said she hoped that they could all make it to the party Saturday night. She did not see Maggie before she left the hospital.

Chapter Eight

Friday Morning, October 29, 1976

Shane and Shelby were happy to see their mother. They all had breakfast together. The children were dressed in their costumes for their class party. Kate asked Mary to take the children to school and pick them up as well, if she didn't get a call from Kate by 11:30 a.m. Even though she slept well at the hospital, that sleep would do little to eliminate the exhaustion that would surely over come her before the end of the evening if she didn't get at least a few more hours of sleep.

Kate left the kitchen and went immediately to bed. She was tired but she was having trouble falling asleep so she started reading one of her anesthesia journals, always a good hypnotic. Within thirty minutes she was asleep but not a good restful sleep. Her dreams, full of disturbing thoughts and frightening images, kept her tossing and turning. When she awoke at noon, she thought she felt worse than she did before she went to bed. She couldn't remember her dreams but she had an uneasy feeling that she attributed to the recent deaths.

Kate called her mother, who had just returned with the children from their school. She asked Mary to give the children their lunch and allow them to stay in their costumes. She would be there is a little while. She had to shower first.

Rather than walking, she drove the short trip to her parents' home because she needed her car to take the children on their surprise outing. When she entered the kitchen, the children were just finishing the last bites of their peanut butter and jelly sandwiches.

The twins spent the next fifteen minutes telling their mother about the events of their class party, including the parade of costumes around the school. Kate pulled her camera out of her purse and starting taking pictures of the kids. Mary also took a few pictures so that Kate could be in them with the twins. After pictures, Kate asked the children to settle down so she could explain their surprise to them.

"I hope Big Bird and Cookie Monster are ready for an adventure. We're going to the apple orchard to buy cider, donuts, and caramel apples."

The kids were excited and eager to get started on their trip. They grabbed Kate by the hands and started pulling her toward the door.

Kate looked at Mary. "Do you want to go with us, Mom?"

Mary declined the invitation saying that the kids needed time alone with their Mom. With that, Kate took the kids and left.

Kate, Shane, and Shelby headed for the Parshallville Cider Mill south of Flint, just off US 23. Even before they arrived at the mill, they noticed that the smell of the apples and donuts permeated the whole town. The town's folk were finishing the last minute preparations for the events celebrating the Halloween weekend. Tables were set up for pumpkin carving contests. Wagons were decorated and ready for hayrides. Water tubs were ready for the apples to be added for bobbing. An empty house in town had been transformed into a haunted house by the local parents association to benefit the children's playground fund. The twins were too young to enjoy most of the entertainment that was aimed at the ten and older crowd but they didn't mind. They weren't too young for apples, cider, and doughnuts. While standing at the counter waiting to pay for their selections, the staff talked to them as though they really were Cookie Monster and Big Bird. The kids did their best to imitate the voices of the famous characters.

Kate bought enough food to have some for now and some for later. They sat at picnic tables down by the water wheel while they ate their treat. Shane and Shelby mentioned that

Kate didn't have a costume. She explained that she was saving her costume for Saturday night when Nick, Uncle Brian, and Maggie, a friend of hers from work, came over. They were all going to a costume party at the hospital. The twins thought it was rather strange that big people had dress-up parties like little kids and that their mother would actually go to such a party.

They finished their snack and walked around the town a while before they headed home.

Between the candy and treats from their school party and those that would be eaten this evening, Shane and Shelby would more than meet their sugar limit for the day. Trying to head off a period of hyperactivity followed by complete exhaustion after a "sugar high," Kate insisted that they have a short nap or at least, lie down and rest for a while before dinner. It also gave her a chance to call Brian and get his impression of Maggie.

"Hi, Brian. How's everything?"

"You mean, how was my dinner with Maggie?"

"Boy, am I that transparent?"

"Yeah, Kate, sometimes you are but I like you anyway. But that's not what you want to hear, is it?"

"Come on, Brian. Quit teasing."

"Okay, already. I was just trying to have a little fun with you. Where's your sense of humor?"

"The facts, Brian. Just give me the facts," she said in her best detective voice. She was becoming impatient with his little game even though she usually enjoyed his sense of humor. She tried not to get irritated and just played along with him.

"I spent about an hour and a half with her. Greg cut me a little slack because I've been putting in so many hours lately. Besides, he thought I might pick up some information from her."

"I think that stinks a little. I mean, you guys are just getting to know each other and you're already keeping secrets from her."

"I know. The thought of that bothered me too, but as it turned out, we had a great time. Greg suggested and I agreed that right from the beginning, I would keep my social life separate from my professional life, as far as Maggie and the Temple investigation are concerned."

Brian decided not to tell Kate that in retrospect, he didn't think that Maggie was very open about herself or forth coming with any personal information.

"I didn't pressure her for any information and I didn't ask her many personal questions. She told me that she came from Florida after the death of her fiancé, and that she had dated a bit here in Michigan during the last year or so, but no one seriously."

Kate was confused for moment. Maggie had told her about a break-up of a relationship, not a death. She dismissed the discrepancy and returned her attention to Brian.

"Maggie told me that she was orphaned when her parents were killed in a house fire while she was still in high school and that as an only child with no other relatives, she has lived on her own since then."

Again something in Brian's story struck Kate as conflicting but she couldn't put her finger on what it was at the moment. It would come to her. Kate was delighted that Brian seemed to enjoy Maggie's company.

Before she hung up, she reminded Brian that he was to pick Maggie up at 5 p.m. on Saturday and bring her over for cider and donuts and to meet the children before going to the hospital for the memorial service and party.

Kate then called the hospital operator and left a message for Nick to call before 6 p.m. if he got a chance. He had to work tonight but he had Saturday and Sunday off. He was in surgery and didn't get Kate's message until after 6 p.m. so he didn't call before she left to take the children to the school for the neighborhood party.

The party was a huge success with the food, games, spooky house, and costume parade. By the time they returned home, the kids were exhausted. Having their classroom party and the neighborhood party both on the same day seemed a bit much but that was the way that the plans had worked out this year. The celebrating had taken its toll on the children. It took all of their energy reserves to bathe and get ready for bed. Once in bed, they were asleep before Kate finished the first page of their bedtime story.

At 9:30 p.m., the phone rang. It was Nick. He apologized for not calling earlier but he had been tied up in the OR. Things at the hospital were quiet for now and he hoped that they would stay that way for a while.

Kate was glad that the hospital was calm. Maybe Maggie would have a quiet night as well. Kate told Nick about her conversation with Brian and his glowing report of dinner with Maggie. She didn't mention the uneasy feeling that she noticed a couple of times during their conversation when some of the details of Maggie's stories to Brian didn't correspond with her recollections of the same stories. She was tired of being the skeptic all of the time, especially when it came to her friends. Besides, if her suspicions stayed on overdrive, they would surely interfere with the mood of her much anticipated weekend festivities and she didn't want that.

Kate said good-bye to Nick and retired for the evening with one of her anesthesia journals. Within an hour, she was asleep.

She had a restless sleep, waking at 2 a.m. and again at 4. Some evil presence seemed to be trying to sabotage her rest. Fortunately, on both occasions she was able to go back to sleep.

Saturday Morning, October 30, 1976

Kate was awake again at 6 a.m. This time she decided to get up. Sitting at the kitchen table drinking a Coke, she began to make notes for the comments she wanted to make at Dr. Dunbar's memorial service that night. In a few short days before to his death, she had become close to him and had come to know some of his story. She wanted to share her feelings of the joy of a new friendship and the sorrow of the loss of that friend. She wanted her colleagues, who didn't know the real Dr. Dunbar, to have a glimpse of him through her eyes.

Her thoughts were of both happy and sad memories, melded together in a heartfelt sentiment. She hoped that the process of writing her thoughts and sharing them with others would have the cathartic effect she needed to help peel away layers of sadness that she had been carrying around.

She was finishing her notes when the children joined her in the kitchen, ready for their breakfast. Of course, they wanted cider and donuts and Kate complied with their wishes. She folded her notes and put them in her purse to be sure that she would have them with her at the memorial.

She spent the whole day with the children, raking leaves and playing in the leaf pile. It was one of those times that wasn't special because of the date, a particular event, or specific occasion but special because it was a family time. It was one of those times that in the future would be recalled in one of those precious "remember when" memories.

Nick arrived at 4:30 p.m. The twins let him in. Kate wasn't quite ready so he passed the time listening to the children tell of their leaf raking adventure. He hadn't spent much time with young children and was finding that he rather enjoyed it. He had actually begun to think of the day that he would become a father. Not that he expected that day to be anywhere in the near future but he was beginning to develop a curiosity about Nick Lecorts, the dad.

Kate entered the living room wearing a set of green scrubs rather than her usual white starched scrub dress. She had her hair pulled up and covered with one of the men's tight-fitting cloth scrub caps. Shelby and Shane, surprised by her attire, roared with laughter when they noticed that their Mom and Nick were twins, just like them.

Mary opened the living room door in the middle of the laughter and the twins rushed to her to share their joke. Kate gave them a few minutes to enjoy the humor of the moment before she tried to calm them down. Maggie and Brian would be arriving soon and she wanted them on their best behavior.

Kate had arranged for Mary to spend the night with the children. It would have been easier for the children to stay with

Mary at her house but tonight was October 30—Devil's Night. Kate didn't want her house to be unattended just in case there was any vandalism, although there had never been trouble in her neighborhood, as far as, she knew. Besides, the neighborhood kids knew that Mike had been a cop and that the police still kept an eye on the McKenna house so she really didn't have to worry about any property destruction.

Mary took the children to the kitchen to start their supper just before the doorbell rang. It was Brian and Maggie dressed in scrubs identical to Kate and Nick. When Shawn and Shelby peeked into the living room to see their mother's guests, another roar of laughter erupted.

"Four twins?" they chanted when they could catch their breaths. "Four twins!"

Brian and Maggie looked at each other with slight embarrassment and then laughed along with everyone else even though they didn't understand the joke. Kate introduced Maggie to Shane, Shelby, and Mary before they returned to the kitchen. When they were out of earshot, Kate explained the kids' little joke to Brian and Maggie.

"They have gone through their life as the McKenna twins. Their definition of twins has always been based on their own experiences and they find it extremely funny that their mother and her friends would dress as twins. They think it's even more incredible that big people would wear costumes to a party like kids do," Kate explained.

The partygoers were all seated for only a few moments when Mary entered the room with a tray holding a pitcher of cider and four glasses. Shelby carried plates and napkins, and Shane carried a plate of donuts. After serving everyone in a dramatic maid and butler routine, the children returned to the kitchen with their grandmother, obviously pleased with their performance.

"Another memory for the reminiscence file," Kate thought.

Maggie was pleased by the attention she received from Mary and the children. "Kate, you are so lucky to have such a delightful and caring mother. I can't wait to meet your father. I'll bet that he's just as wonderful. And your children!" she exclaimed. "I've heard you talk about them so much but I never envisioned such extraordinary little cuties. I hope that someday, I can have such a loving family for comfort and support."

While Maggie was talking, Kate noticed her looking adoringly at Brian when she spoke of having her own family someday. Kate wondered if she was reading a message into Maggie's glance that wasn't really there or was Maggie already envisioning a future with Brian. Kate chalked it up to an imagination on overdrive and dismissed the thought.

By 5:45 p.m., they had finished their snack and had said all of their good-byes. The two couples left for the hospital and an evening of expected mixed emotions. Brian and Maggie went in Brian's car. Nick and Kate went in Nick's.

The two cars were parked next to each other in the resident physician's reserved parking lot and the couples entered the lounge of the interns' quarters together. They were surprised to see at least 200 people already present with more arriving every minute.

Kate and her group greeted friends, colleagues, and acquaintances, as well as strangers, when they made their way through the crowd to an area close to the microphone that had been set up for the memorial speakers.

The service started a little late, about 6:15 p.m., in an effort to include some of the people who were still trying to work their way into the room. Mr. Eggleston welcomed everyone on behalf of the hospital administration before he introduced Rev. Bill Blackwell, who would deliver the invocation. Immediately upon his introduction, the room quieted and the mood became somber. He began with a prayer honoring the combined efforts made on the behalf of and for the benefit of the citizens of Flint, by the hospital staff, the police department, and the fire department. He acknowledged Dr. Thomas Dunbar and noted some of his acts of kindness and generosity to the community.

Mr. Eggleston made a few comments on behalf of the hospital board and administrative staff about Dr. Dunbar's contributions to Temple Memorial and how his presence would be sorely missed. Dr. Scott followed with a glowing commentary on Dr. Dunbar's medical knowledge, skills, and practice. Mrs. Corena Russell, Director of the YWCA, spoke about Dr. Dunbar's dedication and commitment to the Abused Women's and Children's Shelter; his generous donation of time and resources; and all of his efforts to recruit others for assistance, including everyone connected with the Halloween Party fund raiser.

Now, it was Kate's turn to speak on behalf of the nursing staff. She took her notes to the podium but spoke without glancing at them.

"Four or five years ago when I met Dr. Tom Dunbar, I knew him to be an excellent ER physician and one of the most arrogant, egotistical men that I had ever had the displeasure of meeting." Her comment caused a subtle murmur in the crowd.

"How many of the nurses here had to put up with his sarcastic and ambiguous comments when they passed him in the hospital?" The murmur grew louder.

"I remember times when I was so irritated with him that I wanted to slap his face right off of his head to erase that sarcastic smile." The crowd was quiet again, anticipating the next scathing remark.

"Well, that wasn't the real Dr. Dunbar. That was his façade. It took me a while to get to know the real Dr. Dunbar and when I did, he was my friend. I feel blessed to have known him and to have had time with him as a friend. He was kind, caring, and hard working, as those of you who worked with him in the ER can attest to." A round of applause arose from the crowd.

"Just recently, Tom confided to me that after a lifetime of searching for a partner to share his life, he had found his mate. Tom had fallen deeply in love with MJ Iverson." A gasp came from the crowd.

Maggie had no reaction to any of Kate's comments. In fact, she seemed rather oblivious to any of her surroundings, devoting her entire attention to Brian who was listening somberly to Kate's message.

Kate continued. "I didn't know MJ very well but I got to know her through Dr. Dunbar's eyes. He said that not many people made the effort to get to know the real MJ and he was glad that he had. He said that they were alike in so many ways and he was delighted that their future seemed so full of promise."

Kate stopped momentarily to gather her emotions. "Both Dr. Dunbar and MJ died unexpectedly and way too soon. They both need our prayers." Kate bowed her head for a brief moment before she began again.

"The work he did on behalf of the Women's Center was very important to him and to the center. So in his memory the Center is being renamed the 'Thomas Dunbar Safe Haven'." A round of applause arose from the crowd.

"It will be up to us, all of us, to ensure that the center remains successful." With a change in her tone, Kate did her best impression of Dr. Dunbar's southern drawl. "Now, as Dr. Dunbar would say, all of you lovely ladies and kind gentlemen are here for reveling and frivolity. Please enjoy yourselves and leave your generous contributions for the Dunbar Safe Haven with Mr. Eggleston or Mrs. Russell. And of course, you can always mail a donation directly to the YWCA. Thank you so very much to each and every one of you for your kind attention and generous spirit."

A huge round of applause sounded, to the point that Mr. Eggleston's final comments thanking the guests for their donations and wishing everyone a good time, went unheard.

"The Snowbirds," a musical group comprised primarily of Canadian interns and residents began playing. The party had begun. Kate left the podium and made her way back to Nick. By the time she arrived at his side, Maggie and Brian were already on the dance floor.

"Those were very kind remarks. It must have been really difficult for you to speak so forthright to this group when you are still trying to deal with everything on a personal level," Nick said. He gave Kate a light hug.

Kate smiled a distant smile. "No, actually that was my

goodbye to Tom and MJ and I feel some emotional closure." Changing the subject and her tone she said, "This is a party so let's go have some fun. I haven't partied in a very long time but I'm sure it won't take long for me to get back in the groove."

Nick smiled at her in admiration. "Want to dance?" he asked.

"I do but I think I'd like a drink first. I'm really thirsty."

"A drink it is." He took her hand and guided her through the crowd that offered a mixture of compliments and condolences.

Nick ordered a beer and Kate ordered a glass of white wine. Because the party was a charity benefit, local merchants donated most of the food and drinks so there was no posted charge for the partygoers. But almost everyone paid a generous donation knowing that all of the money would go directly to the Safe Haven. Even the DJ, who was making all of the announcements, performing the master of ceremonies duties, and playing records alternately with the band, was donating his time and equipment.

The party was a huge success. By 8 p.m., they had already amassed more funds than they had expected to collect for the whole evening. Plus, everyone seemed to be having a great time. It seemed like the tragedy had passed and a time of healing had begun.

By 10 p.m., Kate was ready to call it a night. Her sleeping habits were so mixed up from her third-shift stint that she suddenly felt as though she hadn't slept in days. Nick assured her that he didn't mind going home early so they got ready to leave. There were a number of people that Kate felt obligated to thank personally before she left so she started making rounds. She wanted to let Brian and Maggie know that they were going home and to wish them a good evening. She found them on the dance floor. Brian and Maggie had been inseparable all night and at times seemed oblivious to any others in the room. They expressed disappointment that Nick and Kate were leaving but Kate was quite sure that her friends really wouldn't know the difference.

Kate and Nick decided to walk to Kate's house, leaving Nick's car in his assigned parking spot in the resident's lot. Hand in hand, they walked through the quiet neighborhood. The sky was full of twinkling stars and the autumn air was crisp and cool. The dried fallen leaves crunched with each step. Occasionally, a gusty breeze caused the leaf piles to blow creating minor whirlwinds. Nick put his arm around Kate in an effort to protect her from the elements.

Kate's emotional circuit had been on overload for so long that her whole body ached. She longed to relax, to let down her guard, to live and love again. Tonight, as she walked quietly with her new friend, she felt the old pressures and reservations begin to fade as feelings of hope and optimism for the future surged forward from their hiding place deep within her soul.

When her house came into view, Nick stopped.

"Kate, I've really enjoyed your company tonight. And now, before I safely deliver you home as promised, I'd like to kiss you good night. Is that okay with you?"

Kate smiled up at Nick. She stood on her tiptoes, reached up, and put both hands on his shoulders. He bent slightly and she, ever so lightly, kissed his lips. She pulled back and gazed into his eyes again. "Does that answer your question?"

"I guess it does," Nick whispered as he pulled her close and kissed her with gentle passion. The floodgate of emotions that had been guarding Kate for such a long time had been lifted. She returned his kiss with such a craving and desire that she could feel his closeness in every cell of her body. She lost all contact with her surroundings and was only aware of the emotional flurry that was pulling her closer and closer to being at one with Nick. Her heart was pounding and she was breathless. Every inch of her body was tingling and her legs felt weak.

Nick broke the kiss and held Kate in his arms. He could feel the heat of her passion that matched his own eager readiness but he was well aware that they couldn't very well make love in the middle of the street. Nick ended the embrace and reached for her hand. They began walking toward her house. On the porch, Kate's hands were shaking so much that she kept fumbling with her key. Nick took the key and opened the door.

"Won't you come in for a while?" Kate asked.

"I really don't think I'd like your mother to see me like this." Nick glanced down at himself and when Kate's eyes followed his gaze, she noticed a very apparent erection. She smiled and felt pleased with herself and not the least bit embarrassed.

"Another time, Kate. There will be many, many other times. For now, good night my sweetheart. Have a good night's sleep and wonderfully sweet dreams."

He kissed her lightly on the forehead and closed the door.

It was almost a minute before Kate realized she was holding her breath. She inhaled deeply then slowly blew her breath away. She'd felt love before, the love of parents, the love of children, and the warm comfortable love that comes from marrying your best friend. But those feelings of love were so different from what she was feeling at that moment. She couldn't even begin to describe the emotional explosion that had just taken place.

"Hi, Kate," Mary said when she entered the living room.

She was startled by her mother's intrusion into her musing. "Hi, Mom."

"You're early, aren't you? I wasn't expecting you for a few hours yet. There wasn't any problem was there?" Mary asked.

"I'm just a little early. We never intended to stay too late. And no, there wasn't any problem. Nick has some work to do in the morning and I was getting tired so we just decided to go home."

"Good, that gives us time for a little chat. How was the memorial?" Mary asked.

Kate thought, "The memorial. Had it really been just a few hours ago? It seemed like she had just spent an eternity with Nick on the sidewalk near her house."

She was deep in thought and didn't respond immediately to her mother's question.

"Kate, what's wrong?" Mary asked in an effort to bring Kate's obviously distracted attention back from her private thoughts to the here and now.

Kate returned to the present. "Ah nothing, Mom.

Everything's fine. The memorial service was a nice tribute to Dr. Dunbar. The Women's Center was renamed the Thomas Dunbar Safe Haven in his honor. The benefit part of the event was a huge success. Even more money than anticipated was collected."

"What a honorable remembrance for your friend." Mary continued, "Speaking of friends, how was your date with Nick?"

"We had a really good time. He's such pleasant company—compassionate, witty, charming. I've only known him for such a short time but already I feel like I've known him forever. Isn't that strange?"

"Not all that strange."

"What do you mean?" Kate quizzed.

"Nothing honey. You've been on an emotional overload for too long. I don't want to add to it by getting into a philosophical discussion. Let's just be happy that you had a good time tonight. And what about your friends, Brian and Maggie, did they have a good time as well?"

"Considering it would have been difficult to slip a piece of paper between them all evening, I would say that they were enjoying themselves. Every time I saw them, they were laughing, dancing, and singing along with the music. It was marvelous seeing them like that."

Mary walked toward the closet to retrieve her coat. "Since it's not too late, I'm going home instead of spending the night. Will you call your father and tell him that I'm on my way home?"

"Sure, Mom. See you tomorrow. I love you."

Kate called her dad to tell him her mother had left for home. She locked the door and turned off the porch light before leaving the room.

She checked on the children who were sound asleep in their beds. She danced to her room to some unknown song that was playing in her head. She peeled off the scrub clothes, washed her face, and covered her hair in preparation for a shower. She was poised to step into the shower when the phone rang. She wrapped a towel around herself and hurried to answer the phone.

"Hello?"

"I just called to say good night." Nick's clear, deep voice resonated through the phone.

"Are you back to your room already?"

"No, I'm in the lobby of the interns' quarters. I decided to check on things at the party. It's still going pretty strong. I'm on the way to my room right now. I hope the music doesn't keep me awake. I'll talk to you tomorrow. Sweet dreams."

"Thanks, Nick. It was sweet of you to call. But now that I've had a chance to slow down, I realize that I'm much more tired than I thought. I'm glad we called it an early night. I'm ready for those sweet dreams."

"Good night, Kate."

"Bye, Nick."

Kate's heart was still racing from the phone call when she stepped into the shower. The water spray upon her skin was like a thousand sensuous fingers. She moved her soapy hands over her body, slowly at first and then in an erotic, passionate rhythm. She pleasured herself to an explosive climax. She heard herself moan at the pleasure of it.

"Nick," she breathed.

Kate had no memory of leaving the shower, drying off, or going to bed. She was asleep immediately and her dreams picked up where reality left off.

Shortly after Nick and Kate left the party, Brian decided that it was time for him to take Maggie home. Both of them had had quite a bit to drink and Brian didn't want either one of them driving. They decided to leave his car and walk to Maggie's house.

Once there, Maggie opened each of them a beer. She invited Brian to make himself at home while she went to change into something more comfortable. She returned to the living room wearing a black slip nightgown and a fresh spray of perfume. She took a long drink from her bottle and set it aside.

She stood in front of Brian where he was seated on the couch and reached for his hands to pull him to his feet. Once standing, he embraced her and they began a passionate dance that ended with them on her bed. It wasn't difficult to loosen the string tie on the top of his scrub pants and they were quickly removed. Soon, they had shed all of their clothes, as well as, all of their inhibitions. After a night of passion, they fell asleep in each other's arms.

Maggie awoke at 5 a.m. and headed for the kitchen while Brian continued to sleep. She made a pot of coffee and fixed ham and eggs with toast on the side. When everything was ready, she woke Brian and told him that breakfast was ready.

He dragged himself to the kitchen and sat down at the table. His eyes felt scratchy, his mouth was sour, and his head hurt a little but, all in all, he didn't feel too bad considering the amount of alcohol he had consumed the night before. He was pleasantly surprised by Maggie's effort to ensure that he was up in time to eat, go home and shower, and make it to the station before the beginning of his shift for the day.

Before Brian left, he invited Maggie to dinner at his house that night. She didn't have to work Sunday night, and Brian had Monday morning off from work for a dentist appointment so the timing was perfect. He gave her his address and she knew exactly where his apartment was located so directions weren't necessary. She agreed to be at his house at 6 p.m.

After he left, she took a couple of sleeping pills, disconnected her phone, and went to bed. It wasn't long before she was in a very deep sleep.

Chapter Nine

Sunday Morning, October 31, 1976

Kate slept soundly and didn't wake until 7:30 a.m., when the twins dive-bombed her bed from opposite directions.

"Come on, Mom. Wake up!" They shook her shoulder. "We made breakfast for you. Come on. Get up!"

Being ever mindful to hold the covers at her chin, Kate made exaggerated yawns and stretches, as though she was Rumpelstiltskin waking from his twenty-year nap. The children continued their barrage of jostling and pleading. She was thankful that they didn't jump under the covers with her, as they often did, because she was nude. She couldn't remember the last time she had slept without her nightclothes.

"Okay, okay! I'm awake! You guys go to the kitchen and I'll be there in just a minute."

The twins scampered off the bed. She put her nightshirt on, pulled on her pale pink chenille robe, and slipped into her floppy slippers before she headed for the kitchen. The table was set with three bowls and spoons, three juice glasses, milk, orange juice, cereal, and one can of Coke. Four slices of bread were on a plate next to the toaster. Kate was pleased. On the seat of Kate's chair was a folded copy of the Sunday morning edition of the Flint Journal.

Shane and Shelby began their twin speak. They used two voices to tell one story while they took turns finishing each other's sentences. "We didn't cook anything yet because we didn't want the toast to get cold or the cereal to get soggy but now that you're here, you just sit there and read the paper and we'll take care of everything."

Kate picked up the paper, sat down, opened her pop, and began to read the news while the children scurried about the kitchen. The front-page story carried all of the latest revelations about the numerous events that were taking place at Temple, including coverage of the memorial service honoring Dr. Dunbar and the benefit dedicated to the women's shelter.

She put the paper aside. She wanted to give the children her undivided attention. They deserved it. She smiled in appreciation for all of her good fortune. She was also astonished and bewildered when she realized that her first thought about the children's surprise was that she wanted to share it with Nick.

She tried to take the children to church at least every other Sunday and often when she couldn't go, her parents took them. But today wouldn't be one of those days. Kate thought that she might be too emotional to sit through a service and she didn't want the children to see her upset. That would require an explanation she was not prepared to give. She hadn't made arrangements with her parents to take the children to church so this Sunday they would stay home.

Halloween and the children occupied her thoughts. The trick or treaters would be coming tonight and there were preparations to be made. It was not unusual for 150 to 200 children of all ages to visit between 6 and 9 p.m. More decorations were added to the ones already in place. The treats, small Milky Way, Butterfinger, Baby Ruth, and Snicker candy bars were placed in Kate's large wooden salad bowl.

The children's costumes were ready, as well as, the scrub clothes for Kate to wear. Nick was scheduled to arrive at 5:30 p.m. so that they could all have hot dogs before Kate, Shane, and Shelby left to go visit their neighbors. Everything was set.

While the children were amusing themselves with one of their board games, Kate decided to call Maggie and get the scoop on her date with Brian.

Kate let the phone ring about ten times but Maggie didn't

answer. Disappointed, she hung up thc receiver. Immediately, the phone rang.

"Hello?"

"Hi, Kate. It's Brian."

"Brian, hi. I was just thinking about you. What's up?"

"I'm at work right now. I had a few minutes so I thought I give you a call and fill you in on last night before your curiosity got the best of you."

"Thanks, that was nice of you. I tried to call Maggie but she didn't answer."

"I'm not surprised. She's probably sleeping. We had a pretty late night last night but Maggie got up at 5 a.m. to fix my breakfast and get me off to work on time. Pretty impressive if I say so myself. I've got to tell you, Kate, Maggie is one the sweetest, most exciting, fun-loving women I've ever met. Why didn't you hook me up with her sooner?"

Kate laughed. "I tried to, if you will recall. So, I guess that you two had a good time last night, huh?"

"You know I'm not one to kiss and tell but...."

"But what?" Kate asked, anxious for all of the information that she could get.

"When we left the dance, where we both had a bit too much to drink, I left my car in the parking lot and we walked to Maggie's house. You know, she only lives a couple of blocks on the other side of the hospital."

"Yes, I know. Keep going," Kate encouraged.

"To make a long story short, I spent the night with her and she really knows how to make a guy feel right at home."

"Brian, I don't really need to know those kind of details."

"I'm sorry, Kate. I'm just trying to explain that I enjoy her company. Let's just leave it at that."

"Good. I think that's a good place to leave it."

Kate could feel herself blushing at his admission.

"I invited her to dinner at my house tonight and I'm cooking."

"Spaghetti, right?" she guessed.

"You know me pretty well, don't you? Yes, spaghetti, garlic

bread, and wine. Neither of us has to work tonight or tomorrow morning so we won't have to get up so early after this date."

"How is it that you got a Monday morning off from work?" Kate asked.

"Not just for the fun of it that's for sure. I have to go to the dentist at 9 a.m., so I don't have to go to the station until noon," Brian explained.

"So I guess that since you invited Maggie to your house for dinner that you really like her?" Kate quizzed him.

"Don't jump to any conclusions, Kate. I haven't made plans to spend the rest of my life with her. It's not like I found my soul mate."

Kate had a slight shudder in response to the expression "soul mate" as if she had been brushed by a feather. A microsecond of honest realization then the impression was gone. Kate had no idea what that flash of premonition meant but it would come to her eventually, it always did.

"We have fun together. She makes me laugh. And she really knows how to make me... Well, you know, make me. Yes, Kate, I like her. Okay, now I have to get back to work. I'll talk to you later," Brian said.

"Okay, Brian, I'll talk to you later." Before she hung up, she quickly added, "I'm really happy for you."

Kate's conversation with Brian reinforced the confident feeling that she had about Brian and Maggie as a couple. She decided not to try to call Maggie again today. She assumed Maggie was still sleeping so she wouldn't be tired during her date with Brian that night.

She would try to call Maggie tomorrow during the day. If she couldn't reach her then, she would just wait until Monday night at work to talk to her.

After Brian hung up, Greg called him over to the conference room. The table in the room was covered with papers that Greg had been studying.

"Brian, I've pretty much finished the background checks on Sargent, McKenna, and MacGregor, and I'd like to give you every thing I have so far. Let's start with Kate. There's nothing in her background that you don't already know, I'm sure. Why don't you look these notes over while I go get some coffee? Do you want some?"

"No thanks." Brian said as he took the papers from Greg and started reading.

Brian had finished reading the report on Kate by the time Greg returned to the room.

"You're right, Greg. I don't see anything here new to me and certainly nothing that would suggest that she should be a suspect in this investigation."

"I agree so let's just set her file aside for now. Okay, have a look at Sargent's file," Greg said as he handed Army's file to Brian. While Brian read the file, Greg reviewed his notes on Maggie.

Brian finished reading Army's file.

"Greg, this guy has an outstanding military record, a good history locally before he went into the service, and a good employment record since his return to town after his discharge. He doesn't even have, as much as a parking ticket. He even does volunteer work with underprivileged kids. He has a relationship with one of the nurses at the hospital. I don't see anything here that deserves a second look at this time," Brian said confidently.

"Good, that's what I thought, too. Now we have to talk about Margaret MacGregor. I know that she's a friend of yours but I want you to set that aside for now because I have some issues with her past. This is a fairly long report so rather than have you read it all now, I'll give you the highlights. You can read the whole report later."

"Fine. What ever you think."

"I found nothing on her in Flint to suggest that she's ever had any problems here. She has a good employment record and she has never had any contact with the police. But I found quite a different story when I contacted a couple of police departments in Florida, one in Orlando where she lived and one in Winter Springs where she worked. I also contacted a woman named Cheryle Cooke who was listed in her employment record as her next of kin.

"It turns out that Mrs. Cooke is Maggie's Aunt, her mother's sister. This is her account of Maggie's childhood. Maggie was not abandoned or adopted as a child. She was an only child, raised by her natural parents in a middle-class family. From all accounts, it was a normal and loving home but the parents had difficulties with Maggie from the time she was very young, like about 4 years old.

"Most of the time, she was just a normal little kid. But there were times when she had trouble controlling her temper. She lashed out at neighbors, classmates, or anyone that she thought had betrayed her. She started to become more and more withdrawn from everyone. Her parents took her from doctor to doctor to find out what was wrong with her. She was eventually diagnosed as schizophrenic with a paranoid personality. Mrs. Cooke read a definition to me that was provided to her by one of Maggie's doctors.

"Schizophrenia – a psychotic reaction which usually begins in adolescence, where the patient has thought disorders and emotional and behavioral disturbances; the patient has a tendency to withdraw from reality and to regress to a deteriorated level of conduct.

"A paranoid personality is a disorder where the patient unrealistically clings to an particular belief that may have little or no foundation in reality. These people often go through life with a very large chip on their shoulder. Their symptoms are often precipitated by environmental stress."

"Wow, that sounds pretty serious," Brian said with concern.

"According to Mrs. Cooke, after Maggie was given that diagnosis, she was given psychiatric therapy and she did very well for a few years, once they figured out a medication regimen that suited her symptoms. But the summer before her senior year in high school, it became apparent that she had stopped taking her medication because she started acting strange again.

"That was also the time that her home caught fire and

burned to the ground with her parents inside. That's when Maggie became an orphan. There was some speculation that Maggie was somehow responsible for the fire and the deaths of her parents but the subsequent investigation didn't find a direct link so no charges were ever filed.

"Mrs. Cooke and her husband wanted Maggie to come live with them but she had herself declared an 'emancipated minor'. Maggie received a rather large insurance settlement that she used to furnish an apartment and live on while she finished high school. She also used that money to finance her nursing education. According to Mrs. Cooke, Maggie would go through periods where she would faithfully take her medication and go to counseling. Then there were times when Maggie decided that she didn't need any medication and stopped taking everything."

"Did Mrs. Cooke say whether or not Maggie acted normal when she was taking her medication?" Brian asked.

"Apparently she lived quite a normal life when she was medicated," Greg confirmed.

"Is that it," Brian asked when Greg finished the report.

"Not even close. There's a lot more that you need to hear," Greg advised.

"Okay, Greg. Give me a five-minute break and I'll be back."

Brian left the room for a few minutes. Greg used that time to organize the reams of paper that covered the table. When Brian returned, he was carrying a pot of coffee and a couple of doughnuts. He poured a cup for himself, topped off Greg's cup, and returned to his spot at the table.

"I guess I needed some coffee after all. Okay, I'm ready. If you've got more there then let me have it."

"Mrs. Cooke is only one of my sources for information. Like I said before, I talked to the Winter Springs and Orlando Police Departments. I also talked to one of the administrators, a MaryAnn Fotenakes, at the Winter Springs Community Hospital. I got the most personal, detailed information from her that she had retrieved from MacGregor's personnel file. She was very accommodating and forthcoming with all information that she thought would be helpful to our investigation because she was on staff during a particular period of havoc at the hospital that she blamed on Maggie.

"When Maggie worked at the Winter Springs Community Hospital, she started dating a prominent physician, Dr. Simon Bolivia, who just happened to be married at the time. This doctor apparently had quite a reputation as a ladies man, a love-them and leave-them kind of a guy. When the doctor refused to leave his wife for her, Maggie created a very public disturbance at the hospital, vowing to get even with him. Everyone thought that she was just venting her anger, playing the part of the jilted girlfriend, and nobody took her threat of revenge seriously. After that, Maggie became withdrawn but she still showed up for work and did her job. Her co-workers thought she was acting that way because she was embarrassed and humiliated.

"About six months after their breakup, strange things started happening to Dr. Bolivia. His patients began to unexpectedly die post-operatively which was very surprising to everyone because he was an excellent surgeon and had never had any problems like that before. Post-mortem exams could find no physiological or pathological reason for the deaths so they were attributed to the surgical procedure. Since these strange deaths affected only Dr. Bolivia's patients he was blamed, not legally, but personally by the general hospital consensus. Word got out into the community and his medical practice went down the toilet. He started drinking. He ended up losing his practice, his money, his family, everything. He even found his dog dead outside his front door one morning. There was a lot of talk about whether Maggie's curse and her vow for revenge somehow had anything to do with Bolivia's tragic circumstances but nothing was ever proven one way or another. Shortly after that, Bolivia was forced off the hospital medical staff. That was the same time Maggie left the Winter Springs Hospital and came to Michigan. Miss Fotenakes added that MacGregor's personnel file was flagged in a way so that if any employer contacted the hospital for a reference none of the personal information would be released, only her work record which was excellent."

"That story is weird. How could Maggie be responsible for all of that," Brian responded. "You know, she told me that she came to Michigan after her fiancé died. Is that doctor still alive?" he asked.

"Yes, and I tried to get a hold of him but with no luck. The word is that he lives on the streets. And then there are the police reports. She was charged with some vandalism and disturbing the peace. There were some other accusations that were investigated but not prosecuted. She ended up with one misdemeanor conviction and she was sentenced to community service which she performed. At one point, Dr. Bolivia had a restraining order against Maggie for his family and him. He was convinced she was behind all of his problems but he couldn't prove anything."

"It sounds like she's had her share of problems and weird happenings but at the same time it doesn't provide any connection to the Temple deaths," Brian pointed out.

"I know that but Brian think about it. This girl, Maggie, has been surrounded by death and deadly circumstances most of her life and it seems that the pattern hasn't changed. I just want you to keep your eyes and ears open and to be careful."

"You know I will. I'm having dinner with her tonight. I'll give you my best impression after I spend some more time with her but based on what I already know, I think you're really over reacting," Brian said, trying to reassure Greg, as well as himself. "Besides, Maggie has been a great friend to Kate this past year and she never asked or expected anything in return, according to Kate. Kate did mention a couple of what she thought were irrational comments or reactions from Maggie in the last few days but given what's been going on at the hospital lately, it didn't seem that abnormal."

"You might be right, Brian. I may just be blowing smoke but I'm concerned. And because of that concern, I'm going to ask you, not order you but ask you, to stop seeing Maggie socially until this case is resolved. I know that you're planning to have dinner with her tonight but after that, please don't see her for awhile. Can you handle that?"

"Sure. She's a nice girl and I like her company but we've only gone out a couple of times. I was a little uneasy dating her during this investigation anyway. I only went out with her as a favor to Kate. She planned this whole party thing," Brian explained.

"Good. Now that that's settled, there's something else. I don't want you to give this information to Kate, not just yet anyway. I think she would have too much trouble hiding anything from Maggie."

"Are you sure Kate shouldn't know? If there is even the slightest chance that what you're thinking about Maggie is true then Kate might be in some trouble," Brian said with concern.

"Don't worry about Kate. We'll keep an eye on her and if it looks like she really is in trouble then we'll tell her everything and get her away from Maggie," Greg assured.

Nick arrived promptly at 5:30 p.m. He wasn't sure if the person who passes out the treats was supposed to wear a costume so he wore scrub clothes.

Because Kate was busy in the kitchen, Shane asked for permission to answer the door. She said yes so Shane let Nick into the house. He came to the kitchen and sat at the table. Kate poured him a cup of coffee and told him that dinner would be ready soon.

She was fixing one of the children's favorite dinners, hot dogs and potato chips. Nick hadn't been too keen about eating hot dogs until his trip to Angelo's with Kate. Prior to that lunch, it seemed that all of Nick's previous attempts to enjoy this American cuisine were less than satisfying. Kate assured Nick that tonight would be okay because like Angelo's, she served only Koegel Vienna Hot Dogs—the best in the whole world.

"You were right, Kate. This is really a good hot dog. What makes it taste so much better?"

"I don't know. I guess that's their secret. And since you like that hot dog so well, next time I'll have another surprise for you from Koegel's—pickled bologna."

"Pickled bologna?" Nick mused. "Never heard of it. I've heard of pickled pig's feet, pickled vegetables, and pickled eggs but never pickled bologna."

"Well sir, you are in for a treat!"

The twins were starting to get impatient while they waited for the evening's events. "Come on, Mom, we need to get our costumes on. It's time, it's time," they pleaded trying to coax her into their room.

"Okay, Nick. I'm leaving you in charge of the door from now until we return from trick or treating. Good luck."

In a matter of minutes, costumes were on, and they were on their way. The air was pleasantly cool with a light breeze that held wonderful fragrances, including the smoke from a distant leaf fire.

Leaf fires were outlawed in the city but occasionally one was lit and the smell brought back sweet memories from Kate's childhood. She recalled a high school project that required each class to construct a float for the homecoming parade. The students worked on the floats for weeks before the big event and the last weekend before homecoming, they would always build a big bonfire. That was such an innocent time. Mike and Kate were moving from childhood and were just begun to explore an adult relationship.

For a second, Kate's heart ached at the loss of Mike. He was missing all of these precious moments with his family. Her only saving grace was that she believed that he was watching from above and was pleased with the way that she was raising his children and happy that she was finally moving past her grief and getting on with her life.

Before she knew it, they had arrived at the first neighbor's door. Their neighbors were like a huge surrogate family and all were delighted to play the game of "guess who?" as the children went from house to house. Since the children only went to houses in the immediate neighborhood, Kate wasn't worried about contaminated treats that some children had received in years past. Even so, she made a point with the children by checking the entire contents of their plastic pumpkin pails before they were allowed to consume the fruits of their labor.

On the porch of their own home, the twins yelled at the top of their lungs, "Trick or treat!" They were giggling when Nick opened the door.

"So who do we have here? Looks like Bert and Ernie!" Nick teased.

"Bert and Ernie!" the twins said with exasperation. "No, we're not Bert and Ernie. We're Big Bird and Cookie Monster. Now you have to guess who we really are."

"Well, I'm not sure. The voices sound familiar but I can't think of the names."

"It's Shane and Shelby," they exclaimed as they lifted their masks. "We fooled you, didn't we? We really did, didn't we?"

"Yes, you sure did."

The children gave Nick a house-by-house description while removing their costumes and preparing for bed. The four sat around the kitchen table checking each piece of candy. Nick and Kate took turns answering the door when the last few ghosts and goblins came to visit. Once finished, Nick ushered the kids to bed and Kate turned the porch light off. When she went to say her last good night to the children, she found them both huddled in one bed. Nick was telling them a not-too-scary ghost story. When he was finished, they said one final good night and the bedroom light was turned off. Finally, there was a chance for Nick and Kate to be alone.

They held hands, casually strolling to the living room where they sat on the couch. Nick put his arm around Kate's shoulder. She was comfortable with that and softly put her head against him and placed her hand on his thigh. It was all so natural.

Nick asked, "Have you talked to Maggie or Brian today?"

"I tried to call Maggie but she didn't answer her phone so I haven't talk to her. But I did talk to Brian. He called me this afternoon. He said that they had a good time at the party and he ended up spending the night at her house. She got up early this morning and fixed Brian breakfast before he left for home to get ready for work. He invited her to his house for dinner tonight. So it sounds to me like they are enjoying each other's company," Kate answered, gloating a little because she was such a good matchmaker.

"Yeah, from what I saw of them, which really wasn't that much, they certainly seemed to be enjoying themselves. And what about you, Kate, did you enjoy yourself?"

Kate smiled. "Yes, I did. I really did. After I got home last night, I thought about the time we shared. I kept trying to understand and categorize my feelings, without much success I must say. I decided to stop trying to analyze and label everything and just live the feelings. Does that make sense to you?"

"Very much so. And I think that's some very good advice that we should both take for now, just live for the day and take care of tomorrow when it gets here," Nick paused. "Speaking of tomorrow, my 24-hour shift starts at 7 a.m. so I'm going to have to leave soon."

"I was going to make us some popcorn," Kate said somewhat disappointed.

"I'll have to take a rain check. I still have to stop by the ER on my way home to check on the hospital's Halloween candy inspection effort. I was on the committee that set up the standards for the X-ray department to use when they examined the candy for neighborhood kids. Besides, I'll bet the kids wake you up very early tomorrow, probably asking for candy for breakfast."

"I'm sure you're right."

They walked to the front door, bringing their evening to a conclusion but not the internal conflict that had been ever present all evening. They had been together for hours with a brief kiss being their only intimate contact because the children were always there. Most of the evening, they had been doing a secretive and seductive dance around each other, bringing their physical and emotional desires to the forefront. Both had been under a self-imposed abstinence for some time. Now they wanted more. They kissed, gently at first then deeply. Her body was pressed up against his and the heat of the moment seemed to melt them into one being.

Kate felt dizzy and weak in the knees. She found herself

sitting on the couch trying to steady her breathing. "How could I be sitting here alone," she thought. "I don't even remember him leaving." Again she tried to put her feelings in a neat reasonable compartment but nothing fit. "Passion? Absolutely, these are the feelings of passion but there's more to it. Desire for a prospective love? Yes, but more. Lust? That definitely fits, too. Maybe I should take my own advice and just let it happen without putting a name on it."

She broke out of her thoughts and headed for her room. She stripped off all of her clothes and prepared to shower. After a cool refreshing shower, she slipped on a nightshirt, slid between her crisp cotton sheets, and closed her eyes in anticipation of sweet dreams.

Maggie spent the late afternoon primping and preparing for her date with Brian. She was anticipating a cozy dinner followed by a whole night of lovemaking. Everything in the past was over and forgotten. She was beginning the next phase of her life that would be her "happily ever after" dream come true.

She packed an overnight bag with toiletries, make-up, perfume, a couple of downers, and her red negligee. She took the bag with her when she left her house, knowing that she wouldn't be returning until the next morning.

Maggie showed up at the door to Brian's apartment building at exactly 6 p.m. She rang the bell and waited for Brian to answer. Rather than using the buzzer to let her into the building, Brian went down and opened the door himself. He greeted her with a gentle hug and a soft kiss before they walked up the stairs to the apartment.

From the hallway, Maggie could smell the aroma of the spaghetti sauce wafting from Brian's apartment.

"Oh, Brian. The dinner smells wonderful. I can't remember the last time I had a good home cooked meal. It was so sweet of you to do this for me."

"It was the least I could do after you took such good care of me after the party," Brian admitted. "Would you like a glass of wine?"

"Yes, thank you. That would be nice."

Brian poured Maggie a glass of wine. She sat on one of the stools at the kitchen counter while he continued working on the dinner.

When everything was finished to perfection, he served her dinner at the candlelit table, while soft music played in the background. His romantic innuendoes captivated her. She was completely entranced until he told her that as much as he enjoyed her company, she would have to leave right after dinner.

Maggie couldn't believe his words.

"Excuse me. What did you say?"

"I said, 'I'm sorry that we can't spend more time together tonight.' I have tomorrow morning off because I have to go to the dentist. When I invited you to dinner, I didn't realize how much paper work I would need to finish tonight."

"That's not what he said before. Look at him, he's lying about something. He's trying to get rid of me for some reason," Maggie thought.

"It's the hospital case. I've got some reports to do," he tried to explain.

"Fine, Brian. You do what you have to do," she said brusquely as she made a 180-degree change in her attitude toward him. She didn't know what happened, when, or why. All she knew was that Brian had joined the other side. Now he was one of her enemies and he was trying to dump her. How could she have been so wrong about him?

Brian sensed Maggie's abrupt about face but didn't have a clue about how to smooth things out and make her understand that he didn't mean to hurt her feelings. He chose to keep his thoughts to himself for the time being. He was sure the day would come when he could explain everything and she would understand. He wasn't sure that she would understand if he tired to explain things right now. If he had learned anything from previous relationships, it was that women didn't take rejection easily. He decided a simple apology for ending the evening early would be best.

"Maggie, this isn't exactly what I had in mind for this

evening but sometimes that's just the way it goes. I'm sorry. I'll make it up to you, I promise."

"You're goddamn right you'll make it up to me, you son of a bitch," Maggie thought.

"Maggie, would you like some more wine?"

"No thanks, Brian. I can't have any more to drink if I'm going to be driving home," she tried to soften her tone.

"Oh, right. Of course, you're right. Would you like to dance?"

"No. Actually, I think I'd better get going so you can get to your work."

"Maggie, I didn't mean that you had to leave right this minute. We can still spend some time together."

"Really, Brian. I think that it's best that I leave right now. I'll give you a call tomorrow to see how you're feeling," she said but she thought, "What do you want, Brian, a quickie as payment for a spaghetti dinner?"

Maggie picked up her purse, kissed Brian on the cheek, and was out to her car within a minute. She was very confused about his change in attitude. On the drive home, she tried to analyze his comments and actions. Maybe she was wrong about him. Maybe he really did have to work and he wasn't just using that as an excuse to get rid of her.

She dropped her overnight case on the floor at the foot of her bed. She stripped her clothes off and put her bathrobe on. She opened a beer and parked herself in front of the TV. She tried to watch a movie but she couldn't concentrate on it. Her mind kept wandering back to thoughts of Brian and the wonderful future that she had imagined. She really wanted to believe in him.

Finally she decided that she must have jumped to the wrong conclusion in thinking that Brian was a betrayer. She would give him one more chance to prove his love and devotion for her but if he failed her again, it would be the last failure of his life.

Maggie spent the rest of the evening planning the scheme that would allow Brian one last opportunity to redeem himself, allowing for a "happily ever after" future with her.

Chapter Ten

Monday Morning, November 1, 1976

Kate was wide-awake at 6:30 a.m. Today, she would have breakfast ready before the children were awake. It proved to be a routine, semi-organized morning with the children safely deposited at the front steps of the school at 8:50.

From there, Kate went straight home and immediately tried to call Maggie with no results. She decided to spend her morning doing errands and visiting with her parents. She planned to pick the children up for lunch, spend some time playing with them, probably going for a bike ride, having an early dinner, and then going to bed as soon as her mother arrived at 6 p.m.

Brian got up at 7 a.m., giving him plenty of time to eat, shower, get ready, and leave for the dentist in time for his 9 a.m. appointment. As he went through the motions of his morning routine, he replayed the events of the night before. He felt a little guilty for putting Maggie off the way he did because he really did like her and he enjoyed her company. Besides, he never noticed anything in her behavior that warranted Greg's suspicions. He hoped that Greg's information wouldn't amount to anything that could implicate Maggie in the Temple deaths.

During Brian's dental procedure, the dentist realized that the work necessary to correct Brian's problem was more extensive than he had anticipated. He recommended that Brian not go to work that afternoon but rather take a couple of pain pills and take it easy for the rest of the day. The dentist assured Brian that he would have his office staff call the station before Brian left the office and arrange for him to be excused for the whole day.

"Flint Police Department."

"This is Dr. Seigel's office. I'm calling on behalf of Detective Brian Goss. May I please speak with Detective Greg Martin?"

"One moment, please."

"Greg Martin."

"Hello, Detective Martin. This is Judy Bourdeau at Dr. Seigel's office. Dr. Seigel is Brian Goss's dentist. Mr. Goss is here in the office right now. The procedure that Dr. Seigel performed on him this morning was considerably more extensive than he had anticipated and he has recommended that Mr. Goss take some time off from work, at least the rest of the day. Mr. Goss asked us to give you a call and let you know."

"Thanks for calling. Tell Brian not to worry about anything. I'll take care of things until he feels better. Tell him to come in tomorrow morning if he feels up to it, and if not, have him give me a call," Greg said.

"Okay, I'll give him that message. It's good that he is excused because once the local anesthetic wears off, he will be too uncomfortable if he doesn't take his pain pills. And if he takes the medication, he won't be fit for work. Thanks for your help."

Brian didn't feel too bad when he left the office because his jaw was still frozen but he could tell that his face was starting to swell. He stopped by the pharmacy and picked up his prescription before he headed home. When he pulled into his reserved spot in the carport, he was surprised to see Maggie standing next to her parked car in one of the guest parking spaces.

"Hi, Maggie. What are you doing here?" Brian asked.

"I thought you might like a little TLC from your favorite nurse after your trip to the dentist. I brought you some chicken soup. It's the universal cure-all, don't you know?" Maggie said sweetly.

"That's very kind of you but you shouldn't have put yourself out," Brian said as he walked toward the door of his apartment building.

"It was no problem at all. In fact, it was my pleasure," Maggie countered while she walked along with him.

When he opened the building door, he invited her to enter in front of him. They climbed the stairs to the door of his second floor apartment. He unlocked the door and they entered.

Brian's jaw was a little swollen and was starting to get uncomfortable. He took his prescription, Tylenol #3, to the bathroom and took two of the tablets. He changed into a T-shirt and a pair of sweat pants.

While he was in the bathroom, Maggie poured the still warm soup into a bowl and waited for him to return. He joined her in the kitchen where he sat on one of the two counter stools.

"Maggie, it was really nice of you to bring the soup over but I can't eat any of it right now. I'm not suppose to eat anything until the local anesthetic has worn off completely. That will be a little while yet," Brian explained. "I was supposed to go to work this afternoon but my dentist got me excused for the rest of the day so I'm going to kick back and take it easy until tomorrow morning. I just took some of my pain medicine so I think I'll just sit here and watch TV until I fall asleep," Brian said as a subtle suggestion that Maggie should leave.

Maggie was impervious to his remark. "I thought you should have a little something in your stomach so your pain medicine doesn't make you nauseated. Are you sure that you don't want to just sip some of the broth?"

"Yes, Maggie, I'm sure that I don't want any broth." Realizing that Maggie didn't get the hint, Brian was more direct. "I think it would be best if you left now so I can get some rest," Brian said as he put his head on his hands and leaned his elbows on the counter. With his back to Maggie, he said with as much tact and patience as he could, "I'll call you tomorrow."

"You'll call me tomorrow," Maggie repeated in low, sarcastic tone.

Before he could react to her change in attitude, she had already reached into the bag that had contained the carton of soup and retrieved a loaded syringe. With one quick motion, Maggie drove the needle into his neck and injected the contents of the syringe.

He tried to pull her hand away from his neck but it was too late. The damage had been done. She peeled his hand from her wrist and backed away from him. He tried to stand and walk toward her but he collapsed after just one step.

"You'll call me tomorrow?" Maggie repeated with a malicious venom-filled tone. "I don't think so. I don't think that you ever intended to call me. I don't know what happened but something changed your mind about me. We were planning to spend the rest of our lives together. I was to be your wife and the mother of your children. Maggie and Nick were going to be our best friends. They were going to stand up for us at our wedding. They were going to be the godparents to our children."

She was screaming at him while he was lying on the kitchen floor dying. Trying to maintain some semblance of control, she lowered her voice. She moved Brian onto his back. His breathing had stopped but he still had a weak pulse.

"He's not dead yet so he can probably still hear me," she thought. She continued the commentary about Brian and his betrayal. Finally, she stopped talking and just stood watching him as the last vestige of life left his body.

Maggie knew when she headed for Brian's apartment that she was going to give him one last chance to prove his love for her. She knew that granting him another opportunity was a magnanimous overture on her part but she felt that she should be generous. After all, she did love him. However, if he failed her then she would have no choice but to punish him for his betrayal and deception. And he did fail. He failed miserably.

She stepped over his body and sat on the stool where he had been only minutes before. "I have got to figure this out," Maggie said out loud. "The first thing that I need to do is take the phone off the hook."

She stepped over him again and went to the living room.

She took the phone off the hook so that if anyone called they would get a busy signal. After all, Brian didn't want to be disturbed, now did he?

The night before, Maggie had decided that she would end Brian's life if he failed to redeem himself but she had made no plans beyond that. She went to the refrigerator and got a beer that she drank right down. Finally it came to her. She had her plan.

She had a well-stocked first-aide kit that she always kept in her car. She had seen so many trauma patients on her job in the operating room, she decided that if she ever came upon an accident, she wanted to be prepared. Over the years, she had taken a number of supplies from the hospital to stock her kit.

She took Brian's keys and her keys when she went out to her car to retrieve her kit. She used his keys to let herself back into the apartment. Once inside, she put her kit down by the door, opened it, and removed a pair of gloves. She put the gloves on and headed straight to the bathroom.

She rinsed her gloves with water to remove any trace of powder from them. Then she located the bottle of pain pills, poured most of them into the glass in the bathroom, and filled it with water.

She took a large bath towel with her when returned to the kitchen. She rolled Brian's body onto his side and slid the towel underneath him. She used the towel to drag him into the bedroom. He was heavier than she figured and she was winded from the exertion but she was pumped up from adrenaline. She only needed a minute to rest.

She began the task of pulling him onto the bed. She posed his body in a sleeping position on his back. She adjusted his clothes and fixed his hair to conceal any evidence that she had placed his body there. Next, she arranged the linen on his bed to look as though he had just gone to bed.

Maggie went to the living room, picked up her kit, and headed for the bathroom. She used her finger to mix the solution in the glass to make sure that all of the tablets were dissolved. She removed a large syringe, a nasogastric (NG) tube, and a stethoscope from her kit. She pulled the solution up into the syringe and took it and the NG tube into the bedroom.

Maggie squirted a bit of the solution onto the end of the tube to lubricate it. She tipped Brian's head back and lifted his chin toward the ceiling. Holding his head in that position with one hand, she used her other hand to insert the NG tube into his nose. She met with only a little obstruction before the tube slid down his throat and into his stomach.

Once she thought that the tube was in his stomach, she attached the syringe to the free end of the tube. She put the earpieces of her stethoscope in place and put the diaphragm of it on Brian's stomach area. She pushed some air from the syringe into the tube. When she heard it gurgle in his stomach, she knew the tube was in the right spot. With the position of the tube confirmed, she pushed the plunger on the syringe until all of the drug solution was emptied into Brian's stomach.

She went to the kitchen where she found a bottle of whiskey in the cupboard. She took the bottle and a glass back into the bedroom. She poured a large amount of the whiskey into the glass and pulled it up into the syringe. She attached the syringe to the NG tube and injected the whiskey.

She removed the tube and carried it and the empty drug solution glass to the bathroom where she put them in the sink. She washed, rinsed, and dried the glass and returned it to its spot on the edge of the sink. She took the prescription bottle back to the bedroom with her.

She carefully applied Brian's fingers to the kitchen glass and whiskey bottle to make sure that his prints were on them before she put them on the nightstand. Next to the whiskey bottle, she placed the open prescription bottle on its side with the three remaining tablets next to the bottle.

She put all of her supplies along with her beer bottle into the plastic bag that had contained the soup. She washed the soup bowl and spoon, and returned them to the cupboard. She made a quick check around the apartment to make sure that everything was in place. She carried the plastic bag and her kit out to her car and left. She wasn't concerned if a few of her prints were found in the apartment. After all, everyone knew that she had dinner with Brian last night.

It was noon. Maggie drove to the back parking lot of one of the local medical clinics that was empty because of the lunch hour. She parked next to the large trash container, got out of her car, disposed of the plastic bag, and drove home.

"Well, there goes another relationship into the garbage," Maggie said to her self with no particular concern because she had been so wrong about Brian. He was a deceiver. "I guess I'd better go home and get some sleep," she said out loud while she yawned.

It wasn't until she got home that she gave any thought to what effect her actions would have on Kate. Maggie knew that she would have to be on her guard the next time she saw or talked to Kate. She decided that she should try to call Kate to let her know that the relationship with Brian hadn't worked out like she had hoped, to see how she reacts. She dialed Kate's number while she sipped on a beer. The phone rang several times and Maggie was getting ready to hang up when Kate answered.

"Hello," Kate said a little breathless. She heard the phone ringing from outside and had hurried to answer it.

"Hi, Kate. It's Maggie," she said with fake enthusiasm.

"Hi, Maggie. It's good to hear from you. I tried to call you yesterday but I guess that you were sleeping. I talked to Brian yesterday morning and he told me that you guys were going to have dinner last night. So how did it go?"

"That's what I wanted to talk to you about."

"Maggie, is something wrong?"

"Kind of."

"What, Maggie? What is it?"

"I guess it really started the night of the party. I mean, I like to have a drink just as much as the next guy but Brian really put them away. I didn't know that he was such a big drinker. He got so drunk."

"Usually, he isn't. I've never seen him drunk," Kate said puzzled.

"Well, he was at the party. We walked back to my house because he was too drunk to drive. I tried to feed him but that didn't help so I put him on the couch where he spent the night. I knew that he had to work Sunday morning so I got up early and fixed breakfast for him and sent him off in enough time to get home and cleaned up and to work on time. Before he left, he begged me to give him another chance and he invited me to dinner at his house Sunday night. I accepted the date and he left. I wasn't convinced that I should see him again but I decided to give him one more chance."

"I can't believe this. It doesn't sound at all like the Brian I know," Kate said totally confused because Maggie's version of the date was totally different from Brian's version.

Maggie was immediately defensive. "Are you calling me a liar?"

"No, no, Maggie, not at all. I just find your description of Brian's behavior so incredulous," Kate explained.

"Good, I'm glad you believe me because it's the truth. So anyway, I went to his house last night expecting a nice dinner. He was making spaghetti when I arrived. He answered the door with a drink in his hand. He smelled like a brewery and was already three sheets to the wind. I couldn't believe it. He told me that he had a dentist appointment the next morning and he was fortifying his courage. Have you ever heard of anything so childish?" Maggie asked.

"No, I haven't," Kate said quietly.

"I stayed long enough to eat dinner and then I couldn't stand it any more so I left. I know you had your heart set on the four of us being lifelong friends but it's not going to happen. I'm really sorry, Kate."

"Oh Maggie, you have nothing to apologize for. If anyone needs to apologize, it should be me. I guess I didn't know Brian, as well as, I thought I did. I should have checked things out better before I put you into such a crummy situation. I am so sorry."

"Listen, Kate. Can we talk about this later? I've got stuff to do around here and then I need to get some sleep before work tonight. We'll talk later. Okay?"

"Yeah sure, later. Bye, Maggie."

Maggie was certain that Kate was persuaded by her description of Brian's boorish behavior. She tried to decide, based on Kate's reaction to her story, if Kate was still her friend or if Kate would betray her for Brian's sake. The only thing that she knew for sure was that she was too tired to make any decisions right now. She went through her usual routine of popping pills and drinking beer to bring on a much-needed sleep.

Kate stood with her hand on the phone several minutes after she put it down. Nothing that Maggie had just said made any sense. A few of the details matched the ones that Brian had told her, but in general, it just didn't make sense. She also noticed when Maggie adopted the defensive attitude, much like she did in the office that time when they were talking about MJ.

She picked the receiver back up and dialed Brian's number. Before it rang, she hung up because she remembered that Brian had to work Monday afternoon. She called the station.

"Flint Police Department."

"Hi. This is Kate McKenna. Would you please connect me with Brian Goss?"

"I'm sorry, Kate. Brian's not here. He had some dental work done this morning. Evidently, it was more extensive than he expected because his dentist suggested that he take this afternoon off. He plans to be here tomorrow morning. I'll leave a message for him that you called."

"Okay, thank you."

Thinking Brian was home, Kate dialed his number again. This time she waited for it to ring but she got a busy signal. She made a mental note to call him again later.

She returned her attention to her children. They played until it was time for her to fix dinner. The kids wanted macaroni and cheese and they wanted to help fix it. They all headed for the kitchen to begin their chore.

After they finished eating, Kate started to get sleepy. She washed the dishes and cleaned the kitchen. By the time she finished, her mother had arrived. Kate decided not to talk to Mary about her conversation with Maggie because she didn't want to start thinking about everything all over again. She had to keep her mind clear of disturbing thoughts because she needed to get some sleep.

Kate talked with Mary for a few minutes. She hugged her mom, kissed her kids, and went to bed, knowing that her mother would wake her in time for work.

Chapter Eleven

Monday Night, November 1, 1976

Kate walked through the ER like she had done so many times during the past year but it wasn't the same any more. She was quite sure that nothing would be the same any more but she couldn't tell if that was a good thing or bad thing. Too many conflicting thoughts, emotions, facts, and innuendoes were causing a serious congestion in her mind. Her intuition wasn't working well.

Kate left the elevator on the tenth floor and knew immediately that the OR staff was in for a long night. A traffic accident had increased business for Dr. Wade, the orthopedic surgeon on call. He had finished all the injured patients scheduled for surgery that night but one. That patient, who had bilateral fractured femurs, was the one that the third-shift crew would work on that night.

OR 7 was still dirty from the last case because the second shift crew had been so busy, they hadn't had time to clean it. Kate, Maggie, and Army dressed and immediately went to the OR. Both teams worked together to clean the room and get the next case set up. While they worked, the patient arrived on a stretcher and was parked in the hall next to the OR 7 door.

When Kate finished with the anesthesia set up, she interviewed the patient and reviewed the chart. She also talked to Dr. Wade about the surgical plan so she would have all of the information that she needed to formulate her anesthesia plan.

The patient was taken into the room by 11:30 p.m. Two

members of the second-shift OR staff stayed over for about an hour to help get the case started. Two separate OR set ups had to be prepared because each leg had a different kind of fracture. Also, both legs had to be scrubbed, prepped, and draped separately so there were two prep and drape tables. Prepping legs can be a difficult process. It was especially hard in this case because the patient was a big guy and his legs were heavy. Once all of that was done, the second-shift people left and Kate, Army, and Maggie assumed the responsibility to complete the case.

Dr. Wade used orthopedic hardware to stabilize one of the fractured legs and he put a traction device that would be connected to weights for a day or two on the other leg. The weights would help pull the broken ends of the bone back into alignment. When the weights had successfully reduced the fracture, the patient would return to the OR and have that fracture stabilized with hardware.

By the time Dr. Wade finished his work it was 5 a.m. Kate and Maggie transported the patient to his room and Army began cleaning up the room. It took another hour for everyone to finish their work and get ready for the Tuesday morning cases. At 6:30 a.m., some of the first shift crew was starting to arrive. Kate really wanted to talk to Maggie privately because she was sure that Maggie must have been devastated by Brian's actions. She found Maggie in the workroom.

"Maggie, are you okay?" Kate said with genuine concern as she placed her hand on Maggie's shoulder.

Maggie turned around in surprise and shrugged her shoulder from Kate's hand. "Of course, I'm okay. Why wouldn't I be?"

"I guess I thought that you'd be upset by Brian's behavior," Kate said a little baffled.

"No, of course I'm not upset. Why should I be upset? Brian and I only went out a few times," she said very matter-of-factly. Maggie watched Kate carefully when she asked her next question. "Kate, the fact that things didn't work out between Brian and me won't have any effect on our friendship, will it?

You don't feel like you have to make a choice between him or me, do you?"

"No, of course it won't," Kate assured Maggie. "And I would never let anything or anyone force me to make a choice between friends."

"Good, because I not going to miss Brian as a friend but I would really miss you if anything ever happened to our friendship," Maggie explained.

"Nothing's going to happen to our friendship, Maggie. I promise you that."

"Thanks, Kate. Thanks for that."

When other staff members started entering the area, Maggie and Kate cut their conversation short.

"See you later, Kate."

"Yeah, Maggie. I'll see you tonight."

Maggie headed for the nurses' lounge while Kate headed for the anesthesia lounge. They both changed their clothes and left the hospital.

Tuesday Morning, November 2, 1976

Maggie was exhausted. She thought that she had gotten enough rest the day before to keep her going for a while but apparently the busy night had taken its toll on her energy level. She had a shower, skipped breakfast, and opened a beer. She pulled out the case containing her drugs from the cabinet under her bathroom sink and poured two Seconal tablets into her hand. She downed them with a big swig of the beer. She scrutinized the bottle before she tossed it back into the case. She noticed she was getting a little low on her Seconal. She'd have to get another prescription soon.

She pulled the drapes in her bedroom and climbed into bed. As she finished her beer, she thought about Kate who had yet to find out about Brian's death. Maggie was sure that by tonight at work, Kate would know.

"What would Kate know?" Maggie wondered out loud and then she answered her own question. "She would know that her friend Brian, who had totally misrepresented himself as an upstanding citizen and all-around nice guy and had totally taken advantage of her very best friend in the whole world, had been a complete idiot and had overdosed on pain pills and killed himself."

Maggie couldn't imagine that Kate would think anything else. But on the extremely remote possibility that Kate had even the slightest notion that Maggie had anything to do with Brian's sad demise then Maggie would have no choice other than to determine that to be an unforgivable error on Kate's part. Kate would have to suffer the consequences.

Maggie was getting drowsier by the minute. It made her sad to think that Kate might betray her. She didn't want to think about that any more. She was asleep as soon as she dismissed all thoughts of Kate's possible betrayal.

Kate was very tired. It had been a long, busy night at work but she knew that sleep would have to wait for a while. She had breakfast with the twins but her mother didn't join them. Mary left to go home and have breakfast with John. Kate helped the kids get ready for school and when it was time, she dropped them off near the front door of the school.

She had a few errands to run and then she stopped by her parents' to visit. While she was there, Kate ask her mother if she would pick the kids up from school at lunchtime and keep them until time for them to get ready for bed.

"Mom, I have some things to do this morning and then I have to get some sleep. I'm really tired. We were busy all night and I think I'm coming down with a cold or something. Before I go to bed, I'm going to take a decongestant. I'm sure that once I fall asleep, I will sleep until I have to get ready for work. Does that sound okay to you?" Kate asked, looking the worse for wear.

"I think that's a good idea. Do you want something to eat while you're here?" Mary asked, hoping that Kate would take her up on her offer.

"No thanks, Mom. I think I'm going to just go home, take

care of my business, and go to bed. I love you guys. I'll see you tonight, Mom." Kate headed for home.

The first thing Kate did when she got home was to call Brian. She dialed the number to the station and waited for an answer.

"Flint Police Department."

"Hi, this is Kate McKenna. Would you please connect me with Brian Goss?"

"I'm sorry, Kate. Brian didn't come in this morning. Apparently, his jaw is still bothering him. I'm not sure when he'll be back, maybe tomorrow."

"Oh, I'm surprised. I didn't know his tooth was so bad."

"I don't think he expected it either. Can I help you with something else?" the dispatcher asked.

"Yes. May I speak with Greg Martin?"

"Looks like your batting zero. Greg's not available right now."

"Okay. Thanks for the information. I'll try to get hold of him later," Kate said, disappointed that she couldn't reach Brian or Greg.

She tried Brian at home but when she dialed his number, it was busy again. She figured that he had the phone off of the hook so he wouldn't be disturbed. She understood his strategy because she certainly had done it enough times but it sure was frustrating.

She decided to soak in a hot bath while she listened to some classical music and sipped on a small glass of white wine. After she was thoroughly relaxed and wrinkled like a prune, she got out of the tub, dried off, and rubbed lotion all over her body. She took a Benadryl tablet to ward off what she thought was a stuffy nose coming on. She pulled the shades in her room, disconnected the ringer on the phone, and climbed into bed. It felt so good to stretch out and relax against the cool sheets. She was so tried that she was asleep immediately. A much-needed deep, deep sleep.

When Brian didn't show up for work Tuesday morning,

Greg wasn't that surprised because the dentist had warned him that Brian might not be up to working just yet. But he had expected that Brian would at least call and check in. When Brian hadn't called by noon, Greg called him at home. Of course, Greg got a busy signal. He put the phone down, a little irritated by the inconvenience. He would try again later.

Before Greg got a chance to call Brian back, he got called about a distraught man who had barricaded himself inside his home with a gun, threatening to shoot himself if his estranged wife didn't come back to him. Greg was one of the best hostage negotiators in the department, and in cases like this, his services could be invaluable. He immediately left for the scene.

It was 6 p.m. by the time Greg had convinced the man to come out of the house and surrender his gun. The man was taken to the psychiatric unit at Temple Hospital. Greg got back to the station shortly after that. He tried Brian's number again and again the phone was busy. Now Greg was pissed!

"What kind of an idiot leaves his phone off the hook for days on end? And what kind of idiot doesn't bother to check in at work when he knows damn well that he's supposed to?" Greg yelled at anyone who would listen. He grabbed his jacket from the back of his chair and stormed out of the office.

The drive to Brian's apartment took about ten minutes. Greg's car jerked to a stop. He jumped out and slammed the door, mumbling and grumbling all of the way to door of Brian's apartment building. He tried the security door and it was unlocked. He didn't bother ringing the doorbell. He entered the building and went up the stairs to Brian's door. He knocked on the door a few times. When he didn't get an immediate response, he started pounding on the door. He was pounding so hard that one of Brian's neighbors stuck her head out of her door and into the hallway and threatened to call the police if he didn't quiet down.

"Never mind lady, I am the police," Greg snapped at the woman. He was running short on patience.

The woman immediately pulled her head back in and slammed the door. As soon as her door was shut, Greg used his foot to force Brian's door open. One kick and he was in.

"Brian? Brian, where are you?" Greg yelled as he darted around the apartment looking for him. He immediately spied Brian on his bed. He didn't look good.

"Brian, oh my God, Brian." Greg touched his face. It was cold. He was dead. "Oh no, Brian, what the hell happened," Greg yelled. He stood there staring down at his friend for less than a minute but it seemed like a lifetime. He felt helpless. He was too late. Brian was gone. There was nothing he could do to help him now.

Greg backed out of the room seemingly mesmerized by Brian's lifeless remains. He was unwilling to look away just yet because he felt that once he did, that would be the point that his friendship with Brian would officially end.

When Greg finally lost sight of Brian, he snapped into his detective mode. He went to the kitchen and used a napkin from the counter to lift the receiver from the phone. He dialed the number to the station and reported the death. There was no obvious evidence of foul play but he wasn't taking any chances. If the death was some how connected to one of Brian's cases, Greg was going to find out. He ordered the dispatcher to notify all of the appropriate police and investigative personal, including the medical examiner, and tell them to report to the scene immediately. He also requested that an ambulance crew be on stand by to remove the remains, as soon as, the crime scene had been appropriately documented. Before he hung up, he told the dispatcher not to identify Brian by name on the radio. Greg wanted to talk to Brian's family before the word got out.

He headed back to Brian's bedroom to look around. When he initially looked at Brian, he didn't remember seeing any trauma or obvious cause of death. He wanted a second look. It was then that Greg noticed, slightly concealed by a lamp, the whiskey bottle, the prescription container, and a few tablets.

"Oh shit, Brian! What the hell have you done? How could you be so goddamn stupid?" He was livid with Brian's apparent overdose and at the same time, he was devastated by his loss. Here he was standing over the body of his partner, not to mention his life long friend and the little brother he never had. Brian had been such a significant part of Greg's life for so long, he loved him dearly. Now he was gone. Why? For what reason? An accident? A stupid goddamn accident!

This was the most indecisive moment in Greg's life. Should he tamper with the evidence a little to eliminate any chance that Brian would be accused of suicide? It was obvious to Greg that Brian's death had to have been an accident not a suicide. The thought that this was a homicide had yet to enter his mind. Greg decided that he had to keep his faith in Brian and believe that a thorough investigation would vindicate Brian from any wrongdoing. Greg realized that Brian's only hope to prevent him from being labeled "a victim of suicide" was for him to preserve the crime and oversee the investigation, making sure that only the very best people worked on this case.

Greg went out into the hall and began pacing. He didn't want to be alone with Brian when the other members of the emergency crews arrived. Everything must remain on the up and up. He had already determined that he would stay at the scene until Brian was taken out and then he would accompany him to the morgue. As the others began to arrive, Greg went back inside the apartment.

Again Greg used the phone in the kitchen. This time he called the station to get Kate's number. He dialed her number but it just rang and rang. "Goddamn it!" Greg said as he slammed the phone down.

While Greg made phone calls, the paramedics examined the body. Since Brian was dead, the paramedics called the medical examiner's office and ask for permission to move the body to the morgue. Their request was approved. After the crime scene investigators took a number of pictures and examined the body, bed, and linen, the paramedics went about their business of bagging the body for transportation.

The police personnel with the exception of Greg Martin proceeded to process the crime scene. Greg continued to make phone calls to people who he felt needed to be notified of Brian's death. He approached the paramedics and asked, "Do you guys know the number at Temple Memorial?" They said the number in unison and Greg repeated it back. He returned to the kitchen to phone the hospital.

"Temple Memorial Hospital."

"This is Detective Greg Martin. I need to speak with Dr. Nick Lecorts. This is an emergency."

"I'm sorry, Detective Martin. Dr. Lecorts is scrubbed in surgery right now. Would you care to leave a message for him or would you prefer to speak with another doctor?" the operator asked.

First he couldn't get a hold of Kate. Now he can't reach Nick. Greg's agitation was increasing by the minute. "No, not another doctor. I'll leave a message for Dr. Lecorts. Tell him that Det. Greg Martin needs to talk to him, as soon as possible, and it's an emergency. Have him call the Flint Police Department. They'll find me. If I don't hear from him in the next hour or so, then I will call you again. I expect to be at Temple sometime in the next couple of hours. Please tell Dr. Lecorts not to leave the hospital until he talks to me. Did you get that?" Greg barked at her.

"Yes sir, I did. I understand the urgency and I'll take care of it personally. When you call back, ask for Brenda," the operator advised him. Immediately after disconnecting with the detective, the operator called the OR and left an urgent message with the ward clerk for Dr. Lecorts to call the operator, as soon as he broke scrub.

It was 9 p.m. by the time Dr. Lecorts left the OR. He had already been given the message so he immediately went to the OR office and called the operator.

"This is Dr. Lecorts. Do you have a message for me?"

"Yes, doctor. Detective Greg Martin called earlier and he just called again. He wants to talk to you and he said it's an emergency. He's down in the ER, waiting for you."

"Thank you. If he calls again in the next fifteen minutes, tell him that I'm out of surgery, I have to change my clothes and write some orders. I'll get to ER as soon as I can." Nick paused for a second. "Operator, instead of waiting for the detective to call, will you please call the ER and make sure he get the message that I'll be there soon?"

"Sure, doctor. Right away."

Nick checked on the condition of the patient while the OR crew prepared him for transport. He took a few minutes to write the post-op orders before he headed to the doctors' locker room where he changed out of his bloody scrubs. Within minutes, Nick was on his way down the stairs to the ER. He immediately spotted Greg waiting by the main desk.

"Greg, what's up?" Nick said slightly winded from running down eleven flights of stairs.

"Nick, finally," Greg said with some relief. "I've been trying to get a hold of you for a couple of hours. Do you know where Kate is?"

"Home, as far as I know. Why? What happened?"

Greg pulled Nick aside to an area that afforded them a little more privacy. "Brian's dead."

"What?" Nick said with bewilderment. "What happened?"

"It looks like an overdose, accidental overdose. His dentist gave him some pain pills, Tylenol #3, after he did some work on his teeth Monday morning. He was given thirty tablets and only three were left. There was also a bottle of whiskey on his nightstand. It looks kind of bad for Brian but to me it doesn't make any sense. Brian never put too much faith in pain medicine. He didn't even use aspirin. And even if his mouth hurt so bad that he did take some pain pills, he was smart enough to know that you don't mix medicine with booze. I wish you would track down Dr. Park and find out whatever you can about Brian's cause of death. Also, how well do you know Maggie MacGregor?" Greg asked.

"I know her from the hospital and I know her as Kate's friend. Why? What has she got to do with this?"

"I don't know for sure but my gut feeling tells me that she might have everything to do with it. Brian had a date with Maggie for dinner Sunday night and based on some information I got about her background, I asked him to cancel it. Brian said that because it was already Sunday afternoon, it was too late to cancel the dinner but he said he wouldn't see her anymore until after the Temple investigation was closed. We both had some concerns about him dating one of the primary suspects in that investigation."

"What are you talking about?" Nick said taken aback again. "When did Maggie become a primary suspect? And just what is she suspected of doing?" Nick demanded.

"A lot of suspicious information turned up when we did the background check on her. Although she was never arrested or indicted, some people implicated her in several deaths in Florida before she moved to Michigan. Now think about this. Three deaths in one week and she was around every time. I just don't like those kind of coincidences. Which brings me back to my original reason for contacting you. I can't get a hold of Kate. I've tried her home several times but she never answers."

"I haven't talked to her since last night. She said she was going to take her children to school and try to call Brian in the morning. She thought that she might be coming down with a cold or something so she was planning to sleep all afternoon and evening until it was time for her to get ready for work. I know that when she's really tired and wants to sleep, she often turns the phone ringer off. I could call her parents and see if they know anything but I don't want to alarm them if I don't have to," Nick explained.

"I know that she's supposed to be to work tonight at 11 p.m. If I don't hear from her by then or if she doesn't show up for work on time, I'll let you know because then I'll be worried," Nick explained. "But I don't think Kate has anything to be concerned about when it comes to Maggie. Kate told me that she is Maggie's best friend. I don't think Maggie would ever do anything that would hurt Kate."

"Okay, listen Nick. I want you to talk to Kate before she goes to the operating room tonight and tell her to stay away from Maggie or at least, don't be alone with her. I don't trust her. If my suspicions about her are true, she attacks those who are closest to her. I don't want Kate to become her next victim," Greg warned.

"Why don't you just arrest Maggie if you think those things about her are true?"

"Because we don't have any evidence on her. Like I told you, it's just a gut feeling. It would really help if you could push the medical examiner a little to do the autopsy on Brian, as soon as possible. If she somehow had anything to do with Brian's accident then hopefully we'll get some proof that we can use against her."

"I might be able to help speed up the post. Dr. Park is a good guy and he's Kate's friend. I'll call him right now and see if he'll come in tonight and get started. How much should I tell him?" Nick asked.

"You don't need to tell him anything except that it would be a favor to you and Kate to get in here right away. He's already been notified about Brian's death and some of the circumstances. I think he might have been here earlier when they brought Brian in so he may have seen him already," Greg explained. "And don't forget about warning Kate about Maggie."

"Don't worry about that. She uses the ER entrance into the hospital and I'm going to park myself right here until I see her. I should tell you that Maggie often uses this entrance so I might see her as well."

"If Maggie does come by, check her out and see if you notice anything odd about her behavior. Talk to her if you can, listen to the tone of her voice, and observe her mannerisms, that kind of stuff," Greg requested.

Nick agreed. He promptly excused himself to go call Dr. Park who explained that he had been at the hospital but he had gone home after he made a preliminary exam of Brian. When Nick explained the situation to him, he was more than willing to come back to the hospital. He had already made plans to do the full autopsy of Brian in the morning and doing it a few hours earlier didn't make any difference to him. Nick told Greg that Dr. Park had agreed to come back to the hospital. Greg knew that both men were going out of their way to accommodate him on behalf of his friend and he very much appreciated their efforts.

"Well, that settles it. I'm staying here until Dr. Park finishes his work. That means I'll be here when the girls come through. I don't want to spook Maggie. She knows who I am and what I look like so I'll need a place that's near but out of sight. What do you suggest?"

"Why don't you go to the small conference room at the end of this hall, next to the waiting area. It's used for grieving families and currently it's empty. ER is pretty quiet right now so no one should bother you there," Nick assured him.

"Sounds perfect. Point me in the right direction and I'll find the room. Come and get me when the coast is clear," Greg said, heading down the hall.

Nick took a seat at the ER desk. He called the floor to check on the status of his most recent OR patient then he picked up a medical journal and sat at the desk reading while he waited for Kate and Maggie to arrive. It was 10:20 p.m.

Chapter Twelve

Tuesday Night, November 2, 1976

At exactly 10 p.m., Mary awakened Kate. She came out of her deep sleep smoothly as though her body knew that it was time to wake up. She yawned and stretched trying to wake up. She asked about her children. Mary assured her that they all had a wonderful afternoon, had spaghetti for dinner, and had played games in the evening. Presently, they were safe and sound in their beds. Mary excused herself so Kate could get up and get dressed.

Kate felt pretty good but still a little drowsy. She knew that as soon as the water hit her face, the last traces of her slumber would be washed down the drain. While she went through the motions of getting ready for work, Kate was reminded that she hadn't spoken with Brian since Sunday and that was before she'd had her little talk with Maggie.

Kate wasn't in the habit of talking to Brian everyday but under the circumstances, she thought they needed to touch base. She decided that she would go to the station first thing after dropping the kids off at school the next morning.

She entered the hospital through the ER entrance. She hadn't gone very far when Nick saw her and immediately went to meet her. He was at her side for only seconds when he spotted Maggie coming through the ER door.

Nick whispered into Kate's ear, "Stay away from Maggie. Don't be alone with her tonight." That was all he could say before Maggie was within earshot of his voice. He quickly changed the subject and his tone.

"So you had a good sleep and for once you feel rested. Good, I'm glad," Nick was saying when Maggie joined them.

"Hi, Maggie, how are you?" Kate asked, not having a clue what was going on with Nick and his dire warning.

"Yeah, Maggie, how are you?" Nick added, trying to remain as natural as he could lest Maggie become suspicious of his behavior.

"Well, aren't you two just the picture of concern? I'm fine thank you. And it's obvious that you two are doing well. I won't intrude on your privacy. Kate, I'll see you upstairs," Maggie said. She walked past the couple toward the elevators.

"No, Maggie, wait up. I'm coming too," Kate said, walking away from Nick. She turned and said to him, "I have to get up to the OR. I'll talk to you later." With that Kate was gone and Nick was sure that either she hadn't heard or hadn't understood his warning. He told her not to be alone with Maggie and the first thing she did was to get on an elevator with her.

Nick could hear an approaching ambulance. He went to find Greg and tell him what had just happened with Kate and Maggie. He couldn't talk long because he was still on call and the patients in the incoming ambulances might need the attention of a surgical resident.

As Kate and Maggie stood waiting for the elevator door to open, they also heard the sound of sirens heralding the arrival of at least one new patient to add to the Temple Memorial census.

On the way to the tenth floor, Kate and Maggie exchanged the usual chitchat. They stepped off of the elevator together and walked to the OR office where they joined Army. In the distant background, they heard the sound of more sirens.

"Hey, you guys. Do you hear those sirens?" Kate asked.

"Yep. It might be one of those nights," Army sighed. He left the office to get started on his assigned chores.

"Maggie, we need to talk but first I have to get report,

check rooms, and set up OR 7," Kate said. She headed for the anesthesia lounge to get changed.

Maggie nodded. Just after Kate left the office, the phone rang. Army and Kate both turned and looked to Maggie expecting it to be the ER calling to schedule a case but she waved them off. Maggie returned her attention to the phone. It was Nick. "Well, she's not here just now. She's changing her clothes but I'll tell her that you called," Maggie said sweetly. She smiled and hung up the phone.

Maggie wasn't sure exactly why but she didn't want Nick talking to Kate right now. She really wanted to keep them apart until Kate demonstrated her loyalty to Maggie when it came to the Brian issue.

Before Maggie had a chance to leave the office and get started on her duties, the phone rang again. This time it was the ER. Two patients with abdominal trauma were just admitted and both needed abdominal explorations, as soon as possible. Everyone had a long night ahead of them.

It was 4:30 a.m., when they finished the last stitch on the second patient. Nick scrubbed on both cases but Kate didn't have a second alone with him. She wondered if she had misinterpreted his earlier caution. She got the distinct impression that Nick had warned her away from Maggie but everyone was acting completely normal. The mood in the OR during both cases was status quo. Even the customary OR dialog among all of the staff members, including Nick and Maggie, failed to give any clue that something was amiss.

"What's going on here?" Kate wondered. She was confused by Nick's behavior. She decided to dismiss all suppositions about a conflict between Nick and Maggie until she had an opportunity to talk with Nick long enough for him to explain.

While Kate had been thinking about Nick, she was also performing the necessary steps to wake her patient and move him to the ICU. Maggie left the room briefly to get the patient's bed.

Nick took advantage of that moment to again warn Kate when he leaned over and whispered in her ear, "Don't be alone with Maggie. I'll be back later to explain."

They exchanged glances and Kate nodded her head in affirmation.

Kate and Maggie delivered the last patient to the ICU. Maggie returned to the OR while Kate stayed to finish her charting. By the time Kate returned to the OR, Maggie and Army had finished cleaning their part of OR 7. Kate had to clean and stock the anesthesia equipment and supplies and put a clean set-up in OR 7 before she could even think about taking a break.

After they finished with all of their duties for the night, Army left the floor to go visit with Joey for a while and Maggie decided to go to the nurses' lounge and rest. She needed to resolve the conflict about whether or not her friend Kate would betray her. She had to find out if Kate's allegiance would remain with her after she found out about Brian's death. Maggie was certain that Kate would know about it soon if she didn't already know. She also knew that some people would be quick to put some of the blame of his death on her shoulders because that's what always happened. Maggie realized that the only way she could ever be sure of what Kate was thinking, would be to look straight into her eyes. Nobody could get away with lying to Maggie if she was looking into his or her eyes. She could look through the eyes straight into their soul. She had the gift and no one could ever fool her.

Kate was confused and very concerned by Nick's comment. She was making a real effort to keep in on a back burner, without much success, until she could talk to Nick to find out what else he had to say. She was trying to clean the gas machine in OR 7 but was having some difficulty because her hands were shaking. Actually, her whole body was trembling. The thought crossed her mind that she may be having some kind of a panic attack.

She was just finishing with the machine when she heard the OR door swing open. She felt a wave of relief. Nick was here. When she turned around it was Maggie standing in the doorway. She tried to conceal her reaction to Maggie's unexpected appearance but she was sure that her face showed some degree of disappointment and surprise. For some reason, she suddenly felt like a prey that had been trapped by the hunter. Her heart began to pound and the pressure in her head increased to the point that she thought it might explode. She took a couple of slow deep breaths in an effort to, at the very least, present a calm demeanor. After all, she didn't even know why she was supposed to be afraid but she was very afraid.

"Hi, Maggie. I'm just finishing here so I'll meet you in the office in a few minutes. Then we can finally have a chance to sit and catch up on everything. Okay?" Kate's voice cracked and the words sounded forced.

Maggie felt like Kate was dismissing her and she resented it. "You know, don't you? I know, you know," Maggie said with no emotion. She looked at Kate with dead eyes.

"Know what, Maggie? I don't know what you're talking about. I don't know anything." Kate was confused and very frightened.

"Kate, don't pull that innocent bullshit with me. I could tell by the expression on your face and the look in yours eyes as soon as I entered the room," Maggie snarled back at her.

"I'm sure that I must have had a surprised look when you came into the room because I was expecting someone else," Kate explained.

"Yeah, right. Expecting someone else. Really Kate, you can do better than that."

"No really, Maggie. I was expecting Nick."

"Why? What's he want with you?"

"Maggie, you know. Nick and I are dating. He was just planning to come visit me when he finished with his post-op checks."

"That's a crock. He's coming up here so the two of you can gang up on me."

"That's not true, Maggie. Why would we want to attack you? We have no reason to attack you. You're my friend. I care about you."

"Don't you dare call me a liar. And don't you throw that friendship crap at me. You're not my friend. You're not my friend and never have been."

All of the time that they were talking, they were circling around the OR table because Kate was making a deliberate effort to keep Maggie from getting too close. Kate felt that it was very important to remain calm and keep talking to Maggie in a firm but reassuring voice and she made a determine effort to remind Maggie of their friendship.

Maggie would have no part of Kate's attempt to divert her attention away from the real issue—Kate's betrayal. She knew, as soon as she walked into the room, that Kate was no longer her friend. That's assuming that she had ever been a friend in the first place which she doubted.

The expression on Maggie's face was becoming so distorted that Kate could hardly recognize this obviously demented person glaring at her across the OR table. Kate was overwhelmed by Maggie's transformation and was becoming more frightened by the minute.

Maggie continued talking in a slow, deliberate monotone, almost as if she were in a trance. "I loved my parents. I loved Simon. I loved Tom. I loved Brian."

"Maggie, I don't understand any of this."

Maggie didn't acknowledge that Kate had spoken.

"I loved them all very deeply. I love them blindly without any reservations. And they all said that they loved me, too. Just like you Kate. They all told me that they loved me. But their love was conditional. I had to live up to their very unreasonable ideals and expectations. I was doomed before I even started because nobody could be that perfect. The truth is they hated me and they just wanted to torture me. My whole life has been one torture after another. I can't do this any more. I'm just so tired of trying to please other people. I only want to please myself."

Maggie and Kate kept their eyes locked on each other as they continued their macabre dance around the operating table.

"And you, Kate. I loved you. You were my very best friend in the whole world. You were the sister I never had. I trusted you. I was always there for you. And you, you turned on me. You believed their lies. You betrayed me."

"No, Maggie. That's not so. I am your friend. You are my friend. I love you, Maggie. It's true, you were always there for me when I needed a friend and I'll always be there for you." Kate was making every effort to placate Maggie's deranged thought process and instill a sense of safety and rationality.

Rather than having a calming effect on Maggie, Kate's comments seemed to amplify her anger and her tone. Now she was screaming at Kate.

"LIAR! You are a goddamn liar! You can say anything you want but I will never believe another word that comes out of your mouth. I can see right through you and you will never fool me again!" Maggie was seething at the thought of this latest betrayal.

Maggie was looking directly into Kate's eyes as she lunged over the OR table at Kate with a loaded syringe in each hand. The one in her right hand met its mark as Maggie drove the syringe into Kate's neck. Kate tried to pull Maggie's hand away but Maggie's strength was so over powering that Kate's effort had no effect. Maggie used her thumb to empty the entire syringe into Kate's neck. Maggie was still raving about Kate's violation of their friendship.

"You can't escape me, you betraying little bitch. I am not your average OR nurse, no ma'am, I am not. I am highly intelligent and very experienced when it comes to eliminating my enemies. And make no mistake about it Miss Priss, you are my enemy."

Kate was aware of the effect that the drug was having on her.

"I thought when I came to Michigan things would be different and for a while they were. I was doing fine until that little slut from the X-ray department starting messing in my business. Tom thought he wanted her. Well thanks to me, they can be together for eternity and they can have each other all they want. Then when you hooked me up with Brian, I thought things would be different. After all, my best friend in the whole world arranged the whole thing. Right Kate? But he only told me that he loved me so that he could screw me. How could I have been so stupid as to get interested in a cop? A goddamn cop who only wanted to have me arrested."

"Succinylcholine," Kate thought. She felt herself sliding to the floor as she listened to Maggie's ravings. "She killed them. She killed them all and now she has killed me, too," Kate thought when she realized that she could no longer breathe. "Please, don't kill me. My children need me. Their father is dead. I'm all they have. Please, oh God, please, let her hear me." Kate prayed her silent prayer.

Her mind was beginning to cloud from the lack of oxygen. She thought she heard voices in the distance just before she lost consciousness.

Nick finally finished all of the required paper work for the evening and his post-op visits. He wanted to go down to the morgue to see if Dr. Park had learned anything yet about Brian's death but he knew he had to go to see Kate first. He had to explain what he could about Greg's suspicions about Maggie but he didn't want to scare her too much until she was off duty. What if another emergency arrived? She had to be able to perform her anesthesia duties until someone was there to relieve her.

As soon as Nick arrived on the tenth floor, he could hear Maggie yelling. He quickly followed the sound to OR 7, where he saw Maggie leaning over Kate with a syringe in her hand.

"STOP! You stop right there. What the hell are you doing? Get away from her," Nick demanded as he charged into the room.

Maggie pulled away from Kate who remained slumped on the floor. She eyed Nick for a split second before she left the room by the other door, the one that led into the scrub room.

Nick rushed to Kate's side. "Oh no. Oh my God. Kate? Kate, please," Nick pleaded.

He checked for a pulse. It was really weak and she wasn't breathing. He gave her two quick breaths mouth to mouth and lifted her to the OR table where he carefully placed her on her back. He located the oxygen flow meter on the gas machine and turned the dial until it registered ten liters of flow. He grabbed the facemask from the top of the anesthesia supply cart and attached it to the breathing circuit. He placed the mask over Kate's face and began squeezing the breathing bag. Too much air was leaking from the machine and from around the mask. His efforts were failing. Kate was dying.

"Come on, Lecorts. You can do this," Nick was telling himself. He tightened a pressure valve on the machine and adjusted the mask on Kate's face.

Again Nick squeezed the bag. This time he could see Kate's chest rise and fall. "Yes. Thank you, God. Okay Kate, now it is up to you. I'll help but you have to wake up. Please, wake up, Kate. I let you into my life. I let you through my barrier. I love you, Kate. I can't imagine my life without you. Please, wake up." Nick kept a running commentary to her while he continued breathing for her. He thought she might wake up faster if she could hear his pleadings and his declaration of love.

Army returned to the OR and he didn't see anyone in the office. He called into the nurses' lounge for Maggie but she didn't respond. "Very strange," he thought. There was no reason for her to be in one of the ORs because everything was already done. He decided to call her name down the corridor.

"Maggie, where are you?" Army hollered.

Nick heard Army's call. "Army, here in room seven. I need help. Please, Army, get me some help."

Army immediately ran to OR 7 and he was shocked to see that Dr. Lecorts was using the gas machine to ventilate Kate who was lying on the operating table.

"Maggie did this. Get someone up here to help me with Kate. Call a code to OR 7. Tell the operator to notify the police down in ER. They need to go find that crazy bitch before she hurts anyone else."

Army seemed to come to attention. "Yes, sir."

He raced to the OR office, dialed the operator, and called a code to OR 7. The responding code team could provide all the help that Dr. Lecorts would need to help resuscitate Kate. He also told the operator to alert the police in the ER that Maggie

MacGregor, an RN dressed in scrubs, was dangerous and was running loose in the hospital. It was imperative that they begin searching for her immediately.

Army started down the hall to begin a search of the tenth floor but was distracted when he heard the members of the code team arriving. He stationed himself outside the elevators and began directing the team members to OR 7.

Army called the operator again and told her to send the police to the tenth floor stat. Before he could hang up the phone, Greg was at the door of the OR office identifying himself as a police detective. He recognized him immediately as the detective who had questioned him about the Temple suicides.

"Hi, detective. It's Army Sargent, remember me from the interviews?"

"Of course, I do," Greg confirmed. "What's going on here? Can you tell me what happened?"

"Well, all I know is that I went to L&D to visit Joey. When I came back, I didn't see Maggie in the office so I went to the door of the nurses' lounge and called for her. When she didn't answer, I called her name down the OR corridor, thinking that maybe she had gone into one of the ORs. Dr. Lecorts heard me calling for Maggie and he yelled to me from OR 7. When I looked into the room, Dr. Lecorts was ventilating Kate who was lying on the OR table."

Greg interrupted Army's narration. "Is Kate okay?"

"I don't know. They're still working on her."

"Okay, go on," Greg ordered. "What about Maggie, where's Maggie?"

"She wasn't here when I got back. I haven't seen her since I left to go down to L&D but Dr. Lecorts said that he saw her and that it was Maggie who hurt Kate. He said that she took off running and I told the operator to have the ER police and the hospital security look for her," Army explained. "Detective, if you're finished talking with me for now, I'd really like to go down to L&D and check on Joey."

"Sure, go ahead but don't mention any of this. No sense

starting a panic if we don't have to," Greg admonished. "Where's Nick and Kate?"

"Just go through the double doors and it's the first operating room on the left. There's a crowd there, you can't miss it," Army assured Greg.

Greg went to OR 7 but the code team was still working on Kate and Nick was in the middle of it. He decided to stay in the background until the situation with Kate had stabilized. Greg needed some information from Nick but it would have to wait until Nick's attention could be diverted away from Kate.

By the time the code team members started to arrive in OR 7, Kate was beginning to make a respiratory effort. She wasn't moving enough oxygen on her own yet so she still needed assistance. But it was a good sign that the muscle relaxant was beginning to wear off. Nick turned the mask and the responsibility of maintaining Kate's oxygen level over to the respiratory therapist when she arrived.

Nick held Kate's hand and continued to offer her words of encouragement while members of the code team attached the cardiac monitor and blood pressure cuff. Doctors checked her heart and breath sounds and one of the nurses started an IV line.

Everything checked out fine and within a few more minutes Kate was breathing deep enough on her own that she no longer required assistance, but she continued to receive some oxygen. She opened her eyes and smiled at Nick, well aware that he had saved her life. As she began to regain consciousness, she could hear Nick giving reports to the arriving members of the code team.

Army checked on Joey and everyone on L&D was fine. They had three patients in active labor so they were fairly busy, plus there were several visitors present. Army figured that Maggie would never try to hide out there because there was too much activity. He returned to the OR in enough time to bring a recovery room cart to OR 7 for Kate. The team members lifted Kate from the OR table onto the cart. Nick and Army wheeled the cart to the recovery room and the code members who had responded to the OR began leaving the area to return to their other duties.

Now that Kate was out of harm's way, Greg's main mission was to find Maggie before she could cause any more devastation.

Chapter Thirteen

Wednesday Morning, November 3, 1976

The head of Kate's cart was raised to a semi-sitting position. She felt sore all over, one of the effects of the muscle relaxant, but otherwise all right. Kate spotted Greg. She looked around the room expecting to see Brian but didn't see him.

Greg motioned to Nick to come speak with him. Nick excused himself from Kate and slid his hand away from hers.

"I'll be right back, Kate. I need to talk to Greg for a few minutes," Nick assured her.

"Nick, I know that it's been a rough night for you and I know that you want to be with Kate right now but I need to know what you know about Maggie's whereabouts. We have got to find her," Greg insisted.

"I came into the OR almost immediately after Maggie injected Kate and paralyzed her. I couldn't go after her because I had to take care of Kate. Maggie ran out of the OR and I don't even know which way she went when she left. I'm sorry I can't be of more help," Nick said with regret. "One thing you should know is that she still had one full syringe with her when she fled."

"Don't apologize. You did what you had to do and it was the right thing because it saved Kate's life. If you hadn't been there to take care of her, she would surely be dead right now. I'll put the word out about Maggie having the syringe so everyone can be on guard. Does Kate know about Brian?" Greg asked.

"I'm sure that she doesn't because she was asking about

him a few minutes ago. She expected him to be here. Did you see Dr. Park after he finished the autopsy?" Nick asked.

"Yeah but he only has a preliminary report. He said that Brian's stomach was full of Tylenol, codeine, and alcohol but he also said that he found a couple of inconsistencies that he wants to check before he gives out any more information. I told him that I would get back to him later today. Of course that was before all of this happened. Kate has to be told, you know," Greg said solemnly.

"I know. I think it would be best if you told her but I'd like to be there with her if that's alright with you."

"That's fine with me. Why don't you move Kate's cart to the far end of the room where it's a little quieter? I'll be there in a few minutes."

Nick explained to Kate that Greg wanted to talk to her but needed a little more privacy so he was going to move her down to the end of the room. When Greg arrived he pulled the curtain around them and formed a little cubicle.

"How are you feeling, Kate?" Greg asked with genuine fondness and concern.

"I'm okay, mostly. Physically, I just feel a little weak in the knees. Emotionally, I'm a wreck. I'm still trying to piece together what happened here tonight. Nothing makes very much sense, especially Maggie's rage. She was so angry with me."

Greg continued. "There's a lot about Maggie that you don't know. I have some information that I need to give you but I need to give some direction to my officers first and then at some point Mr. Eggleston and Rev. Blackwell will be joining us. I want them to hear it, too. Is that alright with you?"

"Sure, Greg. Whatever you think."

When Greg left to check on the search, Kate looked to Nick for a clue as to what was coming. He sort of shrugged his shoulders and suggested that it would be best to wait for Greg to return.

Greg spoke with the officers who had yet to locate Maggie. All exits from the hospital were guarded and the tunnels leading to other buildings were being searched. Everyone was fairly certain that she was still in the building somewhere and in time, they would find her. Greg encouraged them to step up their search of the building but emphasized the importance of avoiding disruption of the patients and interference of their care. Another team of officers was searching the hospital grounds and the adjacent neighborhood while still more were searching Maggie's house. She didn't have a history of harming strangers and the administration didn't think that she would attack any of the patients but she was so fragile mentally that her actions couldn't be predicted.

Nick sat on a chair next to Kate's cart waiting for Greg to return with the others. He noticed that some of the first-shift crew had begun to filter into the area. Kate had requested a Coke earlier and was pleased when Lorraine Thornton, the head nurse of the recovery room, arrived with a can of Coke in each hand, knowing that one might not be enough for Kate.

After Kate took a nice long drink, she asked Nick to please call her mother and tell her what had happened during the night. Kate was sure that the morning news would be full of the hospital happenings and she wanted to make sure that her parents knew that she was all right but she didn't feel up to talking to them herself right now. She was certain that they would want more of an explanation than she prepared to give. He should also tell Mary that Kate would be delayed at the hospital for some time and ask her to please stay with the children. She suggested that perhaps they shouldn't go to school today. Whatever time she finally arrived home, she wanted her children there.

When Greg rejoined Kate, she was sipping on a coke. The IV had been discontinued and she was feeling quite normal. He waited for Nick to return from making the phone call.

When Nick returned, he explained, "I reached your mother and told her that everything here was fine but that you would have to stay for a while. She will take care of the kids. She agreed with you and she's not sending them to school today because she doesn't want them to hear any stories about the hospital until you can be there. She will think of some excuse so that they won't become alarmed. She's going to take them to her house so you can call her there when you get home."

Satisfied that her children were protected, Kate turned her attention to Greg. She felt an ominous dread.

"What is it Greg? What do you have to tell me?" Her eyes fill with tears before he even spoke.

"I'd like to begin with Maggie's history. She was not orphaned and adopted as a young child like she told you. She was born to loving parents who very much wanted a child. They showered her with love, affection, and all of the material things that she needed. Despite all of their efforts, Maggie didn't have a normal childhood. She had periods of severe depression and periods of intense anger that she usually directed to those who were the closest to her emotionally. Doctors examined her but they failed to come up with a diagnosis so she went untreated for a while.

"When Maggie became a teenager she started acting out with defiance and rebellion toward any authority but especially against her parents. It was during that time that she began to drink and use drugs. Her parents took her to a psychologist for family and private counseling sessions. It was determined in retrospect that her problems were of more of a psychiatric nature, rather than psychological maladjustment. At some point, her care was transferred to a psychiatrist. She resented the constant intrusion into her life by her parents. She convinced herself that they weren't her natural parents and they stole her as a baby for the sole purpose of torturing her. Eventually, she came to believe that they were tired of her and wanted to get rid of her.

"When Maggie was 17, her parents died in a house fire but she miraculously escaped unscathed. Although the investigation into the fire proved it was arson, the fire starter was never identified. Some investigators had suspicions about Maggie but nothing could be proven. The authorities kept her under surveillance for a while but they never found anything incriminating.

"Maggie collected on the insurance policies covering the house and the lives of her parents. She used that money to pay her tuition and to live on while she was attending the university where she got her nursing education. She didn't seem to be spending money on any foolishness or luxuries nor did she exhibit any suspicious activities. She even continued with her therapy sessions. After a time the investigation on her was put aside for more pressing issues.

"Eventually, Maggie and her therapist agreed she was remaining quite stable on her medication regimen. The therapist advised Maggie that she would no longer be required to attend therapy sessions on a regular basis. She changed her regular meetings to sporadic sessions. There came a time when she stopped going altogether.

"Maggie completed her education and began working at Winter Springs Community Hospital. She was an excellent nurse and was respected by the other staff members. Socially, she was described as quiet or reserved initially but then she began to come out of her shell. Apparently that change took place when she got a boyfriend.

"Maggie started dating..." Greg paused and flipped through his notes. "Ah yes, hear we are, she started dating a Dr. Simon Bolivia. The story goes that this married doctor had a reputation for having flings with the young nurses on staff. He looked at Maggie as a challenge because she had rebuffed all efforts by other hospital staff members who had vied for her attention. After a couple of 'dates' when he apparently managed to engage her in a sexual relationship, he tried to call it off.

"By that time, Maggie had been feeling healthy and mentally stable for a while. She didn't like taking her medication so she stopped taking the psychiatric drugs. She had convinced herself that Dr. Bolivia was in love with her and planned to leave his wife for her so that they could live 'happily ever after.' She was certain that she would never need medication again because the love of her life was all that she needed to stay well.

"When Bolivia told Maggie that he didn't want her, she lost control because without her medication, she couldn't handle the emotional stress. She recognized that her thoughts and emotions were getting out of control and on her own, she decided to see one of the psychiatrists on staff at her hospital. She didn't give the doctor her complete psychiatric history so he had no idea that she was supposed to be on a regular antidepressive/ antipsychotic regimen. He prescribed some medication to help with her depression and they began having regular counseling sessions. Maggie convinced the doctor that she had just been depressed over a failed relationship and with his help, she'd learned to cope with the situation. After about four to six months, she stopped the sessions and the medication.

"It was about that time that Dr. Bolivia started having problems with some of his OR patients who died unexpectedly post-operatively. The causes of the deaths couldn't be directly attributed to previous physical conditions, the surgical procedures, or the anesthetics. The circumstances of the patient's deaths were very mysterious, especially because only Dr. Bolivia's patients were dying. No patients of other physicians were being affected. Word got out into the community about the deaths, Bolivia's referrals declined, he started drinking heavily, and eventually they kicked him off the hospital staff. He was ruined financially, his health was deteriorating, and his wife left him. He ending up being a social outcast."

Kate finished her pop. She sat quietly listening to Greg.

"There was an investigation into Maggie's activities and there were some concerns about her involvement in the whole Bolivia mess but again, no proof. Then shortly after Bolivia's dismissal, Maggie resigned her hospital position in Florida and moved to Michigan."

Greg paused and Kate took the opportunity to suggest a break. She wanted a little time to digest everything he'd said and make an effort to fit his facts into her recollections of the conversations that she had had with Maggie over the last year and a half. Also, she desperately needed to use the ladies room.

"You must have read my mind, Kate, because I was just going to say that this would be a good time to stop for a little while. This story telling is taking longer than I thought would. What I'd like to do is move to another location before more staff and patients arrive in the recovery room," Greg stated.

When he pulled the curtain back, Nick and Kate saw what Greg had already seen. The first patients of the day had already begun arriving in the recovery room.

"I also want Mr. Eggleston and Rev. Blackwell to join us for the remainder of this discussion because it concerns the hospital." Greg motioned to Kate's supervisor, Leslie Morgan.

"Kate, Leslie is going to take you to the anesthesia locker room and help you freshen up and change into your own clothes if you are feeling up to it. You're probably quite capable of taking care of yourself but I don't want you talking to anyone until I get your statement. So Leslie will be your protector. Okay?"

"Sure, Greg. Whatever you say," Kate replied. It seemed like that was becoming her pat answer but she just didn't feel like any confrontation. It was easier to just be agreeable.

Nick helped Kate off the cart. Her legs felt a little weak but she was sure that she could walk with no problem.

"It's 8:30. Why don't we break until about 9:15 and reconvene in the executive conference room on 1A. Is that okay with everyone?"

All agreed. Leslie escorted Kate to the anesthesia lounge while Nick went to the doctors' locker room for a shower and shave after which he dressed in a clean pair of scrubs. When he left the locker room, he saw Leslie and Kate waiting for him in the OR office.

While the others took advantage of the break to rest a bit, Greg used the time to check on the search for Maggie. He also put in a call to Dr. Park to set up a conference time. When Greg learned that Dr. Park wasn't available, he left a message with his secretary to have him call the administrative conference room on 1A, as soon as possible. Greg wanted any information that he could get about Brian.

When Nick and Kate entered the conference room, Greg was standing by the door. Mr. Eggleston and Rev. Blackwell were seated at the huge conference table. A tray with fruit and donuts had been served, along with a pot of coffee. Nick helped Kate into one of the chairs and then sat next to her at the end of the table facing the two men already seated. She opened her second can of Coke of the day and placed it on the table in front of her. Greg sat at the very end of the table facing all of them. He resumed his story.

"What I'm going to discuss next is our developing theory based on the facts, as we know them to be, and the tips that we've been collecting since the death of Mary Jo Iverson. This information must be kept confidential because it's part of the ongoing investigation of Margaret MacGregor's role in these crimes. When I am through covering the events up to last night or I should say this morning then I will take your questions or comments.

"We believe that Maggie was dating Dr. Tom Dunbar for a brief period. Apparently, he wanted to call it off because he wasn't interested in a serious relationship with her. She, on the other hand, was already planning their future together and refused to believe that he didn't feel the same way. The situation was very similar to the one in Florida. Then Dr. Dunbar began dating Mary Jo Iverson with whom he seemed to be quite infatuated and we understand she felt the same way. When Maggie learned of the relationship between Dr. Dunbar and MJ, she figured that if she could get MJ out of the picture then he would once again turn his attention to her. We believe Maggie caused MJ's fall, maybe with the same drug that she used on you Kate. We also believe that she had a hand in Dr. Dunbar's death. We can't confirm it yet but we doubt that either of those deaths was the result of suicide.

"Our consulting psychiatrist believes if Maggie had sought medical help, a doctor would have recognized that she was in trouble and could have put her back into counseling and on medication. Maybe she could have been stopped with some intervention but she was too out of control to stop on her own. It is evident that she literally crossed Dr. Dunbar and MJ off her list without skipping a beat before she jumped with both feet right into another relationship."

"What relationship, Greg? What are you talking about?" Kate wanted to know.

"Kate, I'm talking about Brian," Greg said.

"Well yes, Brian did go out with her few times but she told me that she wasn't that impressed with him. She thought that he drank too much and she wasn't planning to go out with him again," Kate explained.

"When did she tell you that?" Greg asked.

"Let me think." Kate paused as she tried to get the days straight in her mind. "Maggie called me at home. I think that is was around noon on Tuesday because it was after I did my errands and before I went to sleep for the day. I remember that I had tried to call Brian. I hadn't talked to him since Sunday afternoon. I wanted to know how his dinner with Maggie went on Sunday night but his phone was busy. Right after that Maggie called me, and that's when she told me that she didn't want to see Brian any more."

"Well, I talked to Brian on Sunday. We were both at the station catching up on paperwork. He told me that he had quite a date planned for Maggie, you know dinner, wine, and the whole night together. He said that he had a good time at the party and I think he rather enjoyed her company. I'm the one who told Brian to break it off with her until the investigation was complete because I was getting too much disturbing information from her background check. He said that it was too late to break the dinner date for that night but he said he would make it an early night and then he wouldn't see her any more until after the Temple case was resolved.

"Brian had a dentist appointment Monday morning. His dentist called me at the station from his office and said that Brian needed a little time off from work. I told the dentist to tell Brian to take the afternoon off and the next morning too, if need be, so I didn't expect Brian at work until Tuesday afternoon. When he didn't show up for work by then and his phone was always busy, I decided to go over to his apartment to find out what the hell was going on."

"Yeah, so where is he?" Kate demanded.

All of the men exchange glances. They knew.

"Greg, where is Brian?" This time Kate's voice was less demanding and more pleading.

"Kate, I'm really very sorry to have to tell you this but Brian's dead."

"No, no, not Brian," Kate moaned. "What happened to him?

"We don't know for sure, but it's highly likely that Maggie somehow caused his death."

"All of this is my fault. I had to be the matchmaker. I thought that I could fix up by best friends, make the perfect couple. How could I have been so stupid? Usually, I read people so well, I have such good instincts. How could I have caused such destruction?"

Kate broke down and sobbed. Nick put his arm around her in an effort to comfort her but it didn't have much effect. She just needed to cry it out for a while. She'd been keeping a lot of emotions bottled up ever since very early that morning. The emotional damn broke. She buried her face on Nick's shoulder and her body heaved with each sob.

Greg waited for several long minutes before he began again. "Please don't blame yourself, Kate. It wasn't your fault. You were a good friend. You were a good friend to Maggie and Brian. Maggie fooled all of us. She's sick Kate, sicker than anybody realized."

Kate struggled to bring her emotions under control. She excused herself briefly to go to the ladies room where she splashed some cold water on her face and dried it off. She pushed some strands of hair back and left without looking into the mirror. She felt bad enough without seeing herself in the mirror and feeling worse.

Kate returned to the conference room and Greg continued.

"Kate, I was planning to meet with you at the end of your shift this morning to explain everything to you before you heard anything on the news. I was going to warn you to stay away from Maggie. I thought that we'd have time to develop the leads a little more before we picked her up. She made a move sooner than we expected. I never dreamed that she would hurt you, Kate. I'm so sorry. I take complete responsibility for what she did to you," Greg confessed.

Kate looked up at him with her puffy red eyes. "Greg, it's not your fault any more than it is my fault. You were right when you said that the blames lies with Maggie and her illness."

Greg shook his head and continued. "We need to get a statement from you including all of Maggie's admissions. We have some theories and circumstantial evidence against her for Brian's death but we have her nailed for attempted murder on you, Kate. I swear that when we catch her, she will pay for the rest of her life."

"When you catch her?" Kate said wide-eyed. "What do you mean when you catch her? Don't you have her in custody?"

"I saw Maggie standing over you in the OR just after she injected you. When I came into the room she ran out. I didn't follow her because I stayed to take care of you. She hasn't been seen since," Nick explained to Kate.

"But I don't want you to worry. We will find her and until we do, I'm going to provide you with 24 hour police protection," Greg assured her. "And for your peace of mind, I sent a patrol car to stay with your family."

"Good, that makes me feel a lot better. She knows where I live and I couldn't bear it if anything happened to my children." Changing her focus, Kate asked, "Greg, there's something that you haven't explained yet. How did Brian die?"

Just then there was a knock at the door. It was Dr. Park with the preliminary results of Brian's autopsy. Greg invited him in and asked him to share the results with the group.

"Well, it definitely wasn't from natural causes. Brian was in excellent health. Every organ was perfect. Initially, I suspected that he had overdosed on a combination of Tylenol #3 and alcohol because his stomach was full of it. But when we did the toxicology screen of his blood, no alcohol was present and only a small amount of codeine from the Tylenol #3 was detected," he explained.

"Based on some information from the police detectives, it seems quite probable that Brian's death was a homicide disguised as a suicide or accidental overdose. And in light of the report from Nick, that Maggie apparently tried to kill you with a muscle relaxant," Dr. Park said as he nodded at Kate, "I performed a more detailed examination and I made two discoveries."

"First, I found a needle track in his neck and I believe that he was injected with a muscle relaxant that paralyzed him. That would explain how Maggie could have gained physical control of Brian. Secondly, I found some faint abrasions in Brian's nasal passage and in his throat. My guess is that Maggie inserted an NG tube and injected the codeine and alcohol mixture to make it appear that he overdosed. That would explain the large amount of drug and alcohol in his stomach and the small amount in his blood. Since he was dead when she injected the solution into his stomach, absorption into the blood did not take place. It might have worked under other circumstances but not this time," Dr. Park concluded. "Now if you don't have any questions, I have to get back to the lab."

Greg stood and shook his hand. "I ... We really appreciate how quickly you performed Brian's exam and it was kind of you to come to us to share the results. I'll be talking to you again soon. Thanks, Dr. Park."

When he opened the door to leave the room, they heard a commotion coming from the end of the A corridor. Kate and Nick stayed in the conference room while the rest went to investigate.

A few minutes later Greg returned. Maggie had been found sitting on the floor in a corner of the housekeeping closet on 1A. She had a blank stare on her face and was totally unresponsive to any stimuli.

"She looks like she's in some kind of shock or something," Greg reported. "We'll keep her under police guard here on the psychiatric unit until the doctors figure out what's wrong with her. Go home, Kate. It's over now. Take her home, Nick. She's had more than enough for one day."

Nick called Kate's parents and gave them a very brief summary of everything that had happened in the last twelve hours. He explained that he was going to take Kate home, feed her, and make sure that she had a good solid sleep. He intended to stay with her until she woke up. He asked Mary to fix Kate's favorite dinner, chicken pot pie, and have it ready about 6:30 p.m. Nick would make sure that Kate and he would be there on time.

Epilog

Dr. Park gave Kate the final results from his pathology exams. He concluded that sufficient information had been discovered about the deaths of Mary Jo Iverson and Dr. Thomas Dunbar to determine that their deaths were homicides. The succinylcholine that Maggie had used to paralyze Brian could not be detected in his body but there was enough independent corroborative evidence to rule his death a homicide, as well. There was some circumstantial evidence tying Maggie to their deaths but probably not enough for a conviction. It was verified that the syringe that was used on Kate contained succinylcholine. Maggie could be prosecuted on charges of attempted murder.

Maggie was admitted to the psychiatric unit at Temple. She was diagnosed as being in a total psychotic state and legally insane. Unable to assist with her defense, her attempted murder trial was postponed until such a time that she could be declared sane. Kate went to visit her one time before Maggie was transferred to a state mental facility. She was still in a catatonic state and totally unresponsive.

Maggie's room was in the lock-up section of the psychiatric unit. She was lying in bed with leather restraints on both hands and both feet because she had periodic fits of rage when she threatened harm to herself and others. Kate went to her bedside and took Maggie's hand. When Kate began speaking to Maggie, she moved closer and directly faced her, in an effort to reach her on some subconscious level.

"Maggie, it's me, Kate. I'm sorry I didn't figure out that you were so sick. Maybe I could have helped you. I'm okay. You didn't hurt me. I'm sure you never really wanted to hurt me. I'm still your friend. Maggie, I'm here for you if you need me. I will always be your friend."

Maggie's eyelids fluttered slighter. For a very brief moment Maggie returned Kate's gaze and looked directly into Kate's eyes. Kate was sure she saw a flicker of recognition in Maggie's eyes before they reverted back to a blank stare. Maggie had returned to that far away place where she had to go to find peace from her tormented mind.

Greg lost his partner and good friend but in that loss he gained a new relationship. He adopted Kate as his little sister, much the same as Brian had at one time. He also began to devote some time and attention to Shane and Shelby.

Kate took a couple of weeks off from work at everyone's insistence. In an effort to support her wellbeing and adjustment upon return to work, Kate was given a transfer to the day shift.

Nick had some vacation time saved up so he scheduled some time off during Kate's period of recuperation. Nick and Kate spent a lot of time together, alone and with the twins, getting to know each other.

The weekend after "the event" as Kate labeled her brush with death, Nick cooked a traditional Ukrainian dinner for Kate, the children, and her parents. He was cooking for two whole days before the occasion. The menu included roast pork, cabbage rolls, perogies, and fresh bread. For dessert, he made a bread pudding. Kate thought that they should have invited everyone that lived on her block because he cooked enough food to feed the whole neighborhood.

It didn't take long before Kate was able to put a label on that feeling she had sensed ever since she met Nick. It was love. But not just love. Rather, it was love with a soul mate. A love that declares not the union of two but the union of one soul that had been divided and was now whole again.

ABOUT THE AUTHOR

MICHELE WILLOUGHBY STROCEL was born, raised, and educated in the greater Flint, Michigan area, where she still lives with her husband and three grown children. She holds diplomas in nursing and nurse anesthesia from Hurley Medical Center, and BS and MS degrees from the University of Michigan-Flint. For almost three decades, she held various positions in the operating room from OR nurse to staff anesthetist, and Anesthesia Department Director to instructor at the University of Michigan-Flint/Hurley Medical Center Anesthesia Program. When not writing, she can be found with her family or working on one of her sewing, woodworking, or yard-work projects.

ABOUT GREATUNPUBLISHED.COM

www.greatunpublished.com is a website that exists to serve writers and readers, and to remove some of the commercial barriers between them. When you purchase a GreatUNpublished title, whether you order it in electronic form or in a paperback volume, the author is receiving a majority of the post-production revenue.

A GreatUNpublished book is never out of stock, and always available, because each book is printed on-demand, as it is ordered.

A portion of the site's share of profits is channeled into literacy programs.

So by purchasing this title from GreatUNpublished, you are helping to revolutionize the publishing industry for the benefit of writers and readers.

And for this we thank you.